A Story of Bad

Edward M. Krauss

ISBN: 978-0-9798087-4-6
Library of Congress Control Number: 2007943878

Published by Global Authors Publications

Filling the GAP in publishing

Edited by Esther C. Kash
Interior Design by Kathleen Walls
Cover Design by Kathleen Walls

Printed in USA for Global Authors Publications

Other books by Edward M. Krauss:

SOLOMON THE ACCOUNTANT
A gentle love story set in 1950

HERE ON MOON
A novel of deceit, divorce, recovery

ON BEING THE BOSS
Effective management techniques in stressful situations [co-author]

A Story of Bad

DEDICATION:

For Esther, who is intelligent in the light, and witty in the dark.

AKNOWLEDGEMENT:

The author wishes to acknowledge the assistance of Inspector James Hall and the men and women of the New York City Police Department, and of the Cambodian Mutual Assistance Association, Columbus, Ohio. Donations are strongly encouraged to the New York Police and Fire Widow's and Children's Benefit Fund, Inc. c/o General Post Office, PO Box 26837 New York, New York, 10087-6837, and to the Cambodian Mutual Assistance Association, PO Box 24238 Columbus, Ohio 43224.

CHAPTER ONE

Daroeung Chan found the body. Although early, before the workers were due to clock in, the overhead lights, large bulbs in shiny, half-globe aluminum reflectors, were all on. As soon as she realized what she was looking at Daroeung stopped twenty feet away and screamed a high, almost melodic scream that seemed not to break for breathing. Only three people at work that early, one was Amy, and she followed the screams that led her to her father, Victor Pritkin, face down on the cement floor of the loading dock, dead with a sharp-pointed tin snips stuck deep in his skull, the handles sticking up.

It was a terrible moment for Amy, a terrible morning for the entire staff. Within half an hour the factory was full of police, not just uniforms but a detective in a suit, a photographer, and two people in jump suits wearing latex gloves stretched tight over their hands who covered her father with what looked like an army blanket, thick and dark green, but not until after the photographer had taken numerous pictures. Amy called her brothers. Tony was just about to walk out the door, meaning he would be there, be in his office next to Amy's, in half an hour. She told him to drive carefully, don't speed, there was no reason to hurry. She called Peter and reached him on a pier in Hoboken, the cranes and trucks making it hard for him to hear. He said he'd be right there, and Amy gave him the same message; don't speed, no reason to hurry. The police kept working, the staff milled around uncertain what to do, whether to stay or leave.

Detective Terry Stans stopped another detective, a forensics expert. "Jean, what have we got?"

"Tin snips shoved right into the brain, probably one strong blow, just bam! into the head. Probably dead before he hit the floor. Coupla other same tools sitting around, so maybe the killer just grabbed a handy one. No sign of a struggle, so sneaked up or was walking behind, looks like one or t'other. Preliminary guess death around six o'clock, so he was found real close to the time he was killed, we got the call little after six."

Amy sat at her desk, her hands trembling a bit, trying to screw her thoughts down tight, trying to make some decisions. "Send the staff home till tomorrow... no, Monday" she decided, and started to get up. At that moment the detective walked into her office and she relaxed, somewhat plopped back into her chair.

1

"Ms. Pritkin?"

"Amy is fine, I'm sorry… detective…?"

"Stans. Terry Stans. Can we talk a few minutes? Not long…how do you feel?"

"Weird. Scared. Heartbroken. Yes, we can talk, but I've got to decide what to do about the staff, they don't look like they'd be much good today, guess I'll tell them to go home. Maybe take tomorrow off too….start again Monday. Start again without Dad." She was crying, wiping away the tears as she spoke. "Who would kill my dear sweet Daddy?"

Gently, Terry continued "You didn't find him, right? Not the one who discovered the… who discovered him."

"No, it was Daro, Daroeung Chan, our sewing supervisor. She hasn't stopped crying for a minute, don't think she's ready for an interview."

He frowned a bit, still speaking in a soft voice. "I really need to talk to her as soon as possible, while everything is fresh in her mind. Time works against us, gives whoever did this time to start covering up."

"Sure. I understand."

"Will you help me, please?"

"Of course, but what about the rest?"

"Do you know who came after he was found? Is that possible?"

"Almost everyone; there were only three of us here when I heard her screaming. And screaming. What a sound. I'll never forget it."

"Three besides your father?"

"Me, Daro of course, and our bookkeeper, Rose Mabris."

"If you're sure, then all the others can go, but I want to talk to her, to Rose Mabris, and Daro. Sooner the better."

Amy got up from her desk. He followed her as they walked down a brick wall corridor and through an open area and back to a large room the employees called the loading dock. Daroeung Chan, a woman in her early thirties with a gently rounding face and body was in a corner, sitting against the wall in a tight ball as if trying to use up as little space as possible. She was crying and talking to herself in occasional bursts of rapid speech.

"What language is that?"

"She's from Cambodia, as are about half the girls in the sewing shop."

"How's her English? Do I need an interpreter?"

"It's rough, but no, you won't, she does fine."

"Ask her if she can talk to me, please. Tell her it's important if we're going to catch whoever did this to her boss."

Amy squatted down next to the crying woman, held her hands, talked softly to her. The crying lessened, then Terry saw her lift her head slightly and glance at him over Amy's shoulder, look back at Amy, nod and start to stand. The two women stood up together, holding hands, then hugged briefly.

2

"Detective Stans, this is Daroeung Chan. She goes by Daro. You can use my office if you like."

He nodded thanks, then motioned to Daro to go first. She looked puzzled, so he said "We go" complete with finger and thumb pointing and indicating gestures.

"Sure Mr. Police," but when she still didn't move he realized she was waiting for him to go first. He did so, and they went to the front of the small, crowded factory, back to Amy's office. He didn't shut the door.

The detective pointed to the one chair in front of the desk and she sat carefully, gingerly on it. She was, besides distraught, obviously terrified, although he didn't know if it was fear of the murder and lurking murderer or fear of him, or both. He looked around, paused for a moment, but realized he needed to sit behind the desk, sit in Amy's chair, or else hover over the woman in the small, crowded office. That wouldn't work; he didn't want to intimidate her, he wanted her to relax and remember, so he sat in Amy's chair on the other side of the desk. He got out his notepad.

"Please tell me how to spell your name."

"Is better maybe me think I write you page. I learn make me name" she said, holding out her hand.

"Sure, thanks." He waited while she carefully printed

D A R O E U N G C H A N

and handed his notepad and ballpoint back. "Thank you. Now, please tell me what happened, what you saw."

She paused a moment. "Me need know have enough white make white shirts, no got too many no make white, make blue, plenty blue maybe wait more days white come on truck."

Terry Stans nodded emphatically. "Please tell me if I understand you. You wanted to know it you had enough material, cloth, to make white shirts, or else make blue ones."

She smiled a little. "So good."

He returned the smile. "Thank you. Please go on, tell me everything you remember."

"Box material be all over place, some here, some there, got to go see, maybe someday get new place, boss say maybe someday new place this small make problems, now boss dead." She cried a moment, took some tissues from a box on the desk, wiped her face. "Sorry, talk more. Me OK."

"I understand, you don't have to be sorry. So your boss, Mr. Pritkin say…said that there might be a new factory someday because this one's too small. And you were looking for some white material….."

"Be many boxes some here some there, you know?" she said, her hands moving, pointing with small, delicate gestures.

"Yes."

"So where white? Go loading dock, look before sewing crew here, he on floor. All" she said, shrugging.

"Did you touch him?"

"No, stay away, maybe ...." she shrugged again. "Stay away many."

"You saw him, you stayed away… did you call for help? Run for help?"

"I shout…no…. so loud… what word? Like" she tilted her head back and said "Eeeeeeeeee" with her eyes wide.

"Scream?"

"So good. Scream many. All come. Amy Come. Rose come."

"Do you know who was in the building first?"

"Rose. No, maybe him. Mr. Vic."

"Do you know why Rose was here so early?"

"All time make here early. Make lock. Go home maybe three."

"You're being so helpful. Thank you. Just a little more. You said 'make lock'….?"

Daro pantomimed turning a key in a lock, back an forth. "Me word…. word…. what you do thing make lock….little…." Again she pantomimed poking then turning.

"The key? Keys?"

Daro clapped her hands together in a gesture of frustration. "Make key lock. Rose make key lock be here early all time, go home three." This time she held up three fingers.

"Last question, but I really need you to think hard on this one."

She took in a deep breath and let it out slowly.

"Do you remember anything just before you found him, anything unusual? A sound, a voice, a strange noise, or something out of place, something different, strange…. you understand?"

Softly. "Yes."

"Take a moment. Think.."

She sat unmoving except her eyes, darting about, searching her brain. "Sorry, sorry. All make same."

"And no sound or voice."

"Sorry sorry sorry."

"No, don't be. If the killer was quiet and careful that makes our job harder, but you can only tell us what you know. Please don't feel bad. You've been very helpful."

Daroeung Chan sat, waiting.

"That's all for now. Thank you."

She nodded shyly, sighed a bit, rose and left the office.

It occurred to Terry that if she were telling the truth, then the killer knew the building, knew how to get in and out without being seen or heard. Or hid in the building overnight? Or, of course, had been let in by one of the three...no, four people in the building, the fourth being the victim himself.

Rose Mabris, the company bookkeeper was at her desk, working.

Terry approached her, sat down on a wooden chair with spindle legs. It was black, but in a few places where the paint had chipped a light yellow showed through. Somebody's old kitchen chair. Rose was in her late forties or early fifties, her hair a mixture of reds and browns as though the same coloring was never used twice. She wore a large, forgiving flowered dress with a surprise of feminine lace at the cuffs and neck.

"Can I talk to you now?"

"Sure, just keepin' busy, waiting to talk wit' you, see what happens, ya know?"

"Did you open the doors, unlock the front door this morning?"

"No, da boss was here. Somedays I getshere foits, somedays he does. Used to be always him, before me, last year or maybe two it back and forth who's here first. Today him first. Then he gets killed. Miserable, ain't it?"

"Is there an alarm system?"

"Sure, right over there." She pointed to a keypad next to the door.

"So whoever is here first shuts off the alarm."

"Right."

"How about the lock? Does the first person leave the door unlocked?"

"No, not that early. Kinda what we do is shut off the alarm but leave the door locked until time for the crew, ya know, sewers, the cutter n' helper, ya know when people start showing up we unlock it, leave it that way rest of da day."

"Take a moment, please be sure. Was the door locked when you got here?"

"Yep."

"You're sure because...."

Rose Mabris bent to her left, opened a bottom drawer in her desk and pulled out a large cloth purse, beige, with a print of deep red roses in the fabric. She opened it and took out a single key on one end of a bright yellow, florescent plastic key-chain with a silver dollar encased in plastic at the other end. "Gotit in Vegas. Keep my other keys on this" she said, taking out another, similar ring with car and house keys on it. "So this way I've got da key ready when I get outta my car, put my car keys in my purse, take out this key, close my purse, get outta the car, ya know? Always the same way, move fast. Never been a robbery, holdup, thank goodness, knock wood" she said, doing so firmly with her free hand on top of her desk, "guess da punks don't want to get up so early to purse snatch, ya know, grab this old thing.... so I open the door. If I'm first I close the door, turn off the alarm. If second just open the door, come in, close. So if the door was unlocked I'd know soon's I turned the key in the lock, wouldn't click, ya know? That ever wasta happen I'd stop right there, go get a cop. No, it clicked, door locked like always."

"So turning the key doesn't.... it unlocks it for the person with the key,

5

but when it's shut it is still locked, right?"

"Right. You gotta push a button on the side, when the door's open, ya know?"

"Yes, and someone would push that button when it was time for the rest of the workers to show up."

"Usually me or Amy, sometimes Mr. Vic."

"And the alarm was off."

"Yep. Green light, like now. Red when it's on. Green light, I figure the boss got here first, like he does sometimes."

"The rest of the workers don't get here until seven, right?"

"Seven-thirty. They get half-hour lunch, we don't pay, two breaks, should be fifteen minutes but you can guess how that is." She glanced at Terry, looking for some understanding, some recognition of the abuse of break times, but he sat impassively, waiting. "So start seven-thirty, half hour unpaid, half hour paid breaks, in the building, ya know, eight and a half hours, paid eight. Ya know?"

"Does whoever gets here first…no, let me start over. Are all the lights turned on by you, or Mr. Pritkin, whoever gets here first....does that person turn on all of the lights or only some of them?"

"Why d'ya ask?"

Terry smiled a bit. "You first."

"Depends who gets here first, ya know?"

"Depends how?"

"Me first, I just turn on the front, just the front, the desks, offices, but the boss he likes to wander, see it all, ya know, so he comes in and bang! all the lights, walks through the place lighting it up. He doesn't have an office like his children, coulda, he's the boss, no, he likes…. gone, ain't he. Shit. Sorry. Well, what I was saying is he *liked* being out there" she pointed vaguely towards the production area "kept a ratty old desk, army surplus, old metal thing must weight five hunerd pounds, ya know? But he liked it, it's out there near the loading dock, telephone, papers, everything whizzing around him, people comin goin, he liked it just that way." She paused. "A good man. A really good man. This makes no sense. I sure hope you find the guy what did this. I'm gonna miss that boss of mine, ya know?" A few tears, a wan smile.

"Yes, I think I do. So he got here ahead of you today."

"Like I told ya, but now you sound sure. How come?"

"All the lights were on."

"Mr. Detective" she said, tipping her head in salute.

"Did you see him, talk to him?"

"No, but that's the usual, ya know? Like if I come in first and I'm here he'd sure say hello, chat a minute, but just a minute, go back into the shop, turn all the lights on, mess with stuff, look in boxes, get tickets and shipping stuff ready, like that. So he don't bother me, I don't bother him.

So if he's first I see all the lights on, what I'm gonna do, go find him say hello? We see each other lots of times every day. So if he gets here first, I see lights on, I just sit down, start working, ya know? Once everybody gets here it can be nuts, plain nuts. Phones, people in and out, everybody needs Amy, ask me where she is like I'm a mind reader, people callin' can't speak English, gotta go get someone talk to them, nuts. So before seven thirty is best time for me, get lots a'stuff done. I told them they want stuff done on time best deal is I come in early quit early. Deal. So I get here six to six-thirty, not hard, go home around three, take a nap, can still play canasta with my friends later on."

"All right, let me walk through this one more time. Tell me if I've got it. You or Mr. Pritkin, one of you, is the first person here in the morning every day."

"Maybe four, five times a year Amy, but otherwise, yes."

"You, Amy, Mr. Pritkin, have a key. Who else?"

"Just Tony. He's a son, other one Pete, Peter but most call him Pete... Tony works here. Peter's in trucking, shipping, we're one of his customers."

"I'm sorry – Peter does or doesn't have a key?"

She shrugged. "He started out here, probably did, but he has his own business now, wouldn't need it."

"So you four, Mr. Pritkin, Amy, Tony, you, not counting Peter, the ones we know for sure have keys, also know the alarm code, right?"

"Yes."

"Anyone else know it?"

She shrugged, a large gesture. "Alarm company, a'course. I think at's all."

"And this morning you were second or third?"

"You mean Amy ahead of me? No, she... she was fourth. Counting the boss."

"Mr. Pritkin, then you, then Daro, then Amy, right?"

"Yeah, but Amy like one, two minutes behind Daro, at's all."

"How did Daro get in?"

"I opened the door. Not unusual she gets here early, set up the sewing. Conscientious girl, does a great job."

"Can you remember how long after Daro got here she started screaming?"

Rose paused. "Maybe five minutes, most, no more."

He thought about asking her about someone staying in the building, hiding overnight, but decided that might permanently spook her. Instead he asked "Is there a night-time janitorial service?

"After work? No. They come every day about three, clean the restrooms and break room. Once a month they come on a weekend, usually Amy or Mr. Vic here with them, I done it a few times, get some paperwork done, ya know? They do all the windows, dust and polish, if ya gotchur desk cleaned off they'll polish it, otherwise not. Go out in the loading dock, up and down between here and there, sweep it up good, anything we want. They're here by the hour, we want some extra cleanup they'll do it. The floor's all this tile" she said, pointing to the floor "or linoleum or cement, no carpet anywhere. But they still gotta vacuum some, cloth dust builds up, bits of fabric, ya know? Sewers got to spend the last fifteen minutes cleaning their area, get rid of scraps, sweep up, everyone does it, no production last fifteen minutes, everyone shares da cleaning. Nope. This building is locked up all night long."

Detective Terry Stans nodded. "Thank you."

He got up and walked the few steps to Amy's office. She was back at her desk.

"You sent everyone home."

"You saw them leaving while you were talking to Rose. Yes, I told them to take off until Monday. I also told them we would pay them something for today and tomorrow, not sure what, but some part of their usual pay."

Nice, he thought. "Can I take just a few minutes?"

"Sure, sit down. Learn anything?"

"Yes. I think the killer was either let in by your father or was hiding here overnight."

Her eyes widened. "Why?"

"The alarm, the door lock. There is only one alarm pad, right?"

"Yes, front door."

"We'll sure check, but I'm betting the alarm worked right, is working fine. So he was let in or hid here. Is that possible?"

"Wait, wait, let in... he could have come in with my father, right? Let in doesn't have to mean after my father was already here."

"No...I mean yes, that's right, came with or let in after. But whether he walked in the door with your father or came in, was let in a short while later, it was your father who admitted him. They were the first two in the building this morning, ahead of Rose."

"A robber? Guy with a gun waiting at the door?"

"To do what? Take his watch, his wallet? Both still on him, wallet still had money and plastic. Someone forces his way inside to walk all the way to the back of the building and kill him with a tool kept in that area?"

They sat a quiet moment. Amy spoke. "So it was someone he knew, trusted."

"That's my guess. But we haven't finished the hiding scenario."

She shook her head. "Maybe, but hard to imagine. I mean, you're talking about a stranger. Look around. This place is jammed full, only one story, people in every inch of this place, back and forth all the time. Plus the other doors....not the truck doors.... there are only two other doors, one's next to the truck doors, goes to the truck loading apron, the other is a fire door next to the sewers, both have those push bars, locked from the outside. Permanently. Keys locked away in one of these file drawers, have to dig for them. Sometimes the dock door will be held open for a while by a cement block we keep there, but that's only when someone's going back and forth, maybe doing something with a truck... and of course, smoking breaks, that's where they smoke... but that's when people are right there, sitting next to the door or going through it. When they're done they close the door again, everyone knows that, I don't ever remember it being left open with no one around, Dad made a point of that, everyone knew. So if someone came in the back way he would have been asked what he wanted. So two locked doors, really only way a stranger can come in is through the front door, and he'd be seen right away by me or my brother or Rose, or my father.... We sell to only about six, seven companies, have only a few suppliers, hardly ever see a strange face in here. And even if he got in the back door, or somehow got past the offices through the front door, where would he go? Like I said, look around. We don't even have a janitor closet, that's where the computer server is now, the janitorial and maintenance stuff is in a plywood cabinet we had built, sits outside the restrooms. No spare rooms, no place people aren't in and out of all day long. No, I don't think so."

"So your father let someone he knew in with him, front door, maybe they came in together, they walk to where he was killed, then the killer goes out one of the two other doors."

"My guess would be the back door. There's a small light over it, but unless he stopped and posed, or someone happened to be looking at that exact moment and has great eyesight, he wouldn't be seen."

"What's back there?"

"Large parking area, big enough for trucks to maneuver. Alley. Houses on the other side of the alley."

"We'll ask the people in those houses if they saw or heard anything, but I'm not counting on much. I think I'm going to earn my pay on this one. I have to ask you, where were you between five and seven this morning?"

"Waking up, taking a shower, eating a small breakfast, coming to work. I got here just before Daro found Dad."

"You're not married."

"Actually, I am. Wedding and engagement rings off my hand because we are split and I think it is going to be permanent. Really don't feel like looking at them right now, don't want to see them on my hand. I'm living alone in a one-room apartment, he's still in the house. He wasn't ready to bail, so I did. If we get back together... long if... I'll put the rings back on."

"You took back your maiden name?"

"Never stopped using it. Too many people, customers, vendors, know Dad... knew.... this is so hard....."

9

"We can stop now if...."

"No, let's finish, let me answer your questions, it just isn't easy to all of a sudden be using the past tense."

"I understand."

"So it was just people knew Dad, me, our last name, so I just kept it for business purposes more than anything. No kids, if that's your next question."

"So you were alone this morning."

"You're just doing formula, right? You don't really think I killed my father then, what... went out the back door, around to the front, and walked in cool and calm?"

"No opinions of any kind, way too early. Formula. Good term. Gotta ask."

"Sorry, Detective Stans, no early morning alibi. Empty Bed Blues."

"You haven't mentioned your mother. Were they divorced?"

"No, no.... deeply in love... she's been gone six years now. He never got over it... tried dating a few times, mostly because me and my brothers nagged him to, but nothing stuck. Old-fashioned love story, those two. Ended way too soon." Amy Pritkin folded her hands in front of her. "Can you solve this riddle?"

"I don't know. But I'll tell you this... I don't quit."

In the middle of his interview with Rose, as the employees were filing out past him, Terry noticed a man dressed in a shirt similar to Amy's coming in, looking quite distraught. Several of the employees touched his arm or said "Sorry" as they passed. Terry assumed it was one of the brothers. Now that man appeared in the doorway. "Detective, let me introduce my brother, Tony Pritkin. Tony, this is Terry Stans." Terry rose and they shook hands firmly.

"Sorry to interrupt."

"Just finishing up. I'd like to talk to you next, but if you need some time with your sister I sure can do something else for awhile. I'm trying hard to not be too heavy-handed, this was your father, I know, I'm sorry, really...so if I'm running a little too fast and you need a breather please just tell me."

"I appreciate that. Just... well, Sis, how are you? You all right, need anything from me?"

Amy paused, considered, shook her head slowly. "No, staff's gone, when the police leave we lock it up, start again Monday. Few things to do...change the message on the answering machine, see what trucks were scheduled for tomorrow, call them... except Pete, you or I can tell him."

"You reach him yet?"

"Yeah. Hoboken. Here probably next half hour or so. That's it... no, gotta call the janitorial crew. Don't need them today or tomorrow."

"Why don't you make those calls and then go home. I'll lock up."

Tony turned, faced the detective squarely. "I'm all yours."

"How bad is the coffee in the vending machine?"

Tony nodded slowly, up and down, as if approving, while saying "Pretty terrible, but better than the last vendor's brew. That was too weak. This at least you can dilute. Quarta milk's about right."

Terry smiled, bowed his head a bit and said "Lead the way." He turned slightly and said "Thanks again, Amy."

"Catch'um, will you, Terry?"

"I'll try hard as I can, and that's a promise."

The two men walked to the break room, Tony buying two coffees, adding two shakes of a powdered creamer, Terry's black. Tony was right, it was strongly awful, but if the body wants caffeine, the body gets caffeine. "Mind sitting here? I spend a lot of hours in my office."

"Not at all."

"Could you please take a moment, tell me…who found Dad, what……anything, I guess."

Terry got out his notebook but laid it flat on the table, not opening it, speaking from memory.

"I'm going to mix what I know with what I think I know, suspect. Lay it out as I see it. I'm hoping something will jump out at you… unusual, not regular practice…. something. But there may not be anything, so don't strain to find the missing clue." He shook his head, a small gesture. "May not be a missing clue." He took another drink of the black brew, sat up straighter, and began talking a bit faster. "Your father opens the door this morning, turns off the alarm. At that time the killer, known to him, that is, your father was comfortable in his presence, came in too. Either with him or your father let him in very shortly after."

Tony opened his mouth as if to speak and Terry paused. Then Tony frowned slightly, "No, sorry, do the whole thing. You're right, just roll it out like you're doing, then I'll ask questions."

"Good. I think that will work best. So…. so the two, let's say two men, although the killer could be a woman, but for now…. OK, the two men go into the building, turning on lights, as was your father's habit. They go, directly or not, all the way to fairly close to the truck bays when the other person kills your father with a tin snips, one very hard blow to the head. I'm guessing that is a tool found here, so it was a weapon of opportunity, which could mean a spur-of-the-moment act. Are they?"

"Sorry, my head is spinning. Are…."

"Are tin snips found here, are they a tool you keep in that area?"

"Yes, almost all the fabric we get comes in long corrugated boxes bound with flat strapping, metal or plastic, sometimes round wire, depends on who's shipping it. We use them practically every day."

"So the killer kills him with a tool found here. Have to wait for an autopsy, but I think one massive blow. I really doubt your father heard or felt anything beyond a split second."

Tony was a bit pale. "Wow" he said softly. "Wow. Fucking unbelievable. Why?"

"Sir, when we know that we will know the killer. Probably learn them both at about the same time."

"Because......"

"Because unless he was hiding something, forgive me, we have to check, but unless he was hiding ....something?.... I don't have a guess what that was, probably nothing....so, wait, this is getting backwards. Plain English. I don't think your father was hiding anything, I think he was a straight arrow, good citizen, people liked him. A lot."

As he said that Tony began to cry a bit, wiped his eyes with the back of his hand, nodded.

"OK, so a good guy walks to the back of his factory with someone he knows and trusts who kills him right there and then, and appears to have done it with a tool found here, so he didn't bring the murder weapon in with him. Which means, possibly, he wasn't planning on killing your father when he walked in the door, but something changed his mind. What? Why? Unless it was a fit of insanity, when we know the reason we'll know the person."

"You're sure it was someone he trusted. Not a... I don't know, a robber?"

"Watch still on, wallet still has money, and way back there, not closer inside, or even outside the door, or where he parks his car."

"It could be so many people, he knew so many....."

"It could be you."

Tony sat, unmoving, a long moment. "Was that police technique? That was good. My stomach feels like ice."

"Tony, I don't think you killed your father, but anyone who your father would readily admit is a possible. Not a suspect, please don't misunderstand. A pos-sible. May I ask where you were between five thirty and six this morning?"

"Sound asleep, alarm is set for six-fifteen."

"Your wife can vouch for that, I'm sure."

"Actually, no. We have two children, the youngest is just four months. Libby... that's my wife, Libby, her mother has been too ill to come from Tennessee to see the baby, so Libby flew there, took both kids, be gone a week."

"I see." It was said with complete neutrality, a neutral look on the detective's face.

"Not the best of alibis, is it?"

"No, but unless something pops up that bothers me I'm assuming it's the truth. I've found that lots of innocent people have no alibis; at the library, the Laundromat, went out for an ice cream cone...all alone, no one remembers them. Absolute truth, happens all the time."

"That's some comfort, but my stomach still isn't happy. Maybe it's just the coffee."

"I had to ask."

"Sure."

"Well, that's about all I know. There is no way of telling whether Rose got here just before or just after the crime, but it was close. Given the distance, and the walls and corridors and boxes between her desk and where it happened, she might not have even heard a gunshot. Not important, anyway, because I think he went quietly out the back door, the one by the truck doors. He knew the alarm was off, and probably knew Rose's hours."

"Staff?"

"Perhaps, or someone who got information from a staff member, or someone on the janitorial crew…or a delivery person, driver…… she ever chat with the mailman?"

"Sure, he's had the route for years, bad weather he'll stop for five, she loves to gossip. Harmless."

"Bet he knows what time she starts and quits."

Tony nodded rapidly, thoughtfully. He rubbed his face with both hands. "I see your point."

"Not long after your father gets here Amy arrives, stays in the front office. Daro arrives, wants to check the stock of white fabric before the day starts. She walks back there, screams, your sister… wait, left her out, I did. Rose, I left out Rose. OK, first your father and the killer. Not long after that Rose, then Daro, then your sister, those three in short order, and they're the ones in the building when he's found. Doors are still locked, and as your sister explained there really is no way someone could just come in during the working day, some stranger, and not be seen or challenged, so I don't think he was hiding here overnight. No, he was let in by your father."

They sat, both with about a third of a cup of rapidly cooling bad coffee in paper cups. Neither spoke for a time, and the detective opened his notebook and jotted in it, deliberately keeping his eyes down, not wanting to challenge, giving Tony time to think. After a long while, Terry opened his notebook and looked up.

"Ideas?"

"Zero. I mean, come on! Someone he felt he trusted does this for no reason in the world I can see, kills him? How do you investigate a no-reason murder that makes no sense?"

Terry Stans looked at him evenly, calmly. "You find the reason." A slight pause. "Why don't you tell me how things work here, who does what, help me picture the company."

Tony seemed relieved to be back on familiar ground. "Well, Dad, as founder, was the genius. He had to do everything at the start, and so as the company grew and we got involved he became the all-around helper. He just was an all-purpose pair of hands, probably the last ten years or so. It's a little hard to explain.….."

"You're doing fine."

"He just knew so much. Best way to do a temporary repair on a sewing machine. How to deal with cloth that was a bit musty when we unpack it. How to schedule shipments, keep the stuff flowing. He learned what the fire marshal's limits were, too, and kept us in check, which you can see is a problem. Pretty much the hour-by-hour manager of everything back of the offices. Not really manager, more like... what's that buzz word? Flow-through? Yeah, director of flow-through. Sure wish I'd thought of that while he was alive. Dad would of loved it, maybe a sign on his beat up old desk." He smiled a slight, crooked smile, wiped a few tears. "We don't do enough, say enough, for each other, take it all for granted. Now he's gone, and I can't tell him......"

"Human condition, sir, taking each other for granted. I'm sure he knew you and your brother and sister loved him."

"Thanks."

"Your sister said he lost your mother about six years ago, and that he wasn't dating anyone. Was that your impression, no one special in his life? I'm just trying to make sure I explore everything. Dead ends are a regular part of this job."

Tony smiled a bit at the memory. "Starting the day of Mom's funeral, Dad's been asked over for dinner by various widows and divorcees. He dated a little, once in a while, but just never had his heart in it. No girlfriend, if that's what you're asking."

"Please tell me more about how things worked, like you did about your father's duties... about yours, your sister's."

"Well... no, one more thing...don't know if it means anything.... the last year we've been sorta looking for a new place, and Dad's been…. he was working with the real estate people, looking at buildings."

"Why 'sorta looking'?"

Tony shook his head slowly, frowning. "Because we all know it will be a real pain, major major headache. How long are we closed, what do we pay our workers while they're out of work, who moves us, notifying suppliers... and how much do we let supplies go down? The less we have to move the better, but if we get too low in raw inventory then we could sit here twiddling our thumbs for a coupla days waiting for the moving van. And some of the sewing machines are getting old... will they be damaged in the move? Should we buy new ones? And how many more square feet? Some of the places are two stories, which is great, really expands the floor space, but the risk from fire goes way up with people on a second floor, so you have fire escapes to maintain, stricter regulations.... on and on. Sorta like a teenager getting braces; you know it's good for you but you'll be glad when it's over."

"Yeah, it does sound like a headache."

"And bankers and lawyers... we own this building, probably have to get a mortgage. Ah! So that's why we sorta look."

"I see. I don't see any link to the crime, but all information is good information. Thanks. And anytime something hits you, give me a call" he said, extracting business cards from his shirt pocket and handing them over. "If you would, here are three more, for your sister, Rose, and Daro."

"Sure. So you want to know my role, and Amy's, how we worked with Dad."

"Please" he said, picking up his pen again.

"I went to college, got a degree in business, generic major, some accounting, marketing, like that. Not sure I wanted to go into this business. Worked for the company since I was a teenager, of course, like my brother and sister, helping out, lift, carry, clean, learn the business. Dad always paid us...and Mom made sure we had lunch, and that we had time to be kids. So not a lot of hours, but some time. In college I worked here part time, helped out, but just wasn't sure. I guess it was too easy, you know, go to college, get the diploma, come home and they hand you the keys to a business."

"What happened?"

"Sometime around my sophomore or junior year the business really started to cook. It was doing alright until then, but always on the edge, only two or three customers, half the volume, no, less than half today's volume. But we do good work, low cost good work, and the reputation was growing, and about that time it just boom! took off, hiring more people, lots of orders, time demands. Dad stressed maintaining quality, turned down some orders, controlled the growth. He had only a high school education but a natural business sense, a gift. He said that quality, low-cost quality was the reason the business was taking off and we had to protect her. Talked like quality was a woman. She was the reason we were doing well, and we had to take care of her."

"Dance with who brung ya."

"Perfect. I guess I'm going to spend years hearing and saying things I wish I'd told Dad when I had the chance." He shook his head. "Don't suppose you want more coffee?"

Terry looked at the blackish liquid in the bottom third of his paper cup, which was beginning to absorb and soften. "No thanks, this will last about a week, I think. Tell you what. I want to hear about your duties, and your sisters, but I also want to walk out the back door, look at that area, the alley. Could we?" he said, gesturing.

Tony picked up both cups and threw them away. They started to walk through the silent small factory.

"Well, story short, I just said hell with it, why not settle into a business

I know and see where I can take it in my lifetime? So I graduated, went to Europe for the summer, risked getting killed on a motorbike on a small mountain road and contracting syphilis or AIDS or who knows what, spared by the fates, came home alive and well and....I said it, didn't I? Settled in. Made the right decision. Married man, doing fine. Until today, that is."

They walked in silence a few more steps, turned a corner and walked into the near end of the shipping and receiving area, the long room ending in the truck doors, a smaller door next to it. Although the floor was cement, dark and stained in spots, the sketched outline of the body showed which stain was Victor Pritkin's blood. Tony stopped, stared.

"I....I hadn't..."

"I'm sorry, Tony, clumsy of me. I should have asked, or warned you. My apologies."

"No, that's OK. I mean, we're going to have to walk right over that spot when business starts up again, aren't we. It's just... how, man this is hard to say.... how do we get it cleaned? Do you... do the police do it?"

"I wish we could. We can't even recommend companies, against policy, might seem like we're favoring somebody. Best I can tell you is look in the yellow pages under haz mat… hazardous material cleanup. They understand, though, so if you ask them to rush they can usually respond pretty quick."

Tony nodded, looking, not looking, at the spot.

"Daro must have been standing about where you are when she saw him. Yes. Came in this way, saw him, screamed, later sat down against this wall" he said, pointing to a nearby spot "and sat there until your sister introduced me so I could talk to her."

Tony nodded, solemn. They continued towards the smaller door. Terry looked at the push bar, paused, then pushed it and held the door open for Tony. Outside he let it shut and then pulled hard on the unyielding lock, looked up at the one-hundred watt bulb in the rusted light fixture, then turned and looked out at the gravel area and the alley and houses beyond, some with small backyard gardens, some with swing sets, a few with unkempt, weedy lawns.

"You didn't bother about fingerprints on the push-bar, reason being he was someone Dad knew, so the guy's fingerprints were probably there and on his desk and other places already, even before today. That right?"

"Well, yes, but more it's just that the bar must have thousands of partial fingerprints and palm prints, dust, maybe some oil from the truckers hands.... not going to be a help."

"Want me to continue?"

"Yes, let's walk, but sure."

"Well, that's about the end of my story. I'm married, two kids like I said, and I do the business stuff, work with the accounting firm, any legal stuff, usually the one signing the contracts, balance the checkbook....money management, cash flow, contractual obligations. Business one-oh-one."

They walked away from the building, the large gravel pieces moving and crunching under their feet. An industrial dumpster, a few pallets, gravel and struggling weeds. A rusting low chain-link fence, more to mark the property lines than to keep anyone out or in. At the alley Terry stood and looked in both directions. Just an alley in a long block, connecting both side streets. Just an alley.

They turned and started back, this time walking around the side of the building, across the paved employee and customer parking area.

"But my sister's got Dad's gift for this business. What I do could be done anywhere... doesn't matter if we were making refrigerators or pizzas or sports clothes, cash management is cash management. But Amy... Amy gets it, the whole clothes making thing. How to hire, how to train, how to maintain quality, working out piecework bonuses so they're a good incentive, not too easy but not too hard.... she's good, real good. I'm a manager. She's a clothing manufacturer."

"And your brother?" They had reached the front of the building. It was getting warmer, and neither made a move to go inside, but instead stood in the sunlight on the cement walk that lead to the front door.

"On his way here, should be any time now."

"No, I mean, I probably won't wait, your sister gave me his cell phone number, I'll just call, meet him someplace. Doesn't have to be right now. I meant, what's his role, why isn't he in the business? If I may."

"Sure, no family secret. He took some junior college but wasn't really interested. What happened is that we had been hiring trucking companies to do some pick up and delivery work. Who moves the material from the docks to here, then who moves it to the warehouses or truck terminals, it's not always the same trucking firm... it varies depending on how the deal is structured, who pays freight charges, who moves the freight. Pete always loved trucks, had a lot of them as a kid, like most boys, I guess, but he just kept loving them. So one day he says could we work out a deal? The company buys him a truck, or loans him the money, he becomes our trucking firm. Like a private, fully committed short-haul firm. We look at the numbers, talk to some leasing people for comparisons, work it out. So he starts with one kinda beat up but decent truck, at first works just for us, soon figures out he can transport some goods for nearby companies at the same time, idea is to keep the truck from ever moving without some kind of load on board. We said as long as we came first..." Tony shrugged. "'It was his truck, his business, but our stuff got first priority. That was about six, no, maybe seven years ago. Things sure have changed. I don't think he drives trucks at all anymore. He owns most of them, still mostly short-haul trucks, but he's got a coupla independents, tractors, the kind that pull the big trailers, under contract. We still use him some, but we're too small'a potatoes now, not big enough loads. Story short, he now has this fancy apartment in Manhattan, don't want to know what it costs... a few big trucks going out of state, mostly short haul between docks in Jersey and New York, port authority, airports, warehouses, customs. Like that. Same trick he learned here, have the truck moving empty as little as possible. Some story, huh? Maybe eight, ten employees, seems like a ton of money, and according to him too many girlfriends. Don't know about that last, Saturday nights I'm home watching some Disney movie for the six billionth time." Tony paused, listened. "Isn't it funny how every vehicle has its own sound, if you just get tuned into it? Methinks I hear Pete about two blocks away."

The sound was already getting louder, a combination of a high-revolution whine as the driver downshifted and the burble-rumble-burble of a tuned exhaust. In seconds an astonishing sports car in arrest-me red came into view.

The car turned into the lot, moving a bit fast, the turn of a driver, comfortable behind the wheel, who has made that entrance so many times that it is an automatic motion. The driver turned again, into the now empty employee parking area, just past that reserved for customers. The car stopped, the engine was turned off, and Peter Pritkin got out.

Peter was a bit taller than his brother and sister, who were within an inch or so of each other, but his height was enhanced because of his chest and arms. They weren't body-builder's muscles, but the biceps, back and chest of a dock worker, lifting and pushing, lifting and pushing. He walked along the side and around the corner of the building to the front, where the other two waited. He held out his hand.

"Detective Terry Stans, I assume?"

"Hello. My regrets on the loss of your father. We're going to try hard to solve this, I promise you."

"Thank you." He turned towards his brother. "How's Amy?" He glanced around the parking lot. "She's gone already."

"Yes, we let everyone go, no sense trying to organize anything today, or tomorrow, start again Monday. She was going to call anybody doing delivery or pick up today and tomorrow, head them off, reschedule, then she was going home. She's... she's doing all right, I guess, but she may have been keeping it together for the crew. For me too, I guess. Probably going to let go at home. She's going to miss Dad the most, don't you think?"

"Maybe. Yeah, I guess so, but we all will. Everybody, his friends....Mr. Stans, any ideas?"

"Please forgive me, time's getting tight, I've got to get back to the office, so if you don't mind I'd like to give you the quick version."

"Sure, of course."

"I think your father let someone in with him, or opened the door for him, voluntarily, that is, someone he trusted, very early this morning. I think they were the first two in the building. Not much more....really nothing. Tell you what, Tony and I just went over this, I laid it out for him, he can give you my reasons, tell you how I came to them."

"That'll be fine."

"Can I ask you where you were between five-thirty and six this morning?"

The three men stood on the sidewalk in front of the small, one story factory, the sun warming them and the concrete and the building front. Warm, not yet too warm. They were aware that from time to time a phone rang inside, rang only twice then stopped as the answering machine kicked in. Amy had set the system on night service before she left.

"Leaving my place in Manhattan, getting going. Kind of a pain to live so far from the docks, place I got my trucks parked, barbed wire lot, ya know? But I don't wanna live in Jersey, decided to live in Manhattan, party hardy, love it. Expensive as shit, but I love it. Deal is I gotta get up early, beat the traffic. Usual thing, doin' that today, this morning."

"Anyone see you, anyone with you?"

"Nope, struck out. Two nights ago, you shoulda seen her, tits like melons, hair to her waist. But nothin' last night. So I can't prove where I was, can I? Guess you gotta ask that, right?"

"Right." The detective smiled a small smile.

"So you ask mister businessman here?" Pete said, gesturing at his brother with a thumb.

"I did. Like you said, gotta ask."

"Amy too?"

"By the book. Actually, the word Amy used was formula. Do the formula, ask the question. Peter..."

"Pete, please..."

"...Pete, I appreciate your understanding, taking the short answer for now. And Tony, thanks for taking this time, going into so much detail. I know it wasn't easy. I'll keep you posted."

"Thank you. And good luck."

"Yes, good luck, Detective." Turning slightly, Pete said "I'm still trying to get my head around this. Dad is gone. No more having a beer with the old man, no more hearing his stories of how he started the business. I know it's going to be tough on you and Amy... hard to believe. Let me know if you need anything." He shook his head, looked down sadly. "Hard to believe. Who's going to take care of funeral arrangements?"

"Dad had most of that set, paid it in advance, said he didn't want us to worry about it. Let me talk to Amy, one of us will call you."

Peter nodded and gave a half-wave of his hand as he turned and walked around the side of the building, towards his car. The other two watched him. Tony spoke.

"That's a whole 'nother point, 'nother problem, isn't it?"

"Sorry?"

"Dad did a million things, just kept it moving, kept it all moving...one of them was call the truckers if we were responsible for the shipment, get the stuff in and out quick as possible. Someone's got to pick up that slack. Maybe have to hire, train someone......can't do this now. My head hurts. But it's a real problem... got to get together with Amy soon's she feels up to it... anything else?"

"No. I'll be in touch." Detective Terry Stans turned and walked back to his dark brown four-door sedan with the black wall tires. Tony Pritkin stood in the sun, feeling warmed, sun warmed yet sad and a little scared, and watched him go.

CHAPTER TWO

Two Weeks Later.

WYHAM popped up on June Replyn's computer screen. A WYHAM from Tal. He sent that same message at least once, sometimes three or four times a day, to each of his reporters. WYHAM. When You Have A Moment. Of course it really meant now, really meant, at worst, as soon as possible. If you were on the phone you could finish the conversation, if typing you could finish the paragraph, or at least the sentence, save the document, then grab your pad and pen and get in Tal's office. The reporters agreed that WYHAM was better than an editor sticking his head out of his office and bellowing a reporter's name. The Keystone Grill, a favorite diner one half block from the paper, offered *The Layout*, a tuna patty-melt, *The Masthead*, a double cheeseburger, *A Letter To The Editor*, a rare roast beef sandwich with gravy all over it and hot horseradish on the side. June thought of suggesting the restaurant add *The WYHAM* for a sliced ham on rye but thought better of it.

When up popped the WYHAM June was looking at the latest outrageously expensive slick advertising brochure from one of the newer Los Angeles fashion houses, a fashion house that had been trying to get more notice from New York newspapers and stores and customers. The photographs were of beautiful young women, faces pouting, frowning, or stunned, eyes made up to look as if they hadn't slept in days, all in hair cut surprisingly short. Their bodies ranged from thin to very thin, and they crouched or leaned against walls or sat with their legs apart, the silk dresses with dramatic but attractive prints tight to their upper bodies and spilling loosely over and between their legs. June recalled how her mother commented once, upon seeing such a marketing piece, "Didn't their mothers teach them how to sit?" They came to June's desk almost every day, and the senders, the fashion companies' publicists, all wanted June to write her very next column about the New! Fresh! ideas and patterns and shapes and sizes and is none of the knee shown or the whole knee or some upper thigh and it is the latest length for fall or spring or….

As she was deciding what to do with the undainty ladies, her computer chimed as the WYHAM arrived. Pleased with the interruption, she dropped the brochure on her desk. She picked up her pad and pen and walked to Tal's office.

"Morning. What's up?"

"Morning yourself. Got something different for you."

"Men's clothes? Men in clothes?"

"Well, dead men. One, dead man. Sorry."

"The latest in burial fashions?"

"Witty today, hmmm? This should calm you down. You read about the murder at ComFitter, two weeks ago? Founder of the company, they find him one morning in the shipping department?"

"Yes, I saw that. ComFitter. Cute name. Wonder if the founder thought that up."

"You get to ask. How about you get over to there and do a story on how they are coping, how a business created and built by one man carries on after he is suddenly ….. tin snipped…."

"Your witty turn."

"But seriously, folks….. no, really June, this could be a great story, right up your alley, something that's both fashion and business. Victor Pritkin builds up this little company, takes some of his kids into the business…. so here suddenly he is gone, not just gone but murdered. So how do the kids, the managers, keep the business going? Do they lose customers because customers liked the old man, but without him they go someplace else? Or maybe the business does fine, you know, sympathy, or just the fact that they get publicity. And who picks up the slack, takes over the duties? It's the suddenness of the loss, and how they were forced to adjust quickly, and are they sinking or swimming? That's the story."

"Sure. I like it. I'm there, although I may stay out of the shipping department."

June went back to her desk and pulled up a copy of the story on her screen. She typed Victor Pritkin in the "search for phrase" line, hit return, and up popped four items. For not the first time she thought about how time consuming - and dusty - it must have been to check archives before there were computers. Now it took about as long as a deep breath; inhale, exhale, articles ready to read. Four items. The first was from eight years ago, a story about the twentieth anniversary of the company. The story told about the founding of the company, and that it often offered opportunities for employment to recent immigrants with limited English ability. Victor Pritkin was shown in the finishing area holding up a pair of running shorts, surrounded by women at sewing machines. His was the only male, and the only Caucasian face in the picture.

The second was the story of the murder, the third the obituary, the fourth coverage of the funeral. She read these three in reverse order.

Victor Pritkin Laid To Rest

Victor Pritkin was buried today at Peacefield Christian Cemetery in Queens. A life-long resident of the community, Mr. Pritkin was laid to rest by his three children, Amelia, Anthony, and Peter. He was buried next to his wife, Irene, who preceded him in death by six years. Mr. Pritkin was the founder of ComFitter Sports Clothing, also located in the community, and was the victim of a homicide. Police report they have made little progress on the case but are actively pursuing leads.

Victor Pritkin, 56. Founder of ComFitter Sports Clothing, Bazervia Avenue, Queens. A graduate of West Technical High School, Yonkers. Mr. Pritkin served four years in the U.S. Army and six years in the Army Reserve, retiring as a Technical Sergeant. Recognized for his employment practices by the Asian Assistance Organization of Greater New York. Proceeded in death by wife Irene, mourned by daughter Amelia, sons Peter and Anthony and his wife Libby. Burial at Christian Peacefield Cemetery Sunday. Call Coumer & Sons Funeral Home for visitation and funeral service hours. Those wishing to make donations in Mr. Pritkin's honor are requested to support the Asian Assistance Organization of Greater New York.

Factory Owner Found Slain

Victor Pritkin, founder and owner of ComFitter Clothing, was found dead Tuesday morning in the shipping area of the factory at 2113 Bazervia Avenue, Queens. Mr. Pritkin was discovered by employees reporting for the first shift. Although details were not disclosed, a police spokesperson said that the death clearly was a homicide, and that a murder investigation is underway. Persons with information may call 770-6767 in confidence.

Mr. Pritkin founded his company almost thirty years ago. Initially the firm made sports-logo T-shirts and shorts under contract, but gradually moved into making low price sports and casual wear under its own logo, CF. In addition to Mr. Pritkin the firm is co-managed by Mr. Pritkin's children, Amelia and Anthony.

June called ComFitter and asked for Amelia Pritkin. There was a noticeable pause and then "Can I tell Amy who's calling?"

"Sorry, this is June Replyn, I'm a business reporter with the Courier. I only need a moment of her time. Thank you." Again there was a pause, then "hold on" and the line went dead. No music, but no dial tone either, so June assumed she was on hold. After a long minute and a half "This is Amy Pritkin. Can I help you?" Neutral but on the cool side.

"Ms. Pritkin, my name is June Replyn, I'm a business reporter, New York Courier. My editor has asked me to write an article about how your company is getting through this difficult transition period."

"Why?" Much cooler; this was slipping away.

"I assure you that anything I write will be respectful of your father, in fact will honor him as the founder of a successful firm, a firm which has provided employment to many immigrants. I read the article about the twentieth anniversary, nice story. And when I searched our archives for your father nothing came up about underpaying them or hiring illegal immigrants, not in all those years, and we certainly have stories like that about other companies."

"Yes, I know. Dad was always scrupulous about that, and about taxes. 'It isn't worth it to lie to the tax man,' I've heard him say that so many times. Every time a story would pop up about someone being indicted for tax evasion or hiring illegals or cheating them on their pay he would use it as a lecture and warning."

"And that's my story. A good man, an honorable man is suddenly gone, and the company must carry on. Who carries that...banner, that message, now? There was no time for transition from the founder's guidance, vision, so how does a company mourn, and of course a family mourn, and still carry on that vision while being forced to make a sudden, unexpected, painful change in leadership? That's what I want to tell."

Enough selling. At first there was no response. June wondered for a moment if she had erred in not making an appointment to sit down and say it in person, the phone approach might be on the pushy side, when Amy said "I really didn't tell his story, say it right, in the obituary. He built this shop from nothing, and did it the right way. I can't, none of us can imagine why someone would want to kill him."

"I'm sorry...."

"Here is my offer. I'll cooperate, give interviews, even let you talk to employees and tour the shop, but you have to make part of the article a celebration of him. It can't be just where do we go from here, but some of it has to be about him, about how he built the company, about what kind of a man he was."

"Absolutely. This is going to be a feature piece, Saturday or Sunday Business Section, maybe front page. I've got lots of column space, within reason. I can make you that promise."

"When would you like to start?"

Thinking "nice save" June said "This Friday? Next Tuesday or Wednesday?"

"Next Tuesday? We start at seven-thirty, so give me some time to get things going...does nine work for you?"

"Thank you. Nine next Tuesday, the seventeenth. I look forward to meeting you."

"Me too. Goodbye"

"Goodbye."

ComFitter was a small dark one-story brick factory, located in a section of Queens with similar companies lined up one after another. They were all about the same size, as small as seven thousand up to about forty thousand square feet, the larger ones two stories, not the modern large one-story factories found in industrial parks. These were buildings built when the word parks referred only to green places where children played and families picnicked, and if a production facility needed to be large it was built on a rather small footprint, two or on rare occasion three stories tall. Most had paved parking lots, although a few were gravel, and all had various ways of greeting visitors and receiving raw products and shipping their finished goods, although all were by truck; no rail sidings running behind these buildings, such service was provided to heavier industries in another neighborhood over a mile away. There were copying and printing plants, companies that made ball point pens and ice cream and the bright metal handles that people push to flush toilets. And ComFitter, low cost athletic clothing, shorts and tops.

In the several blocks surrounding this small industrial area were bars, diners, burger joints, pizza shops on corners or occasionally in the middle of a block. There were some churches and groceries and two bakeries, one dry cleaner, there primarily to serve the homes, the local residents, with few customers coming from more than ten blocks away. The rest of the buildings were those homes; almost every one two stories, mostly duplexes either by original design or adaptation. Some of the larger ones had been converted to rooming houses that served the immigrant population, and food items were now sold in the groceries that responded to that changing mix. The community housed people from Cambodia and Thailand and Vietnam, unknown worlds when the neighborhood was new many years ago.

Amy Pritkin was dressed in a white, short-sleeve shirt with ComFitter printed above her left breast. She was wearing jeans and those shoes June thought of as cross-trainers, exercise shoes. She greeted June, invited her into her office. It was old wood with large windows facing the front lobby and the several desks between her office and the front door. On every desk, and along the walls, space was devoted either to paperwork, a computer terminal, file cabinets or boxes that looked like they stored files. The place was so full that the phrase "fire marshal" came to June's mind.

As if on cue, Amy said "Getting pretty full up. We don't pay much attention, we're use to it, but the fire department checked us last week... we have sprinklers and the aisles are clear.... clear enough, that is.... but they weren't happy. Frowned a lot but gave us a passing score. A 'C' or 'C minus' I guess. We're thinking about moving, but losing Dad has put that on hold for a while. So, have you ever been in a sportswear factory?"

"No, although almost every other kind of clothing manufacturing. I recently got to see leather made; stinky process but quite fascinating. But no, never saw this kind of shop."

"Well, we try to produce good quality and high volume at the same time, not always easy to do, although we do have some great employees. By the way, they know you're coming. Anytime we have strangers walking through we like to let them know, otherwise they are all asking each other and spreading rumors and, well, not getting their work done. So I told them, and they're excited...you're already sort of a celebrity. Some of the folks who were working here eight years ago when the anniversary article ran are still here. That was a thrill, I know lots of them made copies to send back home. Many of our employees send money home; mostly Cambodia, a few Thailand and Vietnam. So they sent the article along with the money, and it was a big deal in their villages or towns, where they came from, especially for those who were in the picture. Of course, they had to translate it."

"Why those countries, why not, say, South America, or..."

"Companies like ours, where not a lot of communication is needed, where most of the skills can be learned by observation and a few gestures, and, to be honest, with modest wages...acceptable, but modest... they, companies like ours, tend to attract people with limited English. They bring over their friends and relatives, cousins...I talked to the owner of a company that makes special order pencils, advertising gimmicks, painted strange colors, ads on them, tassels instead of erasers...you know the kind."

"Yes."

"Well, three-quarters of his workforce comes from one tiny village in Guatemala! He hired a brother and sister, they were great workers, and one day he asked them if they knew anyone looking for work. Next thing he knows he's got a pipeline to this place he never heard of. But it's worked fine for him. Same for us. We hired some folks from Cambodia - totally broke refugees, really sad stories - got a good reputation, and it just grew from there. Turned out to be a good deal for us too, they're great employees. And I know a few Asian swear words, and the words in several languages for sewing and shirt, a few others."

A brief pause, then "So, would you like a tour first?"

"Please."

They walked down a hall, Amy explaining as they went. "The material

26

comes in large boxes, mostly manufactured in China. Sad to think that fabrics can be made there and shipped all that way, costs for freight and handling and customs and it's still cheaper than I could buy from anywhere in America. Really sad, but the deal is that if I decided to buy only American goods I'd go broke, have to raise the prices too much. So. So the fabric comes in, we check it, record it, then it goes to a cutting area. That's the most skilled position, the cutter, he has to follow the pattern, get the most out of the material by cutting properly, making the patterns fit like a big puzzle then cutting them out. Then we sew, pack, ship. That's really all there is to it."

Amy and June stopped in an area where boxes of fabric, great sheets of black, dark blue, and white, were stacked up, several opened. In the middle of the space was a large, flat table, about five feet on a side, a shiny metal laid down over wood, with stout wood legs. On top of the table was stacked material, and a man wielding what looked like an oversized saber saw was carefully cutting the cloth in the shape dictated by the pattern template.

They walked through a small archway to the next area, a large room full of sewing machines in rows, each with a small table next to it on the left and cloth bags and tags on the right. On all the tables was material, cut and stacked, ready for sewing.

Amy introduced June to Daroeung Chan. "Daro, this is the reporter I told you about, who's doing a story about our company. June Replyn, Daroeung Chan. Daro supervises the sewing department, which means she runs the company." Daro shook her head no with a shy smile. "She keeps the fabric coming and the finished product going, oversees break and lunch times, watches the quality, works with the cutter, and gives the single girls lectures on not getting pregnant." Again the shy smile, this time with a small giggle.

"Daro, I'm so pleased to meet you. When you have a few moments I'd like you to tell me what it's like supervising this shop."

"Not so good English" apologized Daro.

"That's not important. I just want to hear from you, in any way you want to describe it, about your busy day."

Daro smiled broadly. "So good." Something at the far end of the room caught her attention. "Please excuse" she said and hurried off.

Watching Daro go, looking at her, not at June, Amy said "Daro is the one who found Dad. She was traumatized, although she did calm down enough to talk to the police. But she was crying, shaking, talking to herself in her language.... I was afraid she would leave, but she is so strong." She turned towards Amy "I guess that's why she was able to stop crying and help the detective who was here, that strength. We've all picked up some of Dad's role while we figure out what to do, maybe hire someone, doing what has to be done... and I've noticed Daro is involved more with the shipping end of things, working with me the way he used to do. She's a priceless asset, and we make sure she knows we feel that way."

The entire piecework department was female, as June has seen in the photo in her paper's archives. About twenty women from Laos, Thailand, Cambodia, Vietnam; low income women working hard a long way from home, but living better and, for some, far safer lives than they had in their homelands. In person they were even younger and prettier, far prettier, than they appeared in the black-and-white newsprint halftone picture. They glanced up briefly, saw Amy standing with the reporter celebrity, but only brief glances; looking away could cause mistakes, and mistakes meant lower income. Bent over their machines, sewing seams ZZIIPPPP and joining fronts to backs ZZIIPPPP they worked steadily, worked hard. Their skin was, to a woman, almost flawless, their hair black and smooth and on some almost to their waists. They had tiny bodies and small pointed breasts. June assumed that once they got much past thirty it got just too hard, bending over like that, hour after hour, repeating those motions, ZZIIPPPP, ZZIIPPPP, ZZIIPPPP.... maybe they got married, or found other jobs. Why not ask?

Daro had made a circle around the room and was near them again. "Daro, please, can you answer a question now or is this a bad time?"

"Work so good, no machine broke, happy. OK time to talk."

"They all seem fairly young. Is this a young women's job?"

"It be like that. After while, they go, get 'nother job, work laundry or tailor shop or something, maybe food store. Some few go home country. See, this be good job for new girls, just come here, after follow some more older sister or uncle or someone. Can't speak no words English, got make some money, either sew this work or maybe motel change beds or some other job, few they be street girls, but know INS maybe send street girls back, some street girls made dead, so most work good, keep job here. Good work girls."

ZZIIPPPP ZZIIPPPP ZZIIPPPP ZZIIPPPP ZZIIPPPP A room full, ZZIIPPPP ZZIIPPPP ZZIIPPPP....

Daro continued. "See, this be piece work. We pay base just min'mum wage, that's all, min'mum wage. But we pay bonus, count pieces for day. That fair, people have slow times fast times, slow or fast in the day, so company say maybe you sew these many in eight hours you get min'mum plus dollar per hour for whole day, dollar more each hour, see?"

She waited. June nodded.

"But real most make least two dollar, two dollar fifty more, each hour. Some make more, some few lots more. They don't be gossip, you know, talk much, conversating, cost them work money, cost bonus."

Again she waited. Again June nodded.

ZZIIPPPP. Heads down, fingers moving, seams coming together, ZZIIPPPP, toss in the burlap bags for finished goods, numbered for each worker, take pieces from the other side, Daro and the cutter's helper bringing new pieces and taking away the finished, ZZIIPPPP ZZIIPPPP ZZIIPPPP ZZIIPPPP. All tagged for each worker so the hourly bonus, the bonus they worked so hard for, would be fairly counted. The company, like all piecework employers, had learned long ago that nothing, not clean bathrooms or free coffee or sufficient gravel in the parking lot to keep away the mud, nothing mattered like a fair and absolutely accurate count of the tee shirts and shorts coming off each machine. So two responsible people, two counters who packed the finished product, first counted and occasionally crossed over and counted the other's work. Flawed work was taken by those counters/inspectors back to the pieceworkers who ripped out the seams and re-sewed, but that didn't happen often; once the sewers learned their jobs it rarely happened. The pieceworkers worked fast, ZZIIPPPP ZZIIPPPP ZZIIPPPP went their machines, and having to rip out a seam by hand and re-sew was a time and bonus killer. So after a short time on the job the pieceworkers would go days, often two weeks or more, without any rejects. They would have the movement set, the rhythm; pick up the pieces, line them up by hand, hold them down, lower the needle, ZZIIPPPP, four or six times or eight times, depending on the piece, give it a tug and quick eye check, sew the elastic in the waist band if needed, quick drop in the numbered canvas bag and do it again, head down, steady cranking, earning that bonus.

June suddenly felt very soft, spoiled, and white. Pasty indoor unhealthy white. And older. "Thank you, this has been most helpful and interesting" she said. Daro nodded.

June and Amy walked into the break room. About half the sewers followed for their scheduled break time. The company kept the room clean and well lit and pleasant looking. Coffee and hot water with tea bags were always available, free, as were napkins, stirring sticks, plastic knives forks spoons, salt, pepper, and little packs of mayonnaise, mustard and ketchup. "As you can see, this is our break room. We try to keep it nice, clean, ask all the employees to help in the effort, pick up after themselves. They're pretty good about it." She paused. "I didn't get much of a breakfast. Would you like something?"

"Sure...."

At that moment a woman that June had seen when she came in, perhaps a bookkeeper, approached them looking worried. Amy turned towards her, and June decided to move away; this was business. She tucked her notebook into her large bag, walked towards one of the vending machines, selected a carrot muffin and a container of apple sauce, got a plastic spoon, took them to a table, then decided she wanted something to drink. Amy and the other employee continued to talk. June set her notepad down next to the food and went to the cold vending machines. She stood a moment, considering juice or milk, decided on milk. The machine didn't take her dollar the first two times, but after smoothing and straightening it the bill was accepted and the milk purchased. Returning to her table she saw a small piece of lined paper folded and tucked under her applesauce. She slid it out, opened it and read

i no pursn kil pritkin i cal yu tmoro 6 morgng

She read it, read it again, then looked up to see Amy walking towards her, getting ready to sit across from her at the rectangular table. June was wearing a suit with a fitted skirt, one pocket on her right side. In a gentle, small movement she slid the note into her pocket, then started busily opening the applesauce and milk, unwrapping the muffin. Intrigue, notes about murder in broken English on scraps of paper, were not ever part of June's world. She slipped it into her pocket without thinking; it was given to her in secret and her decision to hide it was almost a reflex. Now as Amy sat down June considered for the briefest moment taking it out, showing it to Amy – "Look what someone gave me" – but she didn't.

Amy had selected an American cheese on wheat bread, to which she was adding yellow mustard. Her drink was a sixteen-ounce bottle of grape-cranberry.

"Amy, how many languages does Daro speak?"

"You mean because of all the nationalities we have here?"

"Yes."

"Well, as far as I know just hers. But she does it, does her job, with a word or two of the pieceworkers' languages that she's picked up, and with gestures, lots of doing something while the others watch. She'll do something and shake her head no, frowning, then do it a different way and shake her head yes, with a big smile. A natural teacher. Very protective of her girls. That's what she calls them, her girls. 'My girls say need make Dr. Pepper in soda machine.' So, we order Dr. Pepper. Every once in a while there's a problem that needs to be discussed, but that really doesn't happen often. She's been with us almost ten years, have to throw an anniversary party for her. Like I said, she's priceless. We couldn't have grown this rapidly without her."

"But when you do have to discuss something..." June had her notebook out again, writing quickly.

"Well, we do the United Nations thing. One person speaks A and B, another B and C, another only C... so we get the right mix together, lots of arm waving and pointing and gestures, Daro right in the middle of it, but they straighten it out."

"That's just wonderful. I love it" June said, head down, writing. Then she looked up and smiled. "That's exactly the kind of thing that makes an article interesting, the human interest, human angle. I want to tell about your father and his vision, and how he ended up with a team of hard working people who have learned to overcome language barriers. Actually, not people, women, young women all a long way from where they were born."

They spoke some more about the company, about it's history, June taking lots of notes. After fifteen minutes Amy said she had to get back to work, so they threw away their trash and headed back towards the front of the factory. June noticed that the tour did not include the back part of the building, the shipping department where the murder had occurred, but she didn't feel like pressing the point. Maybe next visit. Meanwhile the note, like a tiny animal, burrowed warmly into her pocket. It rested against her leg, waiting.

CHAPTER THREE

June hoped she was reading the note correctly. Like all reporters, her usual hours were those that, as well as possible, fit both the newspaper's publication schedule and the schedules of those she reported on. With the exception of an early morning fashion shoot, most activities took place from mid-morning on; fashion shows in the afternoon or evening, phone calls rarely returned before noon. So June usually arrived at her desk at nine and worked until six or six-thirty, although a show could mean anywhere up to midnight. To be sitting at her desk at 6:00 a.m., ready to think and write and ask questions, would not be easy.

Her bedroom was perhaps a bit foo-foo, but it was her bedroom and to her liking. There was an old-fashioned makeup table with a mirror surrounded by small, low wattage lights that she had found in an antique store, and a flowered material draped over the table and down to the floor on both sides. When she bought the table the glass top was chipped and stained, so she ordered a new beveled piece of glass, a special order that cost a startling amount but was perfect. In front was a small chair with small arms, the chair covered in the same material as draped the table. A bit soft for a makeup chair, but just what June wanted, and she sometimes sat in it for a moment, just resting comfortably, before putting on her face in the morning. There was also a large, overstuffed chair and footstool in a different but complimentary flowered pattern, this one with twisting vines and curled leaves. Next to this chair was a floor lamp with a frosted light bulb for soft light. June never read in bed; she fought insomnia from time to time, and found that it worked best for her to read until her eyes were closing and then mark her place, drop the book on the footstool, turn off the light and get in bed. Once in a while she would fall asleep in the chair, but when she woke she would groggily get in bed, usually after a trip to the bathroom.

The bed was a standard double, with lots of pillows, big and small, with a small wooden foot board and a large wooden headboard with a rose carved in it. The headboard was a gift to her from Ted, and after he died she almost sold it because it was so intimate, so much theirs, almost too intense to sleep with. The bedspread had its own bouquets, the sheets and pillowcases were very good Egyptian cotton, 300-count, in solid soft pastels that worked well with all the flowers in the room.

Ted had been divorced less than a year when they met, and for June it was the first time she had taken a lover whom she thought would be her husband. Ted and June spent many but not all nights together. After a year they began to talk about maybe marriage. Then he had a stroke, thirty-four and he has a stroke and dies and she gets a call from his brother at the office and suddenly she is alone again. Alone again, and now that she is past thirty, two years past, trying to get comfortable with the idea of maybe never marrying. He has been gone now about two years, and she has no interest in looking. Being with someone would be fine, looking for someone would be hideous.

June never had to set her clock radio because she always awoke in plenty of time to be at the paper around nine, but now she had to subtract three hours. Thinking that this must be what it is like for people from Los Angeles when they come to New York for fashion shows, June set the alarm for four o'clock, stared at it and sighed, then made sure it was set on a classical station at a reasonable volume. She made decisions about tomorrow's wardrobe; less thinking to be required at that painful hour.

When the alarm went off there was a moment of sleepy resentment, and then for the first time she was really aware of what she was doing; investigating a murder without approval, dealing with a crime without her boss or the police knowing. The exciting anticipation of the phone call and the small warning bells going off, ringing about proper procedures and liability and job security, were enough to wake her up fully within moments.

When she joined the paper she also moved to this new apartment, a bit expensive but a long walk or short bus ride from work, and June had no doubt she had made a good decision. No long commute for her, and the apartment included one underground parking spot for her car which gained very few miles over the years. This morning she left early enough to walk briskly. The streets were much quieter than during her usual morning walk, and she actually felt wide awake and perky as she strode in the early morning light. She was sitting at her desk at 5:41.

None of the desks around hers were occupied, most wouldn't be for hours. June pulled out a story she was working on, spread the papers and clippings on her desk while booting up her computer. She opened the file and began typing, actually getting into the work, trying hard not to watch the clock. She certainly didn't want to sit with her hand hovering inches over the phone. Nevertheless, when it got to be 5:58 she stopped typing and turned, gazing at the papers on her desk, her brain in neutral.

June jumped a bit when the phone rang, told herself to relax and picked it up.

"Humanities, June Replyn."

"Is money I tell you?"

"I'm not aware of any money, any reward, although ComFitter may offer one. We can't pay you. I'm sorry, but newspapers like ours never pay...."

"So why tell?"

June did a quick think before answering. Money first, morality second. "If there is a reward you will get it, I won't. I promise you, that's the way it works. And there is a killer out there, someone dangerous that needs to be locked up." That sounded so corny June winced.

"Want money."

The phone clicked, and then gave a dial tone. June hung up and stared at nothing. That was it, the phone call was over. End of her career as a detective, a rather short tenure, about thirty seconds. Make a good story, laughs, some evening at a party. She didn't feel like laughing now.

June had no desire to be at her desk at one minute past six. She walked to a restaurant three blocks away, buying The Wall Street Journal on her way. She ate much more than her usual breakfast, her appetite sparked by the adrenaline rush, but it was a slow, sleepy day after that. She gave up at four, went home and took a nap, woke up later feeling terrible, upset and weird and yet hungry, ate microwave potatoes right out of the plastic tray, hot on top but undercooked in the middle, and went back to bed.

One Week Later

It had been three weeks since the murder, and it was obvious that the police had run out of leads. June considered telling them, actually telling her editor first, but there was nothing to report. She had gone over the conversation in her head, actually stored it in her pending file, but it seemed to have no value; revealed it might not get much reaction beyond "So?" Then the company issued a press release in the Sunday papers.

The ComFitter Company announces a reward of ten thousand dollars for information leading to the arrest and conviction of the person or persons responsible for the death of our founder, Victor Pritkin. If you have information please call 212 777 4444. All responses are welcome and will be strictly confidential.

Nothing happened the day of publication, nor the next day. The third day an envelope arrived. June recognized the scrawl, the lead thick and slightly smeared as if the pencil were pushed sideways against the paper. She knew it was going to be another six o'clock date before she opened the envelope, and it was.

reward call fridy 6

All right, go to sleep as early as possible. If possible. Two glasses of wine, a leisurely bath, a friendly but unexciting book. June set the alarm, did the wine and bath and book, got to sleep by ten.

This time she got to her desk at ten of, got up and walked around, got a drink from the water fountain, came back, switched on her computer. At six the phone rang.

"Humanities, June Replyn."

"I want this. You get money, maybe bag box money, give me, no person not see."

"I'm sorry, do you mean you want me to get the money, the reward, and give it to you in secret, no one sees us? Do I understand you? I'm sorry...."

"I know no good English. Is OK. Yes, secret. Give reward secret."

The first time it all happened too fast to really get an impression of the voice. This time she was sure it was a woman whispering in a forced, strained manner. What was the real voice like?

"Do you understand that the way the company set things up they have to arrest and convict... convict, that means, they have to prove, they have to go to court and show everyone the evidence, show he... or maybe she...."

"He a man."

"All right, a man, they have to... the word is convict, it means prove, it means...."

"Prove. Make show all village bad man."

"Yes." June hoped it was yes, it sounded like they were sharing, approximately, the same meaning.

"If the man is arrested and convicted, if they....show the village that he is the bad man who killed Mr. Pritkin, and the village, the people, the jury find him guilty and put him in jail, then you want the money in secret, no one to know who you are. I get the money and give it to you and it is our secret. Is that right?"

"Yes."

"Well, I guess that can be done, but I don't know. Look, you should know I'm a reporter, I write about clothes and the fashion industry. Maybe you need a detective, or a lawyer...."

"You. Trust you."

"Trust me? Why do you trust me?"

"Because you no police."

For a tiny moment her brain thought "know police" and she hesitated, then got it.

June slowed her speech a bit, enunciated carefully. "You trust me because I'm not the police, you don't trust the police, but because I don't work for them you believe you can trust me. Do I understand you corr.... right?"

"Yes."

"I'll have to ask some people, my editor, maybe our counsel...."

"Counsel?"

"Lawyer, the paper's lawyers. Have to ask them. But I will certainly try to do what you want." She paused. "How do I reach you? What is your name?"

"Name Pieceworker."

The pieceworkers were the women June had seen bent over their sewing machines, those who put the cut pieces together, sewed and added elastic and sewed some more then passed the garments to the inspectors and packers.

"Pieceworker. Pieceworker, how do I get in touch with you after I talk to my boss? And does it always have to be this early?"

There was a brief, tiny giggle. Now June was sure it was a woman, pushing her voice lower, making it gruff to disguise it. If it really was one of the pieceworkers then it was a young woman, the giggle fitting.

"You phone keep my talk, I not call you there?"

"You mean, if I'm not here, does my phone...."

"Keep talk. What I call say."

"Yes, it records calls. Yes, if you call and I'm not here it will keep it, record it, record your call."

"So good. I call morning, you still sleep" again a smothered giggle "call same day more later. Time you like?"

"I'm guessing you work seven-thirty to four. How about after work, about four-thirty? Or five?"

"Five. Every time five. OK?"

"OK. Look, I know I'll have some answer by tomorrow, so call tomorrow at five. No early call, morning I mean... just call tomorrow at five and I'll be able to tell you what I can and can't do."

"Five tomorrow."

Pieceworker hung up.

June again called up the articles from the newspapers archives, and they blinked on her screen in seconds. She looked at the picture again, the one with that happy white man surrounded by darker skinned women, all with fabulous dark hair. Was Pieceworker in the picture? Was she one of those women, smiling at the camera with their hands poised over their work?

The Next Day

Tal Sheets - editor of the HUMANITIES section that included fashion, art, music, restaurants, events-around-town, philosophy and religion, as well as the bridge and chess columns, the crossword puzzle and the funnies - was thin, six feet even, with thinning hair and a pointed chin and glasses which were forever being taken off or put on or propped on his head or stuck in his shirt pocket. June had long since given up trying to discern what situations, reading or short or long sight, he needed them for. He was a rapid talker but a good listener.

Tal's office reflected the wide range of subjects under his responsibility. It was filled with art work or bookcases on three walls, the fourth being the outside wall with two windows, below which were tables with magazines and newspapers from around the world. There were framed posters from museums and Greenwich Village jazz festivals. The bookshelves held Andy Warhol next to collections of crossword puzzles next to a collection of candid high-fashion photographs from the streets of New York between 1910 and 1920. When working alone Tal kept his door open almost all the time, seeming to thrive on the sounds of people laughing or calling out, phones ringing, cell phones chirping, computers beeping, desk chairs moving and squeaking. June didn't mind the sounds, actually had learned like the rest of the staff to simply tune them out. Still, it was a relief to lower the volume somewhat, to sit in the comfortable dark maroon chairs, and people regularly closed the door to his office.

Tal arrived at his usual 8:15, and June pounced.

"I have to talk to you about something very important. It's about the Pritkin, the ComFitter murder."

"The murder? Got some clues?"

"This is serious. Yes, I have a big clue…no, not a clue, a lead. Someone who claims to know the killer has contacted me"

"OK, serious time. How? Why?"

"Not sure why, I guess she trusts me. For the how......it's been only whispered phone calls - disguised voice, but I think it is a young woman - and scribbled notes … I was given a note when I was in the factory… couldn't see who gave it to me, actually it was left next to my food in the break room when I went to get some milk. And I've gotten a note and two calls, here."

Tal had been sitting behind his desk, but now he got up and walked around it and took his second desk chair, a twin of the one June sat in, and turned it towards her before sitting.

"This sure isn't the kind of story I usually talk about in here. Way outside. June, I've got to talk to the lawyer types, and of course to the chief, keep him posted."

"Of course. I told her that."

"She give you any name?"

"She calls herself pieceworker."

"Pieceworker? What is that, a lousy pun? Did she do it, finish him off herself?"

"No, a pieceworker is the main assembly person in the shop… almost any shop like that…the sewers, young women bent over sewing machines, paid by the finished piece. She says a man did it."

"Or not."

"Or not. Tal, this isn't your beat or mine. Do you want to pass this on? Will Larry make us pass this on to City?"

"To the crime reporters?" She nodded yes. "June, you didn't plan on working here, didn't take journalism in college."

"Closest I came was reading the campus newspaper. Daily Cougar."

"Well let me teach you a highly technical term. Have to know the secret handshake to use it. The term is big story. What you've got going here is a Big Story. If it were me, or any of the reporters here, or anywhere, we wouldn't let go control of this for…for….well, shit, no reporter is going to give up the chance to byline a murder mystery. Why should you?"

June smiled a little, pressed her palms together like shaking hands with herself, leaned towards him. "Guess I shouldn't. Little scared, maybe."

"Of booting the assignment or of dealing with a murder, maybe a murderer."

"Oh you are perceptive, aren't you? Perfectly perceived. Sure, I don't want to boot it…Pulitzer might be a stretch, but I'd like it to read well. And the other, well, heaven knows I've seen my share of murder mysteries and scary creepy killer shows on the tube…"

"You should be watching only fashion or nature channels."

June gave him a wry smile. "Yeah, sure, so tell me; how does watching baseball relate to the world of fine arts under your command? "

They paused a moment. June spoke more softly. "I never imagined myself a lady detective, despite my Texas upbringing I never held a pistol or rifle….hell, never had a slingshot, I don't think… so this is scary. Not thrilling like a roller coaster, just scary." Another pause. "But it *is* a big story, isn't it?"

Tal looked at her briefly, then got up and walked behind his desk, sat and put his hands over the computer keyboard, looked at her. "I'm requesting a meeting today with Larry, later for the lawyers. You gonna be here?"

"Yes."

"Your story?"

"My story. And since you're going to check with the legal folks I do have a question."

"We can wake up one of our attorneys from their morning nap and ask your question, do it right now. Question being…"

"Pieceworker wants to collect the reward without being known. She wants me to get it, in a paper bag, I guess, and work out a secret transfer. Can I do that?"

"Meaning legally can you do that….. well, I guess yes, but I'll check with the suits for you, important question. It seems to me that that could be very risky. I mean, going to a secret place with a bag of money to meet someone you don't know, who might or might not be involved in a murder? Scary at best."

"Very scary at best."

"But the question to be asked now is whether you, and the paper through you, can accept that role legally. How to do it and assure your safety is another matter, and we've plenty of time for that. Remember, the reward is for the arrest and *conviction* of the guilty, which might be a long time from now. Hell, if you get pressed say yes, you'll do it, you can always back out later, claim the bosses changed their minds."

"Thanks. Makes sense. You want I should keep you posted on this?"

"Most amusing, madam reporter. You betcha. Everything."

"Exactly the answer I wanted. Putty in my hands. Bye."

CHAPTER FOUR

June Mary Replyn was born and raised in Fort Worth, Texas, the second of two children not quite five years apart. She understood that her name came from favorite relatives, one a deceased grandmother, the other a favorite aunt, but she never liked the combination, not in that order. Mary June would have flowed more easily, a bit country she thought, sounds like gingham. After trying several combinations between the ages of six and twelve, including just Mary, she finally dropped that name on all except legal documents, not even a middle M. June Replyn, fashion business reporter.

Her father, James C. Replyn, started in retail sales and worked his way up, now employed as the senior vice president for marketing for a department store chain that specialized in comfortable, casual clothing, planning on retiring in just a year or two. Her mother, Sherie, was a retail consultant, working part-time designing layouts for all kinds of retail stores, new ones and those being remodeled. Her touch was so good that she could dip in and out of the market, offering her services and working like crazy on a project sixty hours a week for a month or two and then take a month off. Her older brother, Taylor Tremont Replyn, majored in accounting and marketing, and now like his father was a senior vice president, SVP of administrative operations for a high-tech manufacturing company near Los Angeles. So the parents had one child in LA and one in NYC. Vacations were usually in Texas or California, since Taylor was married with two children, but her parents, and rarely her brother and his family, did come to New York.

Raised in this environment, with her older brother taking accounting and business courses in high school, she spent dinner hours with two grownups and one nearly so, and the conversation was often on marketing and advertising and new product roll-outs; critiques of advertisements on radio or television or cereal boxes was common, not only criticizing the poorly executed or unclear ads but also praising the clever, innovative, and clear ones. June was encouraged to offer her opinions, and she was listened to as a representative of a key demographic group, the young teen female with emerging tastes and buying power.

In large part because of those dinner table discussions June entered college with a vague sense that she wanted to be in business, be part of the business world, although that choice was more from eliminating other career options than choosing a goal. Not teaching, not nursing, not pharmacy, maybe law? Certainly not engineering; words, not math, were her strength. But after one year and three accounting courses she was not sure of business, either; she could perform the required chores to pass the accounting courses but had no interest in doing so. Then in the second half of her sophomore year she took an elective called The World of Fabrics, figuring since, as a teenager, she had done some sewing with her mother, this would be an easy A. The course turned out to be more difficult and far more interesting than she had expected. The idea that people were making garments out of silk five thousand years ago - five thousand! - and using cotton and wool before that, and the first fiber, flax, perhaps seven thousand years ago, well, it was stunning and romantic and a little hard to grasp. In June's dormitory at the University of Houston were several anthropology students and sociology students taking courses on the history of civilization and comparative religion, and they had discussions about how humans lived more than five thousand years ago. They tried to imagine the total lack of almost anything those students knew to be daily life: electricity and toilet paper and running water and paved streets and motors, any motor of any kind, and sanitary pads and books and newspapers and plastic in all its many forms. One of the few things that those students could think of that they shared with those deep in pre-history, aside from the basic human needs and desires -food, shelter, water, warmth, sex - was fabric. Cloth made from a plant or animal, silk or cotton or flax or wool - how did they shear the sheep? - and wrapped around the human body. It seemed logical that soon after people learned how to make the fabrics and wrap them around their bodies dyeing started, capturing the colors of crushed berries or naturally occurring rust where iron-laden rocks were exposed to a stream or dripping water in a cave.

This course resonated with June like none she had taken before. She eagerly absorbed the names and histories of Rayon and Acetate and all the other manufactured fibers. She learned about thread counts and Egyptian cotton and tweeds and corduroy, about the history of weaving and looms and the rugs of Native Americans and Pakistanis and found it all fascinating. She got an A without really being aware that she was doing any work. At the conclusion of the course she knew which direction she wanted to head, something in the business side of the fashion industry, and so completed her studies with a major in marketing having taken every fabric-related course she could find.

After graduation she took a job as a junior buyer with a giant retailer headquartered in Ohio, made an excellent salary while working long hours, never less than forty-five, sometimes over sixty. Then, after eighteen months on the job, she spotted a want ad in a New York trade publication for someone familiar with the fashion business to write articles from the business point of view.

Living in New York, for at least a while, appealed to June, although it was a long way from Texas. But then, so was Ohio, and she had lived there comfortably and happily, so why not? She quickly but carefully polished her resume and wrote a cover letter. She got back a request for a five-hundred word writing sample, due in two weeks, on the marketing of faux fur coats and two potential barriers to success; overcoming both anti-fur and anti-artificial sentiments. One of her senior papers had been on manufacturing fake fur to appear as real as possible. The computer disks with much of her college work were sitting on the shelves of her former bedroom in her parent's home, still there just because they took up so little space that no one cared enough to throw them out. It took her mother a little searching to find it, but when she did the work was emailed to June, who used it to add technical facts to a well-reasoned marketing article. Two rounds of interviews followed, and at the end of the second they offered her the job.

Three fast years followed. June traveled some for the paper, interviewed managers and corporate executives and designers and models, but also sheep and cattle farmers and clothing and shoe manufacturers. She gained a reputation for presenting business fashion, fashion from a business point of view, in a clear and accessible manner; some finance and business management information, but not too much, so her articles were of strong interest to managers and artists, those who controlled money and those who draped fabrics.

Her office phone rang one day. "This is June Replyn."

"June, this is Tal Sheets, New York Courier. I'm editor of the Humanities section. I'd like to talk to you about coming to work for us. Can I buy you breakfast tomorrow?"

"Uh, sure, certainly, I'm surprised.... I'm sorry, Mr. Sheez?....."

"Sheets. Dozens of jokes about my name, all bad. First name Talarand, my mother is too poetic for her own good. Call me Tal. Where do you want to meet?"

At breakfast the next morning they were each served coffee and gave their orders, then Tal got right to it. "I want you to write exactly what you have been writing, no change. We've been working for some time on the concept that the more of the paper people read, the more they will treasure it. It's rough competing with television and radio and all the magazines, and we want people to see the whole paper as valuable to them, as much as possible. Sure don't want people opening it up in the morning and pitching a coupla sections by habit, never looking at them." He picked up the small pitcher of milk, poured generously, stirred it into his coffee. She waited. He made a gesture offering the pitcher to her, but she replied "Always black, thanks." He began again. "I like how you bring business and fashion together. We can give our artistic, fashion-oriented readers a little business information, education, without boring them, and pull some more business types, some suits, into the humanities section. Which is just what your article does, so I really mean it, I want you to come work for us and do exactly what you're doing now. But with greater resources. And for more money, not much, but more. So what're you making?"

June considered lying but told the truth, he offered her fifteen percent more, and they shook hands as their breakfasts arrived.

CHAPTER FIVE

After talking to Tal, June made sure she was at her desk at four-fifty in the afternoon. At exactly five the phone rang. "Humanities, June Replyn."

"OK you get reward give me no one see?"

"Yes, I can do it. We'd have to work out... never mind. Yes. Yes I can, I can give you the money, the reward, in secret, no one will see or know you or know your name."

"So good. Ready I tell name, you tell police?"

"Wait, wait.... well, yes, if you want to tell me his name, but that's not enough. That's not nearly enough."

"He bad man kill Pritkin."

"Remember we talked about proving, about ... you said show all the village. That's right. We have to... the police have to show *how* you know."

"You not make... you not sure I say true you."

"I believe you. That isn't enough. It isn't enough if the police believe you. You have to..... where you come from, people have gardens, grow vegetables, food for their families?"

"Yes"

"Let's pretend I live there. If I have a garden and someone walks through it and steps on my vegetables, ruins them.. you know...."

"Walk in garden, bad walk."

"So I have to show the village who walked in my garden, prove it by... I don't know, mud on his shoes, something... do you understand? Is this silly... I'm sorry...."

"Understand. Need some thing make prove sure bad man kill Pritkin."

"That's...."

"I try." The line went dead, then a dial tone.

June felt instantly bad, very bad about the conversation, almost nauseated. She felt as if she had encouraged a young woman to do something very dangerous, try to get proof, and didn't warn her, didn't even say "Please be careful." She looked at the phone in her hand and shook her head. "Please be careful," she said to the phone.

A Few Days Later

It was her second visit to the factory. When she got to ComFitter she was careful to park in the back, in the area designated for employees, not wanting to take any of the visitors' parking spaces, not wanting to risk offending. This time she spent the first half hour with Tony, learning about his responsibilities, how he missed his father, how the company had changed since his loss. He was polite, but gave fairly short, to-the-point answers, and was interrupted several times by phone calls. Although there was more June would have liked to ask, especially since she didn't get the value of a full half hour's conversation because of those calls, she made herself stop at the scheduled time. The same was true for Amy; as before she was polite and cooperative, understanding the concept behind the article, but this time her impatience was more evident. A busy place, minus one of the key managers. Of course they were stressed, of course they coveted their time. She was an acceptable but certainly not desired distraction. June told herself that this would have to be the last visit for a while, might have to write the article based on these two visits and a quick follow-up call or two.

On her first visit the tour had included the front office and manufacturing area, and the break room where she had received the mysterious note, but not the shipping department or loading dock. She wanted to see where the murder took place, but didn't know exactly how to ask the question. So she waited until the end of her time with Amy then said "Before I leave, would it offend you if I asked to see the loading dock? I want to describe it for our readers."

A quick, tiny frown crossed Amy's face, then she said "Sure, but if you don't mind I'll leave you there, when you're done looking around you can go down the dock steps to your car. Just please don't get in the way of the employees."

"Thank you, I'll just stay for a few moments. And thanks for the help, all the information. I think you'll like the story, I'm going to write about what a good and creative man your father was, and how you're working as a team to keep things going."

They went past the production, the final inspection and packing areas and through an archway. The area for shipping was long and rectangular, leading away from the arch towards two truck bays at the far end. There were boxes of fabrics waiting to be unpacked, a large industrial scale, strapping equipment, label making machines, tools such as screwdrivers and tin snips. Tin snips. And boxes finished, strapped and labeled and ready to be picked up. Workers came and went using hand trucks and a fork lift to move goods, or weighing and opening or closing and strapping boxes. In the middle of the long, cement-floored room stood a man with his back to them, wearing a suit. He was standing quite still, apparently taking in all in front of him.

"Detective, I thought you'd have seen enough of this place" called out Amy.

The man turned around. He was wearing a dark blue suit - "cheap blue" went through June's head as soon as she saw it, an automatic rating reflex - with an out-of-date red and blue rep stripe tie, plain white shirt and black, thick soled shoes. He looked like a cop in a B-grade movie.

But his face was nice. Strong, intelligent.

"Detective Terry Stans, Reporter June Replyn" said Amy.

"Hello" he said, and they shook hands. "Crime reporter, Ms. Replyn?"

"No, Detective Stans, business reporter, fashion, the business of the fashion industry."

"Oh?"

"I'm doing a story on how a company started and led by an entrepreneur deals with the sudden unexpected loss of that person."

He didn't glance around, looked only at her when he said "It looks to me like they're doing fine."

"I agree, but maybe that's the story. How the family, and the other members of the management team… actually the entire staff, pick up the slack, work harder, learn new skills." She turned towards Amy. "I mean it, I think that's the story. You've all kept on going rather remarkably."

"Thank you… well, he left us with a good strong company, set procedures, lots of satisfied customers… in fact, we've gotten some large orders since… since it happened…. We know most of our customers spread their business around, give orders to the competition so we all stay hungry for more, strive to please them.....but now they may feel sorry for us, or a bit guilty…whatever the reason business is booming. No, our problem isn't short term, it's thinking and planning for the future, continuing to grow and change without Dad's vision."

June was scribbling furiously in her small note pad. "Thank you."

"You're welcome. And now, because of that booming business, I have to go. The stairs to the back lot are over there. I look forward to your story, we all do. Terry, anything you need before I go?"

"No, thank you."

Amy turned and went back toward the production area. The two visitors stood there, watched her depart for a moment, then turned towards each other.

"Why are *you* here?"

"You mean beside the fact that I'm a homicide detective detecting this homicide."

"Sorry, better is why are you here today? The murder was three weeks ago, you must have been here many times, right?"

"Sure you're not a crime reporter?"

"Nope, fashion and the business of fashion. Ask me the difference between Rayon and Nylon. Go ahead. Or how leather is tanned. That's my beat. Turf." She paused. "So, why?"

"I'm here today…wait a minute, you're a reporter. Never mind."

"Not crime, don't have the right union card. How about if I pledge on my Girl Scout oath that anything you say will be completely off the record?"

"Girl Scout?"

"Troop 189, Fort Worth Texas."

"So you just want to know because you're curious, snooping around, want some inside skinny?"

"Yes, I admit it. So?"

He turned and started walking towards the loading dock truck bays at the far end. Not knowing whether or not that was an invitation, she followed. They stopped about twenty feet from the doors.

He turned and suddenly looked her in the eyes, deep in the eyes, straight deep down. "Seriously now, this is a private conversation, just us? I have to know, have to be able to trust you. Don't double cross me, you don't want the police department on your case. Or me."

June looked back hard, wanting him to know she was telling the truth. This had started as not much more than an idle question, crime gossip, but now was becoming something else, something critical, emotional, important. "Private conversation."

He paused just a moment, then took his eyes from hers and looked at the floor, pointing. "This is about where they found him. They cleaned it all up, but this is pretty much the spot. Ms. Replyn…"

"June, please."

"June, Terry. This is it. It's very early in the morning, he is often here early, lifetime habit. So he's here and he is walking toward those doors and he is killed. Why? Why here? We can't be sure, but it doesn't appear that he was running, and there isn't any sign of a struggle… he is just killed dead right here. I keep looking around…. Trucks parked outside, fabric coming in, scale, fork lift, hand trucks, strapping equipment, boxes ready to strap, boxes ready to label and seal… what? What is it, what was he going to do or take or look at or…. or does it have nothing at all to do with this part of the factory? Maybe he was killed here but the reason is somewhere else… in the office or at home or a million miles away. Sound like I'm stuck, June? I am." He paused. "I'll be honest, OK? I'm willing to talk to you like this because maybe you will stumble onto something, may already have and don't even know you did, something you were asking or told that I'd never think about because you're coming at it from a totally different angle… you want to know about the business. Maybe it's something about the business. We'll check the books just in case, but my gut tells me that what we just heard is the truth; look around, it's obvious things are hot, lots of sewing, customer's trucks being loaded. So unless someone was skimming money, books don't balance, then it wasn't that, not a white collar crime. But it could be something else, a business slant you could find that I wouldn't because I don't ask the right questions."

"I don't know, but I guess I can share my notes with you. Have to ask my editor, but I think I can, don't see why not. There aren't any secrets, and most of it will be in the paper, anyway."

"Would you like to see what we've got so far? You share, I'll share. But you can't use it, not a word, in your article, unless I approve. Deal?"

"Deal."

She said she could come to his office the next morning at ten, and they agreed. They shook hands, and then she headed for the dock stairs, her feet already starting to hurt from standing so long on the hard cement in her pointed shoes with the spike heels. Next time she came here she would choose footwear with less fashion, more comfort.

CHAPTER SIX

Although June knew there were guns in the world, had seen them in museums and antique shows, and in television and movies, she had never seen so many, real and loaded, in one room. Men had them under their armpits and on their waists; uniformed police came through wearing them, men and women in uniform with black leather holsters and enormous pistol grips sticking out. They all had the power to kill right there, inches, seconds, from being unleashed. How do they feel carrying instant death on their hips? Do they ever tremble at the thought of what is available, ready, or is that not professional? And even being as cool, cold, and professional as possible, doesn't one still tremble at the thought, way, way down where no one can see?

Detective Terry Stans greeted her politely, brought her to a desk that didn't seem to belong to anyone in particular, a stray in the middle of a large area with many desks. He indicated a chair, a battered but comfortable swivel chair with five legs splayed out to five enormous brass-colored coasters that rolled easily on the wooden floor. He handed her a file and said he'd be right back.

June had seen dead people before - grandparents, friends of her parents, her Ted who died far too young - and others, funerals always, but she had never seen police photos of a crime scene. It was shocking but easier to look at than she expected - it wasn't a known, loved person, just a picture. Pictures, many of them, close-ups of the handles of the tin snips protruding from the skull, medium distance, long distance, side angle, front angle.... oh, it was gruesome, but also astonishing; the tin snips stuck deep in the skull, so deep that it remained embedded when he fell face first onto the concrete floor. Just wham! The tin snips crashing into the skull and he is unconscious, dead? before hitting the floor. Yes, that is what it looked like to the medical examiner, one tremendous blow from behind, likely a right-handed assailant. Assailant. Who but the police used that word in the twenty-first century?

So someone with strong hands and arms and total, unwavering determination deals one deadly blow, so severe the victim just crumples and falls and never moves again. Why was his back turned? Didn't hear him coming? Didn't hear *her* coming, June thought. Plenty of women strong enough to do that, deliver that blow. But again, why was his back turned? Didn't hear is one possibility, totally trusted is another. Did the victim have a hearing problem?

"What do you see?"

Terry Stans had returned with two coffees in great white mugs, both slightly chipped and cracked. He reached toward her with one, gave it to her. The heft felt good. She took a sip; the coffee was strong. How did he know she drank it black?

"What do I see? A test of deductive powers?"

Terry drank coffee, looked in her eyes, nodded.

"All right. Well, I did read the report, but I looked at the pictures first, and I really think what I saw gave me the same... ideas, information.... that was in the report."

"Being?"

"I see he was killed with one blow, because his head is unmarked and undamaged except where the tin snips are.... are...." June struggled for other words, gave up. "Where the tin snips are." She shook her head a bit, annoyed with her answer; she certainly could be more articulate than that! Terry stood there, almost unmoving except for his right arm and the coffee mug that was lifted for another sip. She asked, "Did you get any fingerprints?"

"No lab report yet, they're really backed up. But I don't expect anything... here, how would you hold these if you wanted to strike with a lot of force?" He opened a desk drawer, took out a large pair of office scissors and put them in front of her.

"I guess...like this" she said, wrapping her hand around the blades, just below the handles. "Grace Kelly, *Dial M for Murder*, right?"

"Right. Look where your fingertips are.... so there might be a partial, likely not a full print. Now hand it to me like we are working together, like I just asked you to pass me the tin snips."

June turned the scissors in her hand so that she held the bottom of the blades, the handles toward him.

Terry looked at their hands as he took hold by the handles, nodded, then put the scissors back in the drawer. "So there will be partial and full prints and palm prints from top to bottom, probably every inch of the tool... and accumulated oils from human hands, maybe even a bit of light oil from tool maintenance... in short, that's not how we're going to solve this case. And?...." he said, like an encouraging teacher.

"It was done by someone fairly strong, although it probably doesn't take a lot of force to drive through a human skull."

"That's right, it doesn't. Depends on the weapon, of course, a common table knife wouldn't be easy, but a solid pointed tool like that.....anything else?"

"Am I missing something obvious?"

Suddenly he swooped down and sat straddling a straight-back wooden chair the wrong way, facing her from quite near. June noticed he didn't spill a drop although he had moved surprisingly fast. She could smell him, coffee and something, after-shave probably, just a hint. A man smell.

"Fresh eyes. You've got fresh eyes, not use to looking at things like this. That means you don't know what to look for, but that could be as big a plus as a minus. We agree on the first point, he's someone strong….."

"But it could be a woman."

He arched his brows, a slight look of surprise.

June answered his look with "I see women work out in the gym who could do that, plenty strong enough."

"I agree." He was still close. Was he coming on to her, or is this just police station world-of-work protocol; sit close, be intense, think hard. "More?"

"I think it has to be one of two things…situations. Either he is hard of hearing or he completely trusted the killer. I don't think he was hard of hearing, because there isn't a hearing aid in either ear. Of course, we… you…could just check with his family doctor, but…I don't think he was vain; if he needed hearing aids he would wear them. So I vote for trusted person."

"Why don't you think he was vain?"

"Ah, my professional expertise at last. Because this was a man who built up a company from nothing, was quite successful, and still dressed middle class. I saw a picture of him with some of his workers, picture's about eight years old, and he is wearing a rumpled, off-the rack suit and nothing tie. And here…" she indicated the picture "…these look like cotton work slacks, and a short-sleeve shirt. Even if it was too warm to wear a suit jacket, if he cared about his sartorial image he would have been wearing a long-sleeved dress shirt, probably monogrammed, almost certainly with a tie. No, not vain, no hearing aid. He was killed by a trusted employee …or a friend."

June's eyes widened a little as she said those last words. The betrayal suddenly jumped in front of her.

"Excellent work, madam detective, excellent. I give you a ninety-five. You lose five points because you are too nice to say the obvious."

"Too nice to say the obvious? I want my five points. What?"

"Go back to your last conclusion and see if it doesn't need a little more, if there is something else…."

"He was killed…..by a trusted coworker or a friend….or a relative. A member of his family. Maybe one of his children."

"One hundred points." He smiled a bit, set his coffee on the desk and continued sitting close, manly, legs wrapped around the chair.

June was so aware of his closeness, so aware he was inside her space, although he made not one gesture or facial expression or leer or quip that was in the least flirtatious or even man-woman. All around them the police station noise of phones and conversations and laughter and shouts and desk chairs squeaking and drawers and doors shutting firmly continued. June and Terry sat, tight in conversation, so close.

He reached for a pad and pen. "OK, now what do we do?"

"Don't detectives always have partners? I know police work, I've watched television, you know" she said with mock haughtiness.

Terry smiled, nodded. "Usually, yes, but we're so short handed. Had some promotions and retirements hit, some transfers, some guys injured and not back yet, so several of us older hands are working alone for a while. Backup when we need it, never go on an arrest alone."

She wondered how old this Older Hand was. Close to her age, but how close? And which side?

"Any lady detectives?"

"Sure, quite a few, some of our best. One just made lieutenant, got promoted and transferred to the one four. Why, thinking of changing professions?"

"No, just asking a professional woman question. Almost a reflex, sorry, anytime I see lots of men in power I want to know if the sisters are getting a fair shake."

He sat staring at her, a long pause. "If the sisters are getting a fair shake? Chocolate, strawberry, or vanilla? Or peppermint, one of my favorites."

"Never mind, never mind, can we just rewind and delete the last few moments? Please? You asked if I am thinking of changing professions. Do you really want to know?"

"Well, it was just a wisecrack, so now *I* apologize. Let me ask it this way….how do you like being a reporter?"

"I feel like I'm learning every day. No, not feel like, I *am* learning every day…. thanks to my editor, mostly. He keeps pushing me to expand, explore. I appreciate that, appreciate the support. Obviously he could have taken me off this…I write about the business of fashion, not murder…but he said go for it, he'll back me. I've got a business education, not journalism, but I always could write clearly, always did well in English Comp and… composition, I mean…"

"I know what comp means."

He said it in a neutral, informative manner, but June felt sudden heat, embarrassment from having insulted him.

"Yes…of course, well… guess you're thinking I hope she writes better than she talks…."

"You like ribs?"

A sudden shift in the conversation, and June was feeling a bit fuzzy; the aroma of coffee and manbody and after-shave and sitting so close, his legs wrapped around the chair, open to her…she usually was articulate but now was stumbling over words.

"Ribs?"

"If you don't mind getting messy, sauce on your clothes, licking your fingers… I know a great place in Jersey, bit of a drive but worth it. Maybe Friday after work?"

June was aware that she had just been asked on a date, the first time in a very long time. He was so close, yet pleasant… not scary, not intimidating. "Uh, sure, ribs, guess I'll have to pack a change of clothes if it's that messy."

"Sure, old jeans and a shirt you don't mind staining. If you don't end up wearing some sauce you weren't digging in hard enough. I mean, ribs and potato salad and black-eyed peas, greens and cornbread. What time?"

"Six?" Things were happening so fast.

"Yes, no, make it six-thirty, let the traffic cool down a bit. Pick you up in front of the paper?"

"Maybe you should pull up in back, there's a place you can sit near the rear entrance so you won't have to worry…. oh…" June scrunched her face and shook her head in exasperation.

"What?"

"I was going to say, if you park near the rear entrance you won't have to worry about the police making you move… you know, if you're in front…. dumb…."

"In front, 6:30. The police come I'll just tell them I know you." Suddenly in one smooth move he stood up, reversing the motion that had deposited him spread-leg on the backward chair, a graceful, athletic move. June wondered about the strength of his body, his legs. His legs.

He held out his hand and she shook it, it was warm and dry and firm. "Gotta go, my lieutenant is giving me the 'enough with the conversation' look, something cooking. See you Friday." He gave her a warm smile while looking right down into her eyes, then was quickly gone. June realized her nipples were hard.

On Friday June packed a change of clothes in a duffel bag, figuring that would cause less interest in the office than a suitcase. She was right, no one noticed it or commented, and when six o'clock came many of the desks were already empty, so she just picked it up and headed to the ladies' to change. Two voices were starting to get fairly loud in her head, persistent and annoying. One was how happy she was to be going out on a date, a date with this man. She was attracted to the calm detective who liked to sit close and look into her eyes, mentally attracted, sexually attracted.

The other voice, worrisome, nagging, spoke in stern tones about the information she had that she wasn't sharing. Withholding evidence, interfering with police business, obstructing an investigation…. perfect way to start a relationship with a policeman. Perfect way to *end* it. Forget about a romance; he finds out he'll be so angry that he'll walk away from her. Worse, arrest her! Throw her ass in jail. Read her her rights, handcuffs... which thought suddenly crossed to another part of her brain which reminded her that she had read about handcuffs and bondage and other make-believe bedroom games, but never tried them.... She shook her head, clearing the thought away. Back to the problem. This is something that has to be disclosed. It might be valuable, help him ... the police..... him... close the case. Solve the crime.

And yet, thought June, and yet....this could be a big story, a story of bad, bad people and bad deeds, murder by tin snips in the head and maybe, likely, tin snips swung by a friend or family member. A Big Story. June realized when talking to Tal that she didn't want to give it up, give it to the city desk, and revealing Pieceworker to Terry might drive Pieceworker underground, so that June would end up on the outside of the story, or maybe with no story at all. What to do?

June decided to leave the duffel and dress and shoes it held folded and locked in her credenza, a light brown piece of heavy furniture she didn't use much. Take them home Monday. She walked out the front door promptly at 6:30, and he was parked right in front of the newspaper, a no parking zone, leaning out the window chatting with a motorcycle policeman ... police*woman*, June realized. She hesitated a moment, then walked toward the passenger side of the car...knock on the window? But the policewoman raised her eyes, and Terry understood and reached across the seat and opened the door a bit. Was the officer looking her over, judging, rating? Perhaps. Terry waved goodbye as he pulled away.

They made small talk on the way to the restaurant, Terry not volunteering information about the lady in uniform, June not asking. As soon as they got there and opened their doors the smell of barbecue and wood smoke and crisping fat hit them, and June was instantly starved. They ordered great plates of food and cold beers. While waiting he asked her about her career, how she got into newspaper work, and she told him, then asked about his career. He started to answer as the food was served, a brief but most welcome introduction, then told her between bites.

"My father is in the security business. He wanted to be a cop but had dropped out of high school to help the family, my grandparents had been divorced, grandma didn't have much...and even then they required a diploma. So he became a security guard, Osmus Security, ever hear of them?" June nodded, mid-bite. "He did a good job, got promoted, been with them for over thirty years now. He's in charge of recruiting and training, goes out on spot checks at night. A good man."

"So you caught the bug from him."

"Yeah, although he never pushed me.......always talked about police and respect for the law as important, and I admire him, so I guess it just happened, sort of naturally."

"What a fine role model to have growing up."

"Want to hear one of my favorite stories?

"Sure, but I want you to have a chance to eat."

"I eat way too fast, bad habit, and police work adds to the problem… I can eat a double cheeseburger and chocolate milkshake in about two minutes."

"You don't look like you eat cheeseburgers and milkshakes."

He looked right into her eyes with that way he had that was deep and piercing but not threatening.

"Been looking at my body, have you?" How could he say that as he did, calm, not blushing? He might as well as been asking her to pass the ketchup. June got only as far as "Uh…" and then stopped, stuck. Inarticulate again! He picked up the thread as if nothing had happened.

"I'm the oldest of four, and the next one, my brother, is almost five years younger, then next year a sister, then the next year another sister, so I was always the Big Brother to the three of them, helped raise them. So here's the story. My father had an old friend, Mr. Zazimin, Zazzy everyone called him. Mr. Zazimin owned a used car lot, one of those small corner places, twenty or so cars at a time. Every December he'd let the number of cars start to go down, sell them and not replace them, until he had about half the lot cleared, then he'd set up a Christmas Tree lot. Neighborhood place, neighbors bought there, regulars, nice little business for him and fair prices for the folks. Anyway, he and my father had a deal. My father would wait until the last day, until the 24th, and then Zazzy would sell him any tree for half price. The best trees were long gone, of course, but the half price let him buy a big one, and we'd keep it up for at least two weeks. It was a good time, getting it home and quick dressing it up but not turning on the lights. Then we'd go to sleep and in the morning there were presents and the lights on."

"Sounds like great fun for you kids, although your parents were probably up late."

"Yeah, then we woke them up early, so they didn't get much sleep." He took a few bites, put down the fork. "This one year, I'm nine, Mom's home with the babies, Dad and I go to get the tree. Well, Dad didn't make much money back then. He made enough, but he was feeding six, and there wasn't much slack. So we get there and Zazzy's out sick, took sick that morning so he got this kid to run the lot, kid that sometimes worked for him cleaning up and washing the cars. He doesn't know about Dad's discount, says Mr. Zazimin said the price is the price, that's all he knows. Dad didn't bring enough money with him, so he tells me we've got to walk home, talk to Mom, decide on a big tree for more money or a smaller one, ugly squat trees but cheap. The lot's going to be open another four hours, and we only live three blocks away, so no time problem, but the few half decent trees might be gone by the time we get back."

They both ate a bit more. June was trying not to hurry, she didn't want to finish way ahead of him, so she kept putting her fork down, not easy to do because it was delicious.

"So we start home and it starts snowing, getting colder…then we turn the corner one block from our house and there is this tree, this beautiful, beautiful Christmas tree, half in the street. Looks like it might have fallen off a car or truck, but there isn't any string or rope around it, no broken branches, just there in the street. We go look at it, look at each other, I don't know what to say. But my father did. He says 'someone must of lost this, be back for it. If they don't come in one hour it's public property.' Said that like it was a known law, like 'don't go in swimming right after you eat,' like that, a rule for everyone. Got to wait one hour, then public property. So we wait. Me and Dad, snow coming down, cold, we moved the tree a bit so it wasn't in the street, then started to wait."

"This is all one block from your home."

"Yes, but we couldn't leave it, give up our claim. And there was never a question of my leaving. I mean, I never considered it. This was our adventure, we two men, we hunters, and we had found our quarry and would not abandon it for a little cold and snow. So we sat there on a stone step. Every once in a while Dad would get up and walk in a slow circle, stamp his feet a bit, sit down, then I'd do the same. I was freezing and had to pee so bad I thought I'd die, but I wasn't going to quit. Neither of us said a word, all that time. Then finally he looks at his watch and says 'fifty-eight minutes.' I had this vision of a truck tearing around the corner, reclaiming the lost tree with sixty seconds to spare, but it didn't happen. Then Dad just said 'Yep' and we walked to the tree, he picked up the trunk end and I got the top and we waltzed it home. It was the most perfectly shaped tree we ever had, in fact that I've ever seen. And my mother was in the bathroom, so I just ran out into the back yard, into the alley, and peed up against some bushes by the garage for what seemed like ten minutes. What a night."

He smiled at her at the conclusion of his story, returned to eating. She did too, and for a few moments they ate in silence, comfortable, comfortable with the food and the spicy, slightly smoky atmosphere and each other.

"Might I inquire into your marital status?"

He put his head back and laughed out loud, looked at her and laughed some more, coughed a bit and took a long pull of his beer. "Might I inquire into your marital status? Isn't that cute. Sorry, the formality struck me as funny."

"It was a bit formal. Want to hear the best way?"

"Sure!"

"Secrets of the sisterhood. The best way is.... if you ask a man if he's married it's too easy for him to say no, even if he is. So instead of a yes-no question you ask 'How long have you been divorced?' and see whether he stumbles around suspiciously."

"I'll remember that one, nice interrogation technique. Well, my marital status is divorced, married five years, decent lady, just didn't work out.

Fortunately no kids, she's long gone, living in Maine I think, married, two kids last I heard. Haven't talked to her or any mutual friends in quite a while. Ancient history. Present status not married. And you?"

"Was engaged to a fine man. Stroke, of all things, never thought people our age had strokes. Gone in an instant."

"Sorry. How long ago?"

"Little over two years."

They talked some more, a bit of family history, food favorites, music favorites. Agreed they were both far too full for dessert. He drove her to her door, parking right in front of the apartment, in front of the No Parking Loading Zone sign. He walked her to her door, they shook hands, he waited until she was safely inside.

CHAPTER SEVEN

Detective Terry Stans hadn't had time to talk with Peter Pritkin at the factory on the day of the murder, so he called and made an appointment to meet a few days later on the harbor docks.

Every day sixteen thousand or more sealed containers arrive in America, disgorged from the holds of giant vessels docking in the ports of New York and New Jersey and Brownsville and Grays Harbor and many other deep water facilities. The total exceeds six million a year, all the responsibility of the men and women who stand between the nation and what might be in those containers. Of course, the majority of items are legitimate and properly paid for, and include almost anything you can find in stores except fresh fruits and vegetables. Almost anything. The problem is that tucked in among those legitimate items are things we don't want to let in; endangered and protected wildlife, foreign plants and bugs, heroin, cocaine, hashish, illegal chemicals or parts for bombs or even guns or bombs, and people, sometimes people who didn't survive being shut up in containers for the long crossing.

Many of the containers hold two thousand or more square feet, the size of an average house, a house with every single room filled as tightly, as compactly as possible, wall to wall, floor to ceiling. This is the challenge facing those looking for contraband, and not having a lot of time to do so, because containers keep arriving. They use high-tech devices to scan and search, sometimes dogs, but the volume is truly staggering, and rarely do more than three or four percent of all incoming containers undergo stringent inspection. But it's not a random three percent; containers from some countries are more suspect than others, simply because of history, of past attempts at smuggling. Others have special seals, electronic and virtually impossible to tamper with or trick. Of course, that implies that the shipping firm is trustworthy, or else the wonderful electronic lock is guarding contraband. But by targeting certain containers from certain shippers and countries, by trusting high-tech locks and scrutinizing some documentation and paperwork more than others, the effectiveness of the inspectors is greatly increased. They may only look hard at three percent of the containers, but that three percent is the most likely to carry illegal freight.

Terry was stopped at a gate that provided an entranceway to the docks.

He showed his badge and was waived through. He drove between two warehouses and came to an area where massive cranes filled his vision, cranes capable of lifting tons of goods, over and over, day after day. Behind those powerful machines were long, dark freighters, ocean-going vessels, some riding higher than others at the side of the pier, depending on how much of their load they still held.

He spotted Peter's shiny red sports car at once. It stood out, the only vehicle like it on a pier full of trucks, large and small, and the occasional older four-door car. The scene almost looked like a commercial, so great was the contrast. He parked next to it, got out and looked around. Everywhere men were moving, lifting, driving, signaling directions to the crane operators, driving fork lifts, moving in and out of the warehouses. Suddenly Peter was at his side.

"Hey, Detective, check it out. Our newest truck." He pointed to a large six-wheel vehicle, dark green everywhere except the lights and handles. On the door, in addition to the required identification numbers and certificates, were the words COTTON FAMILY TRANSPORT, INC.

"Cotton family?" said Terry.

"So Tony or Amy didn't tell you the story?"

"Nope."

"Haven't told this in a while, most folks I work with know it. Anyway - so I decide to incorporate, ya know, form my own business, like that, so I do the stuff and go to the government office to register the name and suddenly I realize I don't have a name for the company. You know, I was going to call it Pritkin Trucking or Peter Pritkin Trucking or something, but I'm standing in line and I start thinking what the hell, I'm all grown up, don't want business cause people know my family, want it on my own, you know? So I get to the clerk and she asks me what the company name will be and I stand there, thought I knew the answer but now I'm stuck. The line's getting longer, people are getting antsy, and so the clerk says so what does your company do and I sez it transports cotton fabric between the docks and my family, the family business. So she says why don't I call it Cotton Family Transport for a while till I think of something, I can always change it, but other people want their turn, I got to finish and get out of line. So I call it that, never went back. That's the story" he said, opening his hands, palms up.

"So you get letters addressed to Mr. Cotton."

"All the time, ads, magazine promotions, yeah, all the time."

"Pete, let me ask you a few questions. I got a lot from your brother and sister, maybe just fill in some for me."

"Sure. Want to go inside that warehouse? Quieter there."

"No, thanks, I think it's interesting, all the cranes and trucks, people moving all that cargo."

"Yeah, those things can lift tons and tons, pick up heavy cargo containers like you'd pick up an orange. Got to be careful, though. You get several tons moving, even a few miles an hour, it hits you it will toss you like a limp rag."

"I'll remember that. Pete, as I told you I think someone was let in by your father, someone he knew, then for some reason that person killed him. Any thoughts about someone your father would view as a friend, or at least a trusted person, someone he knew..."

"Who really was mad at him, sort of a secret enemy?"

"That's good, yes, a secret enemy."

A man on a fork lift inside the nearest warehouse shouted something. Suddenly a driver appeared in the Cotton Family truck cab; he had been slumped down, resting. He started the truck, backed it up to a platform on one side of the warehouse. As soon as he set the brake on the truck the loaded fork lift began moving toward it, ready to transfer the goods from warehouse to truck.

"Do you need to take care of something?"

"No, everything's fine, shipment will be on it's way to Moonachie in just a bit. Had some things to straighten out, get some things set for next week. Could do this over the phone lots of times, use email some, but I gotta tell you I like being here, salt air and diesel exhaust, big machines... I like it." He stared up at the closest crane starting to lift another sealed metal container then looked back at the detective. "Sorry, back to.... well, no, answer is no. Can't imagine someone that angry at Dad. Just can't. Oh he was tough on some things, but always honesty things, you know? 'Good quality is everything, customer always right, do it right the first time, take care of the pennies and the dollars will take care of you, your good reputation is your greatest asset.' Probably a dozen more, over and over and over to me and Amy and Tony. Damn thing is he was right, right as rain, I run my business that way, find myself saying exact same things to my drivers, sound just like him. But you know what? I'm making money, and I'm doing it Dad's way. He was right. So did that deal about sticking to quality and not cutting corners make it a little hard sometimes? Yeah, but not near enough to get mad about, certainly not crazy mad to kill him over."

"Anything suspicious recently, your father say anything about an unusual problem......"

"Man, I have been thinking and thinking. Not one, nothing, sorry. Business as usual, he was his same old self last time I saw him."

"Where and when?

"That Monday, the week he was killed. At the shop. Just talking shipments, just business. We don't do as much with them as before, more into units, larger shipments, going to just one or two places. Leave the smaller drop-offs to package carriers, like that. Still, sometimes we pick up their stuff, especially if it's going from the factory to a warehouse or wholesaler in this area."

"And it was just a regular Monday."

"Yep. Talked to him, my sibs, had some cookies one of the sewers baked, left. Regular Monday."

"OK, thanks, that doesn't surprise me, fits with what your brother and sister, and Rose, all said. So far not looking like an easy one to solve, but I'm on it, we're going to work this one hard for quite a while."

"Still having trouble thinking about it, getting my head around it."

"I'm sure you are, and I really mean it, you have my condolences. He was obviously a good man, honest businessman. Can't have too many of those."

Peter Pritkin nodded his head in agreement, stuck out his hand, they shook firmly. Detective Terry Stans turned, walked to his car, got in, backed and turned and drove away. Peter watched him until he was out of sight.

CHAPTER EIGHT

The invitation came in the stack of mail that dropped into one of June's in baskets. She was going through the envelopes and flyers and bulletins and catalogs and announcements, a necessary but somewhat tedious chore, when she came to the invitation, opened it and two tickets fell out.

The Cooper Hewitt National Design Museum is not nearly so well known as the larger and better funded and better advertised museums in New York, and tourists find it as much by wandering by after visiting a nearby more prominent museum as by seeking it out deliberately. Yet it is a jewel of a museum, housed in a wonderful mansion that was once home to Andrew Carnegie. It is beautiful inside and out, and has a collection that focuses on the importance but also the style and grace of the items we use every day. Chairs, necessary for sitting, but chairs that are also clever and original and charming. Other items for the home, of the home, presented so that the visitor can consider them in a new and different way. Consider them as art.

The Cooper Hewitt National Design Museum of the Smithsonian Institution is pleased to present a dramatic and nostalgic look back.

You and your guest are invited to a premier showing of STYLES OF THE CENTURY, a sampling of men and women's clothing from 1900 to 1999.

Thursday, July 10, 6:00 p.m. RSVP (212) 849-8380

The nice looking detective with the moderate price suits had been on her mind. She wanted to see him again, and had been considering just calling him up and taking him to dinner, her treat this time, one of her favorite places. But this seemed even better. She had been with him on his turf, noisy police station and smoky ribs house, so let him spend some time on hers, see if he can maintain that cool, unruffled manner when surrounded by sequins and boas and zoot suits.

She called the station. "New York Police, Station Nineteen."

"Detective Terry Stans, please."

"One moment."

The phone rang three times, then she heard "One Nine, Detective Stans."

"Hello, Terry, this is June Replyn. How are you?"

"Fine, thanks. And you?"

"I'm well… would you like to go to a museum with me? Exhibition, one of those events before it opens to the general public."

"Wine and thin crackers and artists?"

"First two, probably yes. No artists, well, designers as artists, maybe. It's at the Cooper-Hewitt, clothes from nineteen hundred to nineteen ninety-nine. Sound interesting? Or not? I mean…

"Sounds interesting. Ever go to a car museum?

"When I was a kid, don't remember much."

"I like doing that, seeing cars from different eras, so sure, let's see the clothes they wore when they rode in those cars. And carriages, too, if it goes back to nineteen hundred. Thank you. When?"

"Week from Thursday, the tenth, six o'clock."

"Tenth….yes… would you mind if I meet you there? I have to testify at a trial that day, not sure when I'll be called, but judges don't keep things going to six, so I'll be there.. might be a bit late, but sure, thanks."

"I'll leave a ticket in an envelope for you at the door.

"Six or soon after, Thursday tenth, the Cooper-Hewitt."

"Yes. Good."

"Goodbye."

"Goodbye."

June wondered what to wear. After all, it was the second date. That meant something, as did the fact that she called him, as did the location itself, a museum exhibition of clothes. A careful check of her closet yielded no inspiration, so she purchased a simple summer dress, well made and flattering. Hem just above her knees, softly moving material to draw attention to her shapely legs. Tempting and easier to ride the bus, but she often took the long walk to and from work, and her legs benefited.

On the day of the show she got to work early, left early, showered for the second time that day and spent extra time on her hair. She topped it off with a few drops behind each ear of an outrageously expensive perfume saved for special events. A quick final check in her mirror. She smiled at herself, said "Looking good, I like the dress," picked up her small purse and left the apartment.

The wait for a taxi was less than a minute, and she was at the museum at ten to six. She looked around, no Terry, actually not a lot of people yet. At the door to the exhibit sat a woman in an expensive light gray suit taking tickets; obviously a volunteer. June showed her ticket and asked that the other be held, handing her a small envelope with T. STANS on it. Now, where to wait? The answer was obvious, go on in, look at the exhibit, mingle, don't seem anxious. Don't stand in the lobby nervously crossing and uncrossing her arms, that looked too, too eager.

The exhibit was wonderful. Clothing, about seventy percent for women, had been assembled from museum collections, university and professional prop rooms, and people's closets and their grandparent's homes. There were, as June had anticipated, sequins and boas and zoot suits, also cloches and other hats big and small, padding here and there, waists more or less thin and fixed low on the hips or almost to the breasts. People were coming in, the room was filling. She tried not to glance at her watch but did so a few times, very quickly.

It was ten after six. June stood in front of a mannequin dressed as George Raft or Humphrey Bogart would if they were portraying a tough detective in the gangster era; dark suit, white shirt with simple pattern tie, fedora pulled down low over the eyes. "Too bad cops can't dress like that today" said Terry behind her. "I would love to wear a fedora. Always liked those movies where everyone's wearing them. Bunch of bad guys, standing around talking tough, going to rub someone out, all wearing suits and fedoras, inside and out."

She had turned when he started speaking. He had come up behind her, so when she turned they were quite close. She took a step back, but just a small one. Still close.

"Yes, and the detectives wore theirs pulled down like this" she said, indicting the mannequin "and the newsmen wore them pushed way back."

He turned and really looked at the mannequin. "Yes, that's it, that's the look. Not much change in the suits, but the hats are gone. Wonder where the word comes from?"

They were now side by side, not quite touching. "What word, fedora?"

"Yes."

"It's the name of a French play, not sure of the pronunciation, fay-dora maybe, around eighteen-eighty or eighteen-ninety. Starred Sarah Bernhardt... lots of fancy costumes, and she wore a hat in the play, something like these, center crease, brim…. actually it was picked up by women first, called by the play's name. Didn't become a man's hat until many years later, but the name stuck."

He grinned at her. "That is one of the finest pieces of trivia I ever heard outside a sports bar. Don't know if I can ever use it, but it's a winner."

"You aren't making fun of me, are you?"

They had turned towards each other again, still that small distance between them. "Not at all, no, I love trivia. Did you know the term gumshoe was originally used for people who snuck around in shoes made of gum rubber, usually sneaky thieves? It wasn't till later that the term came to mean the people who caught the thieves, the police."

"Not gum on the shoes from walking the beat?"

"Popular misconception. Original meaning long lost, like fedora."

A hiccup in the conversation. Now what? "I don't know how much detail you want, or if you just want to wander. I can no doubt tell you far more about these fabrics and eras than you'll ever want to know."

"Let's wander, see what there is to see."

It was a well designed exhibition. People pointed to garments and said that their mother or grandmother had worn something similar. There were various items scattered about that went with the era being shown; an early electric iron, shoes, LIFE magazines, wallpaper, photos of old autos as backdrops. Terry the detective and June the reporter walked, looked, commented, sipped white wine. Unstoppable professional reflex, she noticed his clothing choice for the day: blue sports jacket, tan slacks, light blue shirt, tie with brown and blue stripes, dark brown shoes. "Sort of" was her assessment.

After forty-five minutes they had made the complete circuit, read the plaques, done the exhibition. It was past seven, and June was starved. White wine on an empty stomach, time to eat! She turned to him. "I'm very hungry. Tell you what... these tickets were free, so far this has been a pretty cheap date. How about I spend some money on you? How about we go to dinner and I pay for it?"

"Sure, lead the way."

They discovered that they both had come in taxis, June from the newspaper and Terry from the court. They walked five blocks to a Greek restaurant, had Ouzo with an ice cube turning it from clear to milky, big salads with crisp lettuce, deep red tomatoes, lots of feta and mysterious, wrinkled, wonderful olives.

She asked him if there was anything in the exhibition that caught his eye. He answered he really liked the cream zoot suit from the forties and her dress. They took a taxi to her apartment, and the driver waited while Terry walked her to her door. The kiss was easy and natural.

CHAPTER NINE

At ComFitter business was strong; as Amy guessed it was a combination of regular customers and sympathy customers and the tragic mention of the company's name, which was nonetheless free publicity. Things weren't going smoothly, however, because Victor was no longer there, and his duties of working with the truckers and customs agents and freight forwarding companies had to be picked up by someone. After a while Amy and Tony hit upon hiring a college student part-time, a major in transportation and logistics. It turned out that the duties could be taken care of in about twenty hours a week, and with their support the student could coordinate the goods moving in and out of the factory. But Amy and Tony couldn't replace what Victor had done during the rest of the hours he was there; poking around looking for problems to solve, quickly fixing the sewing machines when they faltered, having coffee or a beer with old clients to keep the relationship personal, not just business. Being a friend, a warm presence, a nice guy representing a nice company. Victor was missed, and in some ways would never be replaced.

June sat in Tal's office, going over the list of ideas and stories she was working on.

"How's the ComFitter story coming?"

"Been there twice. I think it will be a good story, sort of as we outlined, decent man starts and builds a small business, becomes a family business, suddenly he is murdered, how do they carry on?"

"Family cooperative?"

"I had to assure that it would be not just the murder and the aftershock, how they carry on, but also praise of him, Victor, the kind of person he was. Since it looks like he was near sainthood I'm glad to do that."

"Who would murder a saint?"

She looked at him, shook her head in puzzlement. "Got a guess?"

"That's easy. Any number of evil folks, crazies. The big question is why? Why murder a saint?"

June shrugged. "Don't know, and since there haven't been any arrests, I think the police are stuck. But I'm moving ahead on the story, want to get it written soon."

"Good, good. Have it ready, but hold it, might be a break in the case and we could run the two together... City story about catching the bad guys and our story about carrying on. Anything new?"

"Lord and Taylor changed advertising firms after six years. I'm hoping they'll tell me why. So far they've just said 'business reasons,' but I've got some friends inside, going to poke around, see if I can get a hot quote."

At home at night June thought about Terry, wondered if he would call. He asked her, she asked him, guess that made it his turn. Would he call? Will he call? June sighed. Years without dating since Tim's death, and now here she is, back to "Will he call?" The man was starting to take a bit of her time, occupy a small corner of her mind. Only two dates, small corner, but a presence nonetheless. The museum visit had been on a Thursday. All quiet on the weekend and Monday and Tuesday. "Fun while it lasted" she thought, pushing him away, ignoring, walling off that little corner. Work extra hours, read a book, watch television, go for a walk, go to sleep early. Alone.

"Humanities, June Replyn."

"Hi June, Terry. Sorry I haven't called, really busy. Building up comp time like crazy. I'd like to see you again."

"Me too." She said it without hesitation.

"Dinner and a movie Friday?"

"Yes, sure."

"How about dinner my place, I'll show off my gourmet self."

Quick quick calculation. Take a cab to his place, keeps all options open. The calculation caused the tiniest hesitation. "Thank you, sounds like a good time. And I look forward to your display of cooking skills."

He ignored the hesitation. "Preferences? Things you don't, can't eat?"

"Not real spicy hot, easy on the Tobasco and cayenne. That's about it."

"Fish? Seafood?"

"Do it. May I bring the wine?"

"Sure. Wine for seafood."

He gave her directions, they agreed on the time.

June couldn't help, automatic reflex, appraising Terry's clothes and apartment furnishings; fabrics, color, fashion were her profession and great interest. Like his clothing, the apartment was clean, neat, and done in several shades of blue and brown. And some gray. Not depressing, but certainly not colorful or bright or cheery. Utilitarian, safe, clean, and not a hint of the presence of a woman. It needed a woman's touch. And bright colored throw pillows.

The menu was orange roughy, rice pilaf, a tomato and mozzarella salad with a herb dressing. Quite delicious. They talked some about his work, about being a uniformed officer, they talked about her growing up in Texas and becoming interested in the worlds of marketing and adverting.

"Excellent meal Terry, excellent. Thank you."

"You're welcome. I thought dessert after the movie."

June smiled and nodded. Dessert where? Back at his apartment? "Good idea" she said.

Terry had offered a choice of three movies: an old fashioned western, a spy thriller set in the cold war fifties, a comedy about an on then off then on again wedding. She voted for the spies.

They got to the theater almost twenty minutes early. They spent some more time talking about their first jobs, their early careers. June found his description of being a rookie cop fascinating.

"Tell me some police secrets.

"Like what?"

"Something, I don't care. Just a peek inside that secret world."

"Here's one. If you're on patrol and have to….go…I mean….not just pee but...."

"Number two."

He looked at her, tilted his head, smiled. "'Number two?' Haven't heard that in many, many years."

"I thought I was going to learn something about guns or fingerprints or tapping phones...."

"Look, this is a reality of life. You work in a nice office, air conditioned, ladies room just down the hall, right?"

"Right."

"Well… when you're behind the wheel the better part of eight hours a day every working day finding a safe, clean place is of critical importance. But never mind, I'll talk about guns or fingerprints...."

"No, please, sorry for the interruption. So where do policepersons go?"

"Exactly, that's the question, where do you go? I mean, there you are in full uniform with a thick black belt holding up your pants and over that another belt, handcuffs, mace, gun, other stuff hanging from it, you don't want to go into a bar or restaurant... the greasy places are just too.... greasy... you don't want details, trust me, and if it is a nice place what are you going to do? Just walk past all those white tablecloths and well-dressed people staring at you? They all know where you're going and why you're going there, and since they're paying your salary at least half of them will be timing you in the can."

"Such a stressful situation."

"Hey, you try it sometime!"

"I meant it, not sarcasm... please proceed with police secret."

"Not just police secret. Cab drivers, too."

"I really want to hear. I shall interrupt no more."

"Where is cleanliness important? Answer, same place that there are often police coming and going. Hospitals! Best place for those rest stops, the public facilities of hospitals. They have to care about cleanliness, do a real nice job. Government buildings, too, at least most of them... got to learn which ones. Usually libraries, too."

"Thank you so much. I will probably never ask for a police secret again."

After the movie they went to a small restaurant, he ordering cherry pie and coffee, she a slice of German chocolate cake and cold milk. Dessert there, not back at his apartment. He asked her if she had driven and she said no, a cab, so he drove her home. She felt a bit of disappointment that he hadn't had dessert back at his place, third date, who knows what could happen. He stopped in front of her apartment, double parked, and got out. This time she waited for him to open her door. He walked her to her apartment and put his arms around her and kissed her, a strong firm lasting kiss, but with his mouth closed. When they parted she looked at him, smiled, took his jaw in her hand and kissed him again, briefly, tenderly. "I had a wonderful time, Terry."

"Me too. Let's do this again."

"Oh yes. Oh...yes." June reached in her purse, got her keys, opened the door. As she put the key in the lock she thought about asking him in, couldn't decide, then the moment was lost and he was saying goodnight and she did too and closed the door and leaned against it. It took a while to fall asleep. She should have asked him in.

Two Days Later

June picked up the phone, called Terry, pulse racing a bit.

"I need to talk to you. I've got some good news and bad, to be most original about it. Can we meet at Jones Library, first floor reading room?"

"Most curious. You don't want to come to the station, or meet at the paper? The detective is intrigued."

"I'm glad the detective is intrigued. Can you meet me in two hours?"

"Sure, Jones reading room, two hours, curious detective seeks intriguing reporter."

The Jones Branch Library was a small castle; great stone pieces made up the walls of the two-story structure. The reading room had benefited a few years ago from an endowment by a wealthy businesswoman who grew up in near-poverty. The library was a short bus ride from her home, and she escaped there to read and study, earned a bachelors then law degree, invested wisely and retired a multi-millionaire. In retirement she decided to give away a significant portion of her wealth, leaving a reasonable amount for her children, "enough to help but not enough to spoil them" as she described it. In recognition of the thousands of hours she spent reading and studying there she donated money for a complete refurbishing of the main reading room. The wood-only chairs had been replaced; there were now wooden chairs with small leather cushions on the seats, held in place by flush brass rivets. The tables were either new or renewed by being stripped and re-varnished, and there were beautiful new lamps, brass with goosenecks holding dark green glass shades over the bulbs. A small trust to maintain the room was also part of her donation.

June was already seated when Terry arrived. He sat down across the smooth wooden table from her, folded his hands and looked at her.

"First I want to tell you why we are meeting here. Like I said, I have good news and bad, and if you don't like the bad…. actually, if you don't like the bad, I didn't want anyone from your shop or mine watching us argue."

"But we could have met at the Dairy Inn and had some ice cream and coffee, pump us up."

"Don't forget, there is no raising of voices allowed in a library."

Terry leaned back in his chair. When he did so the bulge of his shoulder holster became apparent. June moved her eyes to it and then quickly away, back to his face.

"So this is really serious bad news, so bad you think I might be mad enough to embarrass you, or me, I guess… maybe I better have the good news first."

"The good news, oh, my, I certainly hope you think it's good news…. well, this is… I want… if after you hear the bad you're interested…. I'd like you to come to my apartment and please make love to me."

Terry did not react to her words, although his eyes danced a bit. Then he slowly sat back up and leaned forward in his chair.

"Unless this is seriously bad news, like for instance you're really a man, I am pleased and delighted to accept your invitation. Can't right now, but tonight? Shall I bring a toothbrush, or is staying the night too bold?"

"Not too bold. The room is a bit girly, but if you can stand it….. mint toothpaste acceptable?"

"Would you please tell me the bad news, right now, right this minute?"

June took a big breath and told him, soft library semi-whisper, about the note, the calls, the almost investigation. "For some reason she trusts me. I'm afraid… I thought she'd stop talking to me if I brought in the police.""And that you'd lose the kind of story that doesn't usually come to the fashion department of a newspaper."

He said it with the most neutral voice and face she could imagine. June couldn't tell if he was agreeing, understanding, angry but controlled. They sat for a long moment, looking into each other's faces, eyes.

"If we are going to sleep together I need to be able to read your emotions better than this. I mean, if I can't tell if you are mad, how can I be sure if you have a good time in bed with me? Are you mad?"

"I could be, but it doesn't seem worth the time. Better use of my time is seeing how what you've learned fits with my information. June, I'm stuck, this case is going nowhere. Your contact might be able to break it open, and I agree that bringing me in, telling her, telling Pieceworker that I'm involved might scare her away... no reason to do that now. You keep the contact going, we'll share."

"Crack the case together."

"Real police people never say 'crack the case.'"

June paused a moment. "But that brings up something else.... confidentiality of my source....I've never run into this before. I work in the fashion world, and those folks want their name used as often as possible, spell it right for goodness sakes but get it in the article, every paragraph if they had their way. So this is all new to me...."

"So far you haven't given me a name.."

"Don't have one.."

"And even if you did... look, she wants the reward, right? Only way to get the reward is to have the bad guy arrested, which means the police. So if you are going to act as her intermediary it means at some point you'll have to pass on the clues, her clues, to us. Fine with me, I don't need to know her name.... Of course, and this is something you might want to tell her, she might have to testify. All depends on how it unfolds. If he confesses, or we find some very strong proof, then she never appears. But if she knows and can prove something that is key to the case, then her earning the award might hang on her getting in that witness box. OK? You comfortable with that?"

"Sure... yes, that makes sense."

"Just because we're sleeping together doesn't mean either one of us has to step over a professional standards line."

"Wait a minute, what's with the present tense? No such has happened yet!"

"Can we get out of here? I've got a toothbrush to buy."

They walked out of the library. As they descended the steps, Terry said "What your editor said about the award, about you doing the delivery, well, let's see. If we get the killer, get a conviction, sure, we could get the award money to her without putting you at risk. And I agree, plenty of time to worry about that. Let's get the conviction."

CHAPTER TEN

Three weeks later.

End of a long day, and no plans to see Terry that night. As June said goodnight to the plant on her desk and shut off the light which shown on it and cast a softening yellow glow on her reading area, she realized that already it seemed wrong, a wrong empty place, to not be with him at the end of the day. Dangerous, dangerous; a few weeks, some nights at her place, some nights at his. Nothing more, no one is in love. No one is falling in love, right? Correct? He isn't, is he? And if he isn't then neither could she.

June decided to walk home, no need to take the bus, no need to rush. A good long walk to exercise the legs, shape the body, burn the time. Her path was not toward the elevators or front stairs close to her desk, out the front door and to the bus stop, but through the building, past the city desk and sports, and down the back stairs next to the service elevator. It was a noisy area. ESPN and FOX Sports proclaimed only fifty feet from police scanners and all-news radio, the reporters having learned long ago to hear only the important, the pertinent, words; pick up "traded to the Packers" and ignore "three-car wreck just north of Lincoln," or hear "pumper 17, ladder 17" and ignore "will be scheduled for arthroscopic surgery and miss the rest of the season."

As she passed through this predominately male area she heard "..... no comment at this time from ComFitter Industries." Then a pause, then a new story started.

"What was that?" June called to the two men sitting at desks on the city desk side. They looked up in surprise.

"What was that... please?" she said, stepping toward them. "I'm working on a story about them, about ComFitter Industries."

The older man answered. "Oh, sorry, didn't get the name, foreign, like Thai or Vietnamese or one of those....some girl... young woman. Shot dead this morning on her way to work. Didn't you hear about it?"

Her brained screamed "NO!" but there was no reason to shout at them, no way for them to know it was important to her. "No. What was the ComFitter connection?"

This time the younger man spoke. "She worked there, part of the sewing crew, I think they said. Didn't catch the rest. Want a number at the department?"

Sewing crew. Pieceworker... could it be? "Uh, no, not now, thanks. Thanks a lot. Good night."

She spun and hurried towards the exit. The two reporters watched her a moment, looked at each other, shrugged as if on cue. Terry had given her his number, and they had connected by cell phones a few times, dinner and after-dinner plans. June stepped into the stairwell, leaned against the wall and snapped her phone open.

"Hello?"

"Why didn't you call me!"

"Are you shouting at me?"

"Is it she, is it my Pieceworker?"

"Tell you what, I'll hang up, you take some deep breaths, maybe have a beer, call me back."

"Wait, wait Terry, I'm sorry, I'm sorry, the woman they found shot, killed, is it she? Dumb question, how would you know. How would *I* know?"

"Honey (part of her head, her heart, felt the surprised, happy zap of the 'Honey,' the first time he had called her that) I don't know what you're talking about. A woman was shot and you think she might be – have been your informant? Why?"

"She was a sewer, pieceworker at the company, a young woman.... so if my Pieceworker is a woman, I think so, I mean I think she's a young woman......sure, it could be."

"Look, I'm in south Jersey, been here all day, whole other case. Can't really talk now. Where are you?"

"Just on my way home."

"I'm going to be here a while. I'll call you soon as I get in my car."

"Wait till you get home, call me, don't want you driving the turnpike one-handed."

"OK."

"Drive carefully."

"Sure."

They pushed the END buttons on their phones.

June hurried down the back stairs, considered walking around the building and catching a bus, instead walked home, walking fast, thinking fast, thinking of murder and another murder and the link between them and he called her Honey.

At home she turned on a radio, no local television news for another 17 minutes. The radio didn't mention the story, she must have missed it. A frozen dinner into the microwave, a quick change of clothes, a cold beer, and she was ready with dinner and drink in front of the television with three minutes to spare. June turned off the radio, on the television, and picked up her fork.

First came the semi-military music and the quick shots of helicopters and cars and trucks bearing the station's logo hurrying about their business while the announcer intoned that it was the six o'clock news, then an earnest blond woman wearing a brilliant lime suit jacket appeared on the screen. There had been a terrible accident, again, on the West Side Highway, so it wasn't the lead story. It was second.

The co-anchor, an earnest, square-built man, spoke as a graphic of a neighborhood map appeared over his shoulder. "An early morning fatal shooting in Queens may be linked to another murder in that borough. Rith Long, 22, was shot at approximately six-thirty this morning on her way to work. Ms. Long was walking to the bus stop with two cousins, a daily occurrence; they lived in the same house and all three are employees of ComFitter Corporation, a Queens manufacturer of sportswear. The cousins stated, through a police interpreter, that a man stepped out from behind a tree, shot twice and ran away. Our viewers may remember that Victor Pritkin, ComFitter's founder, was murdered eight weeks ago inside the manufacturing facility. Police are not commenting on whether the two incidents are connected, and report they have no leads at this time."

June watched more news, picked at her dinner, surfed the channels. The next thing she knew the phone was ringing, ringing, pulling her out of a deep sleep, so deep that for a moment she was disoriented in her own home. The lights and television were still on, she was still seated in front of a mostly-consumed dinner and half-bottle of beer gone flat and stale. She glanced at the clock, 8:37, asleep over an hour. As she rose she half-stumbled and the beer tipped over, fortunately spilling only onto the TV tray, a pale yellow puddle. June steadied the tray and herself, got to the phone.

"Hello?"

"Is that sleep I hear?"

"Gone, sound asleep. Where are you?"

"Disregarding your advice. On the road, light traffic, and I'm so beat I just want to get home and collapse. Learn anything more?"

"Just that it's certainly a murder. Someone waiting for her behind a tree, shot her as she was going to work, ran away. No clues, at least nothing for the public. But I know someone on the force, maybe get some inside info, doncha know."

"Not tonight, but it's mine, alright. I called, gonna meet with the detective that covered it this morning. He's more than glad to hand if off to me if I want it, said I did, that it might be tied to Pritkin. So it's mine."

"Ours."

For a moment June thought the connection had been broken, then she realized that she could still hear faint car sounds. A long moment, then "June....."

"It is still a story, still my story, guess I need to read up on effective crime reporting."

"Dinner tomorrow, red sauce and red wine?

"You just changed the subject, although it was done so delicately I almost didn't notice."

"I'll call you after I see what's up. So, dinner?"

"Sure."

"My place after? I'll scrub the bathtub."

"Think you can get me in your tub in return for red sauce and wine and police gossip?"

"Absolutely. Even with your clothes off."

"The funny policeman."

"The fashion reporter who wants to write about factory tools inside brains."

"Tomorrow."

"Tomorrow."

June was now wide awake, so she did some housework and packed a bag for the next night. She didn't really want to deal with what might be true, likely was true; that someone who wanted to reach her to give her a tip, a name....had been killed for that reaching. And that, of course led to the danger that she, the receiver of the tip, might be facing. What does the shooter know? What does the shooter think she knows? Does the killer even know her, know about her? What does the killer know, her brain repeated. June walked into her living room, checked that the deadbolt was turned, then to the small kitchen and the door that opened onto the back hallway and the garbage chute. That deadbolt was turned, too. She didn't want to feel scared, be scared, but she wished Terry was with her.

The next morning there was a note on her chair "NOW – Tal." June dropped her hat and coat on her chair, put her purse in its usual drawer, then grabbed her clipboard with its yellow lined pad and two pens and hurried to his office.

"Tal?"

"Problem, June. Sit down...no, shut the door, have a seat. Please."

June shut the door, and Tal Sheets came out from behind his desk to sit near her. "Hell of a morning meeting. Rick Jones, you know, city editor, says this is his department's story, they do the crime reporting, what the fu....what in the world am I doing having my girl, he called you that, my 'girl' running around... he said that, too, 'running around' messing in a murder."

"Why Talarand Sheets, I think you're pissed."

"Blank you too."

"Consider me blanked. So what did you say?"

"That you would work in cooperation with City, whoever they assigned. Look, June, there's no way I could have kept this just for you, not with the second murder, public street in front of witnesses."

"No, of course not, that's fine, that's ....of course. Makes sense. But I'm not out."

"No, you are not out. Two-name byline, that's the deal. Besides, you have inside information. If this murder was your Pieceworker, then you're way ahead on the story, and I see no reason for you to just hand over your notes. That's what I said. 'She's not handing over her notes, they work together, got it?' He got it but is really honked big time, I'll tell you. Rick's a good newsman but kind of a jerk. This might get unpleasant, I'll bet they try to cut you out, take it away by....attrition, I guess."

"Plus they'll call me a girl."

"Plus that. Probably try to gross you off the raft."

"Meaning..?"

"Boy is that an oldie, strange how the brain works... probably haven't said it in thirty years. High school, swimming at the quarry, anchored wooden rafts that hold six, eight at a time. Two or three girls on a raft, some guys swim out and join them. If they want to flirt with them that's cool, but if not they start saying fart and sex things and the girls clear out. Gross them off the raft."

"That translates. So they'll call me a girl and talk about blood and bullet holes and try to gross me off the raft."

"Plus all the profanity you'll never want to hear."

"Boys saying naughty words will be no problem at all. What *will* be is that I really don't bring much to the table."

"Why?"

"Pieceworker didn't tell me much. I don't even know if this one was my pieceworker, all though I really am afraid it is, was, her.... won't know unless she left something in writing, and even then the truth is that she didn't tell me a thing. Nothing. Just wanted to know if I could get the reward to her if she gave us the name."

"City doesn't know that, plus you can stay ahead of them by getting the inside from your detective."

June sat and looked at Tal with wide eyes and a slightly open mouth.

"My detective?"

"Tal the wise knows all."

"Please don't tell me you know all. Not *all*."

"Actually, I didn't know a thing until this morning."

"How...?"

"You know Strecta, Joe Strecta, City? Jones said that Strecta told him about you two, says you should stay out of this 'cause it's a conflict of interest, sleeping with the guy'...what's his name, Stans?..."

"Terry Stans."

".....and also reporting, says it should be all his. You know Strecta?"

"I know who he is, but....no, don't know him."

June was angry and embarrassed, both emotions spiraling upward.

"Tal, let me get this straight. Somehow it has been learned that I have a relationship with a detective....."

"Seen in a grocery buying dinner... steaks, wine, I don't know. Buying dinner equals having sex. Sorry."

".....which means I should stay away from the story? Bullshit!"

"Well said."

"So everyone knows."

"My dear reporter, only about half the people in this crazy place are married, and there are nasty rumors about a few of those. As for the rest, it is assumed that they are not celibate.... well, maybe....never mind... but we all know who prefers his own, or her own, sex... point is that it's small news that you have a boyfriend."

Tal sat back, paused, then said "What you have to consider is whether he is putting his career at risk. He is sworn to secrecy, part of his job. He certainly can't be leaking information to the press, bad enough if he just blabs in a bar, little drunk and runs his mouth, something much worse if he has a girlfriend and they pillow talk and it's in the paper the next day. That's his threat. Threat to you is that people will say you're trading sex for scoops. Wouldn't be the first time, although usually it is a reporter paying for a prostitute."

June took in a sharp breath. "Well that was certainly harsh and ugly."

"June, I trust you and believe in you and would bet my last nickel that any man you are dating is being dated because he is good and decent. And intelligent. I'm not your problem, never will be, that was me fighting for you this morning, remember?"

"Sure, but..."

"Problem for both of you is the appearance. As soon as his bosses find out about the two of you he is going to be in the hot seat...he might want to preempt them, walk in and tell them about you and assure them that all is cool. Further problem is they might not believe him, and for sure some people won't believe you."

"The man is adventurous and bold, the woman, the girl, is a whore."

"News to you that there's a double standard?"

"Can we back up a bit? Joe...Strecta? What a name. This is the guy who said it should be all his...this is my new partner?"

"Yep. Wants it all for himself, resents you, chauvinist along with his editor...two of you will make a great pair. At least that's what Jones says."

June sat a minute. After a bit Tal got up and returned to his chair behind the desk, his way of telling her the meeting was over. June got up, started for the door, turned back towards him. "Thanks for taking my side. Always do, don't you? That's why all your staff loves you so."

"It is to puke. Don't you have some work to do?"

They smiled at each other, then she opened the door and left.

The question was what to do about linking up with her new partner. No, the question was who calls first. Sign of weakness it is, calling first to talk about working together; first one to call loses. So instead of walking to where the city desks were clustered June went back to her desk and picked up her copy of the paper. Like many on the staff, she read the paper first thing, used it as a launching pad into the new news day. Some of the staff read almost everything, but others were selective; not everyone read the funnies or the sports section, and certainly not everyone read articles about gowns and fabrics and thin rich men in Paris. But papers were spread across desks throughout the building, coffee stains and doughnut or muffin crumbs dribbling. The one section everyone read was the City section, the local news; it was poor form to be in the news business and not know the latest city council scandal or battle over demolition of an almost-historical site or which local TV newscaster was arrested for drunk driving, so all the reporters made sure they were up on the items reported in that section. As a result, the City staff had a bit of an edge, a tiny swagger point; everyone read their stuff.

June read the article about the murder; it was almost identical to the newscast of the night before. Nothing strange in that; not much was known beyond what had happened in those brief violent moments.... woman leaving for work, walking, man behind a tree steps out, shoots to kill and runs away. The police are investigating a possible connection between her death and the death of her employer eight weeks ago but have no clues at this point.

June thought "I want to get in her bedroom. I want to see if she has any notes, a diary, something. Even if all I can do is look at her handwriting, see if it is the same as the notes I got...is this my Pieceworker?" She turned slightly and suddenly saw stacks of letters and brochures and newsletters and thick packages in her two in-baskets. Of course she had seen them yesterday, and again this morning when the pile had grown some since the night before, but had not wanted to recognize them for what they were. Now she really saw them, acknowledged them, and with a deep sigh reached out and took the one on top of the larger stack. Spend some time in the world she had been hired to cover, to report on. Her world before one murder. Before two murders. Before Terry.

It took most of the day to get through both baskets, but she did, and found in them ideas for several stories and two conferences that she would like to attend if the paper's budget allowed. If only one, maybe the International Wool Conference in London. Terry in a new wool suit in London. She blinked, muttered "Lots of Terry references, my dear, lots of Terry talk. Keep your mind on your work" repeating a phrase her high school computer keyboard skills teacher said to the class at least once a day. Seventeen email messages too, but one of the messages gave her the final bits of information she needed to complete an article about how athletic shoe stores were thriving despite the mega-stores that were crushing other kinds of small retail clothing businesses. She finished the article and sent it for inclusion to Production.

A good day, a good productive day. Did some research, got a start on some new work, wrapped up an insightful article about retailing, emptied both in-baskets, read and handled all the emails. Humanities didn't call City, and City didn't call Humanities, so a stand-off for the day. Time to leave, and.... excited about seeing Terry. Really looking forward, really excited about seeing Terry. Dangerous, dangerous.

June took the bus to her apartment, brushed her teeth and hair, picked up her bag and left. She drove to his apartment, using the time to think about how to approach the matter of seeing the room, seeing handwriting samples. And now there was this terrible complication, so complicating that perhaps she and Terry couldn't detective together; she had a partner who would want to see the same documents, learn the same information. Seemed as if the world of work was offering them a choice: sleep together or detective together. June wanted both.

But wait! Maybe this partner offered a solution to the conflict of interest problem. This reporter, this Joe Strecta, if he had access to, say, the latest victim's bedroom, if he was part of the investigating team, that answered the questions. Then she, as his partner, could state that he, they, were getting information by newspaper work, by investigative reporting, not by favoritism or because of a sex relationship.

Terry was glad to see her. He hugged her, they kissed. June glad that she had taken the tooth-brushing moment. They moved into preparing dinner, each doing chores, he opening the wine and tending the pasta, she making a salad. It was comfortable and easy.

Over dinner she told him about her new partner. "And Terry, I need to see her bedroom. We need to. Got to start saying 'we' when I talk about this."

"Why?"

"Why do I need to see her room?" He nodded, chewing a cherry tomato. "Because I want to know if she was Pieceworker. If I can find any notes, even a shopping list, something I can match to the note and letter I got, that would be a strong indication. Of course, there might be something that relates to Pritkin's murder."

"Got some bad news, June. She was living in a big house, one of those places that started out as a duplex but got turned into a combined...I don't know, rooming house or something. Anyway, after a brief mourning period, perhaps ten minutes, it seems everyone living there who hadn't left for work just helped themselves to the poor girl's belongings. Since it wasn't a crime scene we didn't secure it right away, and by the time I got there this morning the place was bare. I mean *bare;* guess the dresser and bed belongs to the house, the landlord, so those were there, but no clothes, no linens, nothing. If there ever was a diary it's gone."

"Oh that is bad news. That is very bad news. Now I'll never know."

"Welllll.... don't give up just yet. Know what I did?"

"No, what did you did?"

"They pay you well for such English? What I did was check the wastebasket and see if there was anything of interest in it."

"And....."

"And what?"

"Oh we are so amused, we are. Well, time for me to leave, I guess."

"Idle threat. You want a shampoo and backrub, and I'm just the guy. But enough teasing.....here." Terry reached behind him and picked up a plain manila envelope and handed it to her. "There were some tissues, I sent them to the lab but don't expect anything unusual to be on them."

The envelope contained only three items. One was an envelope with stamps such as June had never seen, intricate borders around animals, statues, faces, an empty envelope from Cambodia. The second was a receipt from a drug store for aspirin and toothpaste. The third was a few words on a scrap of paper, perhaps a reminder note or shopping list. A handwritten shopping list, just as June had said. Of course, the writing was in characters and word shapes totally unfamiliar to her, Khmer script, but still there it was, that same pushing, almost smearing handwriting, the style familiar even though the letters weren't. It was she. Pieceworker. June took a deep, ragged breath. "I want to see her. Can I see her?"

"Sure."

June paused. "Terry, where is her purse?"

"Property room, why?"

"Envelope, no letter. In her purse?"

He smiled. "Nice work. I haven't had a chance to look in it yet, but I sure will."

"Who translates it? Who can you trust?....might be part of the....might know something....."

"Easy, easy, this is after work, remember? We use university professors or business people that we have known for years, thoroughly checked out....people we trust who can translate something like a hundred fifty languages and dialects. Comes in handy in wire tap cases. We used one of those professors when the two cousins were interviewed after the shooting, charming guy, Professor Somoeun Kong."

"And this note."

"Sure, but I'll bet it says toothpaste and aspirin."

"Must you be so work oriented all the time? Aren't we here to relax and enjoy ourselves?" June picked up her wine glass. She opened her mouth slowly, widely, making sure he saw her tongue, then raised the glass and drank, her eyes ever on his.

Two hours later she looked at him, sound asleep beside her, and mouthed the words "I love you," making not a sound. Dangerous, dangerous.

CHAPTER ELEVEN

The next morning June called the paper and left a message that she wouldn't be in until late morning. Then she started to call Amy Pritkin, but decided it made more sense just to show up. The intrusion might be resented, probably would be, but at least she could ask a question or two before being dismissed, likely more than she would get on the phone.

June drove to the small clothing factory and pulled into the parking lot, as before parking far from the building so as not to take a space from employees or customers. She walked into the small waiting area that was surrounded by offices. There was no receptionist; one of the bookkeepers or other clerical workers would greet visitors. This time the woman at the near desk - what was her name, Rose? - glanced up from a computer keyboard next to a stack of forms with small squares; it appeared she was loading information into the company's system. June gave a tiny friendly wave and smile and kept moving towards Amy's office as if she were expected. The woman nodded in response and went back to extracting numbers from the small squares.

Amy Pritkin was on the phone, she looked up with both mild surprise and mild annoyance. June held up her right index finger and softly said, a pleading apologetic look on her face, "One minute?" Amy gave a grudging nod and looked down at her desk, concentrating on the phone call. June walked down the hall towards the rest rooms and water fountain, just past the break area where she had received that first scribbled note. But she kept going, quickly through the factory as if on assignment, towards the loading dock where Victor Pritkin was suddenly, terribly murdered with a pair of tin snips.

She stood in the middle of the loading dock. The term was used for the entire shipping and receiving area, probably because it was easier to say, but only the far end was actually a dock; two large overhead doors opened onto a six-foot deep concrete area that included the doors and space between then, plus a few feet on both sides that led to metal stairs, the stairs in turn leading to the parking lot. The truck bays were the sunken kind, designed so that the bed of a trailer backed into it would drop down to factory floor level, allowing fork lift trucks and employees to drive or walk into the trailers.

The rest of the area called the loading dock was inside the doors, inside the building; actually a shipping and receiving area but loading dock was easier to say. The staff knew that "in the loading dock" meant the inside room, while "on the loading dock" was the area outside the truck doors and the building, the concrete apron. There was a large industrial scale and banding equipment and a computer terminal, a few boxes recently delivered and some ready for shipping, and some general storage. One corner contained a stack of toilet paper and paper towels and napkins for the break room, another corner boxes of new tags and labels. A shipping area. A receiving area. A storage area. A loading dock. A place of murder. Why? Why here?

June remembered that this was where she first saw Terry, first spoke to him. He had been wrestling with the same question, 'Why here?' What was here that escaped her, escaped him. Or was it nothing, just that this is where the murderer decided to do it. Or had to do it? June wanted to see it, have the light bulb go on, surprise and please Terry by telling him what she had brilliantly....detected.

Terry! Last night he screamed so loud she was afraid he was hurt, but he laughed afterwards and told her it was a truly astonishing orgasm. She still hadn't spoken to him about the handcuffs. Maybe soon.

Shaking her head, clearing it of last night's hot memory, she said to herself "Come on, now, June, think! It's right here in front of you, just see it! The computer? No, just a terminal, nothing that Victor Pritkin couldn't get to from his desktop. The banding equipment? The scale?"

A scale. An industrial scale. Why was there one in a factory that makes small clothing items? They don't ship by weight, they ship by piece; June had seen the elaborate care that the staff took to make sure the commissions, the piecework bonuses, were accurate. But receiving.....

June turned and quickly walked back into the factory. Amy was still on the phone, and June made a "that's OK" gesture and sat down in a tiny waiting area outside her office, trying to show no disappointment.

In a few moments Amy finished her call, then turned to her computer and began writing. June didn't want to be seen as pushy, so she opened her briefcase and took out a brochure from a manufacturer of leather belts that was introducing a line of suspenders, braces they called them, using the British word, although the company was in Iowa. June remembered that in Britain suspenders are what Americans call the straps on a garter belt. Bet they call braces suspenders in Iowa, June thought, thinking she should check on that, encouraging her mind to wander, to not be impatient. She made herself read the brochure slowly, really reading it, although it was almost impossible to care at all about braces right now. Amy called out "June, come on in."

June walked to her office and stood, implying the briefest of visits. "How are you, how is the staff doing?"

"It's hard. Two murders, maybe connected. I'm sorry, it's really nuts around here, is there something you wanted?"

"And I'm sorry, really, I feel like a....I don't know, a heartless voyeur, but this is such a story now. Actually the same story I first talked to you about, a small successful company surviving, except now it's two shocking deaths. So more of a story. But you probably don't want me or anyone else poking around."

"That's right, but please understand. We are trying to do exactly that, survive, make a good product and fill our orders, business as usual, and meanwhile everyone is...June, sit down, I can give you a moment."

As June sat the phone rang. Amy picked it up. "ComFitter, Amy Pritkin speaking." June worked hard to keep her face blank, to let no impatience show. "Sure, Charley, can I call you back in five, ten minutes? Thanks."

June spoke quickly, sitting straight in the chair, wanting to convey that she knew time was precious and would soon be gone.

"What I mean is that someone is going to write about this. Since we've already spoken, you know me, I told them at the paper that this is my story. One of the city desk reporters, crime reporter, wanted to come see you too, but I just told them that would be too intrusive, to leave you alone. So he will be working with me. We'll write the story together but he'll stay out of your hair."

This was of course a lie, more astonishingly, it was a lie she heard herself making up as she spoke. A great bit of game playing, a crushing gambit, on the fly. She gave herself a mental high five.

"Thank you."

"And I promise you that the slant will stay that way. I mean, when they find the... culprits, that's straight crime reporting, like the trial will be, but my story, the one we'll write together, will stay on the success, the triumph over tragedy, and will be respectful to your father and to Rith Long."

"But I can't talk to you right now."

"No, I know that. What I'll do is...how is this? I'll email you three or four times to get together, and you pick one, we'll do an interview, hour at the most. Maybe I'll need a little more time, but that's OK, no rush to finish. Actually some more time might be valuable. I remember you said you got a flood of orders after his death, and it will be interesting to see if that translates into a long-term gain in business."

"Yes it will. If it does we may have to find a new location. As you know, we are at the thin edge of the fire marshal's good graces. Tell you what. I have to eat. Propose breakfast, lunch, dinner times, bunch of them. Maybe I can commit to two right off, that would be easier for you."

"Thank you. What time is breakfast?"

"Six-thirty."

"Will do. Breakfast, lunch, dinner. One more thing. Can I interview Rith's cousins?"

"They speak almost no English, so you'll need an interpreter. And they are taking a week off...we understand. Not even sure they'll come back, they may be too afraid, and there are other shops that need their skills. We've offered them a half week's wages even though they don't have any vacation coming, partly from sympathy and partly because we want them to be loyal, come back to us. That sounded a bit crass....you won't print that, will you?"

"I'd like to mention the wages. Certainly not the motivation. Just part of a story of a company coping and helping its employees cope, especially the relatives of the victim who were with her when she died."

"Thank you, June. Really, I look forward to seeing your article."

June gave a small laugh. "So do I."

Amy turned to her computer, pushed some keys. "Here are their names and address, you know they live together with some other people from Cambodia. Phone is for the whole household."

"Do you know if anyone bilingual lives there?"

"I think so..."

Time to go. Quickly June asked "Do you know if Rith is going to be buried here or....."

"The Cambodian community donated some money, but we're going to pay most of the cost of shipping the... sending her home. She, her family, are believers in Theravada Buddhism, a faith I never heard of until this happened, but I've learned is widely followed in her part of the world." Amy paused. "The body has to be kept cold for cremation. She'll be sent home as soon as the police are done... when the police release the body."

There seemed nothing to say. The sadness, the shock, hung in the air. "That's nice, Amy. Really."

Amy's glance dropped to the papers in front of her. June took the hint, and as she rose from her chair she said "Thanks for the time."

Amy looked up, smiled a little, said "Sure," and went back to her paperwork.

When she got to the parking lot June got out a tablet and started writing as fast as she could, jotting down questions while they were fresh. She wished she were still inside talking to Amy, it would have been nice if Amy had offered a coffee break and a half-hour talk. But it appeared that cooperation, and the background needed for a well-rounded story, would be forthcoming...but it had to be on Amy's schedule. Fine. Prepare in advance. The notebook page was filling fast: what kind co-worker RL? how long, when hired? who first, RL or cousins? what kind of worker, output? quiet, talkative? English skills? education? where learned sewing/factory skills? June paused, then added: relationship w/Amy? relationship w/Victor? She knew she might not get answers to, or use, all these questions, but for now she didn't edit, just let the ideas flow.

Back at her desk June worked her way through a small list of emails, responding to several, and checked her mail. She was starting to think of her working life as being divided into Regular and The Story. This morning she had been at the factory, working on The Story, now her notebook cooled in her small briefcase while she did Regular work. Having dealt with messages brought to her by computer and mail by the United States Postal Service, she turned to the phone to see what voices were in storage. There were three messages, the first two were fashion consultants wanting to make sure she had received the interesting brochures they had sent about their newest clients, hoping that June would share that excitement with her readers. The third was "Hey, partner! This is Joe, Joe Strecta. Please give me a call, I'd like to buy you a coffee, talk about where we stand on this story." The voice was all warmth and enthusiasm, one old buddy calling another. Interesting.

June pushed the four buttons for an internal call.

"City, Joe Strecta."

"Joe, June. I could use some coffee. Which poison?"

"Keystone?"

"Sure."

"Lobby?"

"In five."

"Cool." They both hung up.

June had several speeches prepared, and she briefly reviewed them; he had no right discussing her personal life, she would not be moved out of the story....and he had to stay away from the factory, she would handle that. She worked up a bit of steam, stoked her determination, set her jaw.

They shook hands in the lobby. June had checked his bio, and knew he was twenty-two years her senior, over twenty years with the paper and some time in radio news before that. He was about four inches taller than she with thinning, graying hair and bright blue eyes. A little overweight.

By unspoken mutual agreement they small-talked or kept silent as they walked, waiting until seated at the Keystone. June ordered coffee, Joe coffee and a toasted cheese sandwich. As soon as he said it June thought that sounded great, and she almost ordered one too, but she was trying to control her appetite, keep her weight under control. Terry worked hard and ate large and burned it all away, and when she was with him it was easy to put a little more mashed potatoes on her plate, have a cookie, two cookies, with the inevitable ice cream. Terry likes her body. She wants him to keep liking her body.

"So, June, where are we? What are you working on, and....." Joe paused, passing it to her, two old buddies.

"What right did you have to talk about my personal life to your editor?"

He didn't blink, didn't pause. "Murder, detective investigating, newspaper reporter also investigating from a different angle, detective and reporter team up..." He held out his hands, palms down, mouth puckered in the "Don't get me wrong" gesture.... "so no disrespect intended, none at all....I'm investigating a murder, my beat, after all, and I've got to talk to my boss. Look, June, he makes us check in anytime there might be something squirrelly, some liability or scandal...." he winced "...bad word choice...see, the rule is that we City reporters have a pretty free hand, but anytime something's up that might involve lawyers or a conflict of interest or a potential embarrassment to the paper, the publisher, we have to tell him now. *Have* to, could be my job, even after all these years. He got caught in some legal mess years ago, almost trashed his career, and he is neurotically careful about this stuff."

"You said I was sleeping with Ter...with the detective. Was that information necessary?"

This time he paused. "June, my boss and your boss cut a deal. We work together on this. OK, we work together. You want to yell at me some first, call me an asshole? Won't be the first time I've received that bouquet. But we're stuck with each other."

"Yeah, yeah....was that information necessary?"

The coffee and his sandwich arrived. The hot cheese smelled wonderful. She couldn't help glancing at it.

He slid the plate to the middle of the table. "Here, peace offering. Half a sandwich. Please. So you want to know how this worked? Here it is, June. Here it is. I tell Rick I saw you together, he says 'doing what?' I say 'talking and holding hands' he says 'oh great, she's fucking the cops for a story.' He said it, not me. Sorry."

She had her hands wrapped tight around her coffee cup. "Really?"

"What, really sorry? Sure as shit. Look, I don't want people talking about me. Hey, I been married thirty-one years, you think I want some guy standing around the paper talking about what me and my wife do? Smack the son of a bitch in the mouth he says anything. So how come we get to say that stuff about you?"

"How come?" She couldn't stand it any longer. She picked up half the sandwich and started eating.

"Best toasted cheese in town. I'm the expert, had 'em in a thousand places like this. How come? Well short answer we shouldn't, long answer buncha stuff about men and muscles and male domination. I'm trying to reform, I am. Old friend'a mine likes to say before you start doing anything positive make sure you've stopped doing the negative stuff. He says it better, more eloquent, but that's the drift. Anyway maybe I don't march in the women's liberation parade but at least I've stopped telling jokes about women drivers and calling all the waitresses sugar."

Joe reached for his half, bit off about a third, and smiled. "Gee I love to eat. You too?"

"So are you going to turn out to be a nice, interesting guy, decent married type, and I'm not going to be able to stay mad at you? Is that what's going to happen?"

Joe sipped his coffee, took another bite. "I read your stuff. Found out I had to split the story with you so I checked you out. You're good. Real good. Not stuff I'm interested in, tell you the truth, but I know good writing when I see it. And Terry Stans is a good detective. This little trio, what the hell they call it, a something a trois..."

"Mana'ge-a-trois."

"I most certainly will not ask how you know that."

"Read it in a book somewhere."

"Without a doubt."

June couldn't help herself, she smiled.

"Anywho, we three just might turn out some fine work, solve the case, cases I should say, and write a kick-ass story."

"You know Terry?"

"Boy I wish I could say 'not as well as you.' But I won't, I won't. Just met him a few times, but I know about him by reputation. He's good, focused, solved some tough cases. Have you done a search?"

"You mean go into archives, search on his name?"

"Sure. He's in there a bunch."

"I can't believe I didn't do that. Thanks, I will."

"You like this guy a lot?"

"You like your wife a lot?"

Now Joe smiled. "Nicely done."

"Let's talk business."

"Sure."

"Joe, I was sent to the factory to do a story about a company dealing with the sudden loss of their founder and leader. They weren't crazy about cooperating, didn't want to take the time, and I think they were....closing in, closing ranks, you know, not wanting the world peeking and poking. It was tough getting the story going." June knew she was making it sound worse than it actually was, but that fit well with what she had promised Amy. "Now they are really skittish, barely let me in the door. I can't get you in, not for a while, maybe a long while. So I'll take that part of the deal, get background." She finished her half sandwich, fought the temptation to order another. "You know, I still have my original assignment, what Tal sent me to do, but now it is more interesting....that sounded a bit cold, I'm talking about another murder. But the question of how a small company copes with tragedy is now plural, tragedies, and... well, I said it, didn't I ...more interesting. You know, their sales are actually up. Might be just because of the notoriety or because people feel sorry for them or something else having nothing to do with the murders, but I don't think so. That's one of the pieces I'm following."

"So how is this going to work? I tell you what I need and you get it?"

"Inside the factory, yes. Outside, well, that's your turf. Look, I'm a business and fashion reporter. I don't have the connections or inclination to hound-dog this, and I have my day job to do. My Regular job I call it. So any way I can help you outside of ComFitter is fine, I hope I can, but you're the City guy. Your story."

"Ours. Two names. Part of the bosses' deal. 'K with me if 'K with you."

"'K."

Joe leaned back, sipped his coffee, put it down with a slight clatter. "Now, new partner, I'm going to ask you a question. If you have an answer I am going to assume it comes from you. I will not ask if you have discussed this with Terry, or even if it is Terry's, but be aware that there are lines that you shouldn't cross and he shouldn't cross. If this relationship stalls..." He pointed back and forth several times, indicating the two of them. "...it will be on this point; what you tell me, what you tell him, all that. There's lots of stuff - potential conflicts, relationship tangles - at work here. First, of course, between you and the folks that give you a paycheck every two weeks, then probably second between you and your detective, and then... well, I guess me. And the profession. And professionalism. And Terry Stans, and his oath, and his career."

"I got a lot of the same from Tal. I feel like I just got two new uncles."

"My daughters are grown, married, live out of state. I may adopt you."

"Uncle Sweet-as-syrup, don't you have a question?"

"You are *quick*. Yes I do. Question is... what's your theory?"

June's brain spun. Every second that went by would build the impression that she was hiding something. But she hadn't had a chance to talk to Terry about her hunch, about the scale. What to say? She turned, caught the waitress's eye, and indicated more coffee. She was fast approaching her daily limit, and if she didn't stop soon she would be jumpy with a sour stomach all afternoon. But the moment helped.

"I have no doubt the murders are connected. There's something you don't know."

Joe reached in his jacket pocket and took out the standard slim reporter's spiral-bound notebook, removed the pen clipped to it, flipped a page and began to write. He barely glanced at the book as he worked, the reporting skills well honed.

June voted and vetoed, self-censored, as she spoke. She told him all about the note slipped to her in the factory, about Pieceworker, the early morning phone calls, her strong hunch that the dead young woman was Pieceworker, that whoever killed Victor Pritkin also killed her. She didn't tell him about the wastebasket, or the scale. Not yet. Then she took another quick mental vote and voted yes, to tell him what was next.

"I thought it might be interesting to talk to her cousins, the ones who were with her. Not police questions; they've already been thoroughly questioned, but it happened so fast they saw, they know, almost nothing."

"I'm sorry, but I have to ask you... do you know that just from the news reports or did Terry verify it?"

"The reports, but I'll check with him." The sharing, the investigation-reporting mana'ge-a-trois had begun.

June continued. "I want to know what she was like, hopes and dreams, if she ever thought she would go back to Cambodia, if she wanted to be a citizen, that sort of thing."

"That's good. The thing is, it might work really well in a City article, especially when they catch the bad guy. Look, what I'm saying is this. I get your point, they'll let you snoop around the factory, not me, and you being a woman, and a familiar face, means you probably can get a lot further with the cousins than I can. I look and act too much like "the man," so even if you introduce me as a reporter they'll smell cop. But June, some of the stuff you uncover might work better in our crime story than in your business story. You know, something like 'Bad guy arrested, killer of young woman with dreams of living the American success story.' So some of the background the cousins give you might get a little lost in a big story about a company's business struggles, but could be a real tear-jerker in ours. So what I'm suggesting, requesting, is that you don't decide what goes where, that we talk over what you've learned and see where it fits best."

"Wise and reasonable." June held up her coffee cup in a toast. "Done." He raised his too and they clinked mugs and smiled.

"So your theory, and it is certainly reasonable, is that they are connected. How about the why?"

She lied. "I haven't a clue. I keep waiting for a light bulb to go on, but not yet."

"So I'll share mine, bounce it off you, see what you think."

"Please!"

"I'm wondering if someone isn't doing something funny with the immigrants."

"Funny?"

"All kinds of things. Illegal immigration, fake green cards, other false documents, who knows what these people's real names are? Someone getting kickbacks from paychecks, hell, even forced prostitution."

"I don't know...."

"Why not? No, if you know something...I don't want to spend a lot of time chasing up the wrong road."

"I did a search, nothing about them, not a single word. Lots of illegal immigration stories in the paper, even in the past year, but no mention of ComFitter. So as far as I know they don't have that kind of a problem. His daughter said keeping legal was a point of emphasis for her father, something he was emphatic about...no, word she used, if I remember right, was scrupulous."

"June, you're thinking like a business reporter, straight facts. Think like a crime reporter."

June paused only a moment. "If it's true...was true...that her father was a straight arrow on this, then maybe he found out something, someone killed him because he was going to go to the cops, the feds."

"Yep."

"And killed her because...."

Joe shrugged. "Because she found out something too, maybe stumbled on it by accident. Because she was the killer's girlfriend and in on it from the start, had a falling out with her guy so he whacked her too, afraid she'd rat him out. Because she was fu... sleeping with old man Pritkin and the killer was concerned about what she knew from pillow talk. Because she refused to hand over part of her paycheck, or screw somebody, or do something that she was supposed to in return for her fake papers, and they killed her in front of relatives as a warning... meaning it was only related to the first murder because they were both about immigration, but they were killed for quite different reasons." He shrugged again. "We don't even know if it was the same person. Different locations, different weapons, very different victims. In fact, the only thing they share is that they worked in the same place, which might mean everything or nothing. Of course, if, *if* she was your Pieceworker then, sure, they probably are linked, but no way of knowing if we have one killer or two. Not at this point."

June remembered the conversation she had with Terry in the police station. "So the killer could be anyone employed there, or connected with the company. Could even be a member of the family."

Joe reached above his forehead, tipped an imaginary cap. "Starting to think like a crime reporter."

"I must confess. Terry helped me see that. Guess I was too innocent, didn't think about children killing their parents. Whacking them, right?"

Joe nodded. "Yep. Children do whack their parents. Sad but true."

They settled up the bill - he paid, she left the tip - and headed back to work. Not quite partners, but well on the way.

CHAPTER TWELVE

Later that day she stepped into Tal Sheets' office. "Tal, I'm going to spend some of your money."

"How much?"

"Taking an interpreter with me to talk to the cousins. I want to find out about Rith Long, the woman who was killed... dreams, plans, what she was like."

"For a crime story or the fashion business story?"

"For City or for us, you mean?

"Ever on point."

"What she was like, what America meant to her, that's for us. I'm still working with Amy Pritkin, and although things are really tense there she has agreed to meet with me.... that means I'm going to meet and eat with her, so you can expect that expense voucher too.... but I think this is going to be a fine story. If I pick up something that might help the investigation....."

"Your detective's investigation."

"Terry. His name is Terry Stans, and I have no ownership papers."

"Sorry. But what if you learn something? What goes to Terry, what to Joe?"

"This is so simple. You are my employer. I am working with City in a cooperative relationship. I have to tell Joe, and I will. If it might catch the killer I have a responsibility to tell the police, and I will do that too. Should the police want us not to print something right away because it might hurt their investigation, I'll just let appropriate authority types deal with it."

"Terry, meet Joe. Joe, Terry."

"Those two, and you and Rick Jones, you four boys can haggle while I go back to writing about whether the knee will be showing under better gowns next year or make sure the world understands the difference between taffeta and tapioca."

Tal frowned a bit. "Was that a pout? Can you work with Joe?"

"No pout, and I can work fine with him. I just don't know where this is going, and I intend to keep checking in, let you make the decisions. Me labor, you management."

"Really..."

"Tal, I want to be straight with you, and with the cops, Terry or no Terry. No employer problems, no legal problems. If I can help catch the killer or killers, help put them in jail, that would be great. And I want to write a wonderful article for us, help Joe write his. Got to tell you, this is exciting and interesting, but I'm not going to ask for a transfer to City when this is over. Tension, sorrow, murder, guns, funerals....nah. I'd rather write about profit margins and marketing plans and go to fashion shows. Better....I'd rather write about company owners who are alive than dead ones with tin snips in the head."

"Glad to hear it. By the way, your article on the shoe stores was, as usual, excellent. Mention that in your next review, will you? When is that, two years?"

"As you well know, three months. Doubling my pay would be adequate."

Tal waved her away, and she left smiling.

Back at her desk June took a few moments to think about her situation, and her conversations with Joe and Tal. She had spoken a personal truth without planning to, and now contemplated her words. This was, as she said, exciting and interesting, but not something she really enjoyed. She was use to working with managers who were glad to see her, who took time showing her around their factories or showrooms or stores, smiling and happy. It wasn't fun to press on Amy, to ask for her words and time when she would so obviously like June to go away. This wasn't a manager proud of a new Spring line and wanting to court June and her precious column inches, this was a manager in pain over the loss, the murder of her father, who was also the founder and soul of the company. Now another murder, possibly linked. Amy was sad and probably a little scared, on top of which, either because of sympathy or notoriety, business was booming. No time for a reporter, barely time for the police.

June had no doubt that people like Joe and Terry had the ability to mentally walk right past that pain, that tension, in pursuit of the story, the facts. And it wasn't a male thing either; she knew that there are plenty of excellent female investigative reporters, detectives, FBI agents. No, just not her cup of tea. Female FBI agents probably don't say "Not my cup of tea."

And Terry. And Terry. And Terry. June knew she was falling hard for him, really in love, but neither of them had said that four letter word, at least not out loud. No discussion of moving in together...hell, she didn't even know if he was seeing someone else. They were together many nights, but not every. Was he sleeping with someone else? Even if not, was he looking? June felt like a junior high girl, her head swimming from the questions launched by her latest crush. But this wasn't junior high, and she had never been married, and she wanted to be married, and...

Almost physically pulling herself out of the spin of questions, June called him at his office. A business call.

"One Nine, Detective Stans."

"Hi."

"Hi."

"Terry, I want to visit the two cousins, ask them about Rith Long, what she was like, what her dreams were, if she planned on becoming a citizen, that sort of thing."

"Well if you stumble on anything you think might help me please let me know. I really don't like how slow this is going. I've got other work, new cases, and this is starting to slip into the 'still under investigation' file."

"Same request from you and Joe."

"Joe? Who is Joe? Does he know about your girly bedroom, too?"

"Joe Strecta, City Desk. My news world is expanding. I need to tell you about it."

"My place or yours?"

"I don't know. I may be offended by that girly bedroom remark."

"I'm glad you're a girly. How about I stop, pick up some salmon and a Piesporter, and you can tell me all about Joe while I fix dinner in your charming kitchen."

"A girly bedroom and a charming kitchen. What else don't you like?"

"I like the kitchen and the bedroom....and the bed... but as you've seen I'm not as much into decoration as you. No... how about ambiance. I don't ambiance like you ambiance. Surely you've noticed."

"You mean your apartment, done up in a variety of shades of blue and gray and mud brown? Who could fault that?"

"You called to insult my muddy blue gray apartment?"

"I called... wait, before I forget, yes to the salmon and Peisporter. The reason I called is to get the number of your translation person for Cambodian. I need an interpreter. And has the letter been translated yet?"

"Not yet, but should be soon."

"There's one more thing. I want to see her. Rith Long. I want you to take me to the, into the morgue. I just need to see her face. Please."

"Sure, but isn't there going to be a funeral? No, never mind, no one knows about her connection to you, so why would you be at the funeral?"

"Not a funeral, a memorial service, her body is going back to Cambodia, but I still can't go. Only reason, excuse for me being there is that I'm there as a reporter, and that might offend someone... make it hard to go further with this... the morgue, can you arrange it?"

"Of course. When is up to you. Want the experience at the beginning or end of a day?"

"Beginning."

"I'll pick you up tomorrow at nine.. no, got a meeting... ten thirty. Ten thirty, does that work?"

"Yes."

Terry gave her the contact name and number of the translator, they agreed on the dinner hour, and hung up. It had not escaped her notice that Terry had reacted to the mention of Joe. A bit of jealousy? Did he like her a whole lot? Right back into junior high.

June called Professor Somoeun Kong at New York International University. The school is known for its outstanding foreign language department and for Professor Kong, a treasured resource. Almost eighty, he carried in his head, and had stacked up in his office and his home library, books and texts and folios of a Cambodia that was long gone, some of it perhaps that could be reclaimed, rebuilt, but most smashed, obliterated, burned into nothingness. The educated, the intellectuals that might remember were also dead, killed in the madness of the killing fields, the red uprising. Professor Kong was working with several students to assemble the materials to be left with the university upon his death, and also to record on tape his memories of the beautiful land he remembered.

June introduced herself, told who her employer was. "Professor Kong, thank you for taking my call."

"My pleasure, Ms. Replyn. How may I be of service?"

"Sir, I got your name from Detective Terry Stans. Have you been following the story of the young Cambodian woman who was murdered?"

"Yes, in fact I have read about it in your fine newspaper. Very sad."

"Remember the two cousins who were with her? You acted as interpreter for the police right after it happened. I want to talk to them, not about the crime, but about what kind of person she was, hoped to be. Human interest. I need a translator, someone who speaks Cambodian. Can you help me?"

"Ms. Replyn, please, the correct term is Khmer, the Khmer language. Sometime perhaps I could give you a bit of a history lesson; Khmer, Kampuchea, Cambodia. But at this moment you need a translator. I'm sorry, I'm really so busy, but we have many bilingual students, and it would be my pleasure to make to you a recommendation."

"Thank you, that would be fine. And Kahmr, thanks for that, too, I'll remember. Professor, as you make your selection, please be aware it must be someone who not only can translate, but who you also feel is of high integrity, since there is still a murder investigation under way, and something might come out. I hope I didn't offend you by saying that."

"Not at all, I certainly understand. Ah, in fact I think I have just the one. Shall I have him call you if he is interested? And if I may, this would be paid, I assume?"

"Whatever the police rate is we will pay the same. That sounds like it will avoid any problems."

"I agree. If he, or another I trust, is interested, I will ask that they call right away."June gave him her number, thanked him.

That night the salmon was fresh and pink, firm and delicious, the wine a Piesporter Michelsberg Spatlese that was exactly right. Fresh baby spinach with a touch of black truffle oil and rice wine vinegar, oatmeal raisin cookies for dessert. June told Terry about Joe, about the agreement to work together on the crime story, about being afraid he would be a sexist ogre but discovering he was not.

"So you're going to see the cousins... for which story?"

"Tal, and Joe, asked the same thing. Got to prep all three of you, guess I should just send multiple emails from now on. I'm doing a human interest story, no crime, nothing about the murder. Joe thinks it belongs in the crime story, 'dead young woman, dead young dreams' rather than in my story about the company, and I think he's right. So if I get a good interview we'll write it together, run it in City. If by then the bad guy has been caught we can make it one big story, killer and victim, lead story. You are going to catch him, aren't you? Catch him, or them, both murders?"

Terry put down his fork, picked up one of the small dinner rolls she had taken out of the freezer and toasted for dinner. So convenient, but no soul to them. He broke off a piece and ate it. "June, the interviews we did with the cousins were next to useless. They didn't see anything except a quick moving man who jumped out from behind a tree and started shooting, then ran away. They were screaming and crying, looking at their dead cousin, and that's all they know. They think he had on a hat. No description of a coat, no good guess on how tall... hell, it could have been a woman. Ground was firm, not even footprints... Maybe they told us all they know, maybe not, although I think they did, which is bad news for me. When something that terrifying happens that fast people generally don't come up with anything we can use, but sometimes we get lucky. A neighbor who saw him without the hat - or a license plate, even a description of the getaway car - not this time. Canvassed the area, doubled back. Nothing. Too early, really, not many people out at that hour, people who are up are getting dressed, fixing breakfast, not looking out the window. We recovered a bullet from the body, we know the gun's a thirty-eight. That's all."

"Terry, I can't ask them about it, they'll think I lied about why I wanted the interview, and I won't get the background I need."

"I'm not asking you to get into the murder. Just keep those reporter ears wide open, and if you hear something that might be a clue, try to go with it if you can, a follow up question or two."

They talked more as they cleaned up, then watched some television, started to yawn about the same time, and got ready for bed. Without saying it they understood there would be no sex that night, and it was fine with them both. Without saying. They got in bed, snuggled up, and soon were asleep. As she was drifting off she thought this was like being married. As he was winding down he thought that maybe one of these days they should live together, or at least talk about it.

Terry was always prompt, and just before ten-thirty he pulled up in front of the paper. June got in and they pulled away. Although it had been a pleasant night and hurried but pleasant morning, now a few hours later June felt weighted down, as if she were going to a funeral. They rode along in silence for a while.

"You OK with this?"

"Not being my usual cool self, am I? Just a lot of emotions, Terry, going to see someone who was killed at a time she was trying to connect to me. I know I have nothing to feel guilty about, but it feels just like that, like I've done something wrong. I almost feel I need to apologize to her."

"I had a snitch killed once. Confidential informant, that's the term. C I, more polite than snitch. Anyway, it's not quite the same thing, but I sorta understand your feelings, can relate. He made his living, such as it was, begging in the streets, hanging in bars, running errands for criminals who were lazy or didn't want to show their faces in the street for a day or two. And snitching, keeping his ears open and giving me tips once in a while. He got killed right after he tipped me about some jewelry from a robbery and the guys selling it."

"How did he know?"

"Simple store robbery, one guy holding a gun while the other empties the cases. They don't even ask about a safe, just grab the easy stuff and go. Except one of the clerks goes for an alarm button, punk shoots him. So they panic, want to unload the stuff fast and get out of town. Try selling it in bars. Real smart crooks, selling jewelry for next to nothing the day after a jewelry robbery and murder. C I calls me, winds up dead. I felt bad, still do. A drunk and petty crook, but mostly stayed out of people's way. Shame, really. So like I said not the same as you and Rith, but I understand."

"Who shot him, the same robber?"

"No, he was being questioned at the time. In fact both robbers were being leaned on when he was killed. I think it was the robber's brother, they did some deals together. I couldn't prove it, though, no proof. In fact, I think he was a lookout on the store job, he and his brother and the other guy, but they insisted it was just the two of them, and that's what they said all the way to their twenty-five to life sentences."

They arrived at the municipal building that held police offices, the medical examiner, the coroner, and other police and public service departments. June wanted to do it, view the body, but also wanted it to be over with. They didn't talk as they showed their identification to the guard and signed in. Since Terry was an officer they didn't need an escort. Terry put his shield on his left jacket breast pocket, June was given a plastic clip-on tag with "VISITOR Escort Required" on it. They were admitted past the guard's desk and walked to a bank of three elevators. Terry pushed the down button, they waited a few moments until one appeared, several people getting off. Terry and June got into it alone, the walls metal, gray, slightly scratched. She noted that there were two lower levels, and Terry pushed the button for the second one.

"What's on the first level?"

"Parking, mostly. Underground garage. Nice perk."

She nodded. Small talk on the way to see death.

The doors opened and they came out into a hall that spoke clearly to what this lowest level was all about. The floor was large white tiles, about six inches square, with gray grouting. The walls were hospital green up halfway and white the rest of the way to the white ceiling. There was a faint odor of chemicals in the air. It was quiet, and their footsteps sounded loud on the tiles and echoed off the walls.

Terry indicated two doors, double doors hinged to be pushed open at the same time, metal plates to absorb the blow of the gurneys carrying the dead as they were transported from the hallway to that room. He pushed one open and held it for her.

It was cool, but not cold. Terry greeted a man sitting behind a desk doing some paperwork. June glanced to the side and saw into another room, a woman in a green gown and cap bending over a body, reaching out to do something. June quickly looked away. The man checked a clipboard, stood up, and led the way to a bank of large drawers, all stainless steel, set into a stainless steel wall. Closer to this wall the coldness of the unit could be felt, this cold storage unit for mortal remains. He clicked a lock and pulled out a drawer. Her face was covered, an old, old custom of respect, still practiced in this modern, efficient, cold place. The man pulled back the white sheet.

There was nothing extraordinary. She was just a girl, a young woman. Pleasant looking, a nice face with lovely smooth skin. June wished she could have seen her eyes, the smile people told her about. June stared at her for ten long seconds, then softly said "Thank you." The man gently returned the sheet, pushed the large drawer in until the latch clicked.

It felt to June as if she couldn't draw a deep breath, as if she wanted to scream but had no air in her lungs to do so. They didn't talk as they walked again down that echoing green and white corridor and waited for an elevator. Next to the elevators was a bulletin board, and June glanced at it, glad to have something mundane to focus on. A federal minimum wage notice, a workers' compensation rights announcement, a union meeting schedule. The elevator appeared, they rode up, signed out, June returning the badge. Calm on the outside, she was almost frantic to get outside and take a deep breath. Not quite claustrophobia, but close.

As they emerged Terry started walking but June took only a few steps and stopped. "Need to sit down?" he said, gently taking her arm, nodding towards some concrete and wood benches on either side of the doorway.

June said no, not really meaning it. "Just let me move slowly for a minute. I need to catch my breath." She began to walk again, slowly, breathing deeply. Terry glanced at her a few times, worried, but it didn't appear she was going to faint. They walked to the car, got in, drove away.

Two days later Terry called June at her desk and asked if she could get away for about half an hour. It had been raining off and on all day, so she grabbed her light yellow coat and matching rain hat and headed for the front door. It was raining steadily by the time she got there, wind picking up, so she pulled her hat down tight as she waited. Soon after he pulled up, again driving his brown Chevy four-door with black wheel tires, a car that said POLICE to anyone attuned to such vehicles. She ducked her head against the wind, half-ran to the car, got in. Between them was a stack of folders, a clipboard, and a half-full box of low price pens.

He was in a serious mood, business. "Hi. Thanks for getting away. I want to give you something, but first an explanation. What I'm doing might seem to be breaking the rules, giving the press information that I shouldn't. But my take on it is you can help the investigation. Maybe. Remember we talked about your interviewing the cousins....got a date yet?"

"Not yet. Professor Kong was too busy to help me, but he said he'd get me someone. He called back the next day. When Professor Kong gave me his name, Salath Doeung, and phone number he told me Salath would be available, called him an interesting student. Sal, that's what he goes by, doesn't have a foreign accent, sounds like any New Yorker. He had a big paper to finish for an architecture class...that's his major. Anyway, big paper, due next Monday, so we're going to meet at the University, Student Union, next Tuesday at 11:00." They were driving north, and after only a few blocks he turned a corner and parked in front of a No Parking sign.

"There's always a place for the police to park, isn't there?"

"Always. I'm glad you haven't seen the cousins yet, because we got the letter translated. Now I know you can't do the interview like a police questioning, we talked about that, but when I said you might stumble on something, be alert, well, I've got to change that. I want you to probe just a little, whatever you can. I'm not asking you to jeopardize what you're there for, and if it doesn't happen, the moment doesn't occur, then it just doesn't. But please try to make it happen."

"What's in the letter already?"

The rain picked up again, wind blowing harder, the water slamming against the car, seeking a way in. Terry picked up the top folder, opened it, and slid out a single sheet, handed it to her. "It's hard to translate a grammatical error from one language into another, hard to translate 'I seen it' or 'ain't' and carry over the flavor....Professor Kong said the language seemed to be written by someone with not much education, so he cleaned it up a little to make it easier to read."

Daughter pretty like stars I writing to you we are all so thankful give thanks you live in America send money help all family. (We are) able to buy five more healthy chickens make eggs make more chickens. (You) remember land behind house family owns all now your father cleaned made chicken home there now we sell eggs not yet soon sell chickens too. So thankful even bought new clothes for all family. I think you should not tell chief (she might mean boss) about him stay away maybe soon he go work another village. You are good daughter miss you cry but happy you are there safe stay safe someday we be together again mother who loves you in the day and night.

"Oh Terry, this is so sad, this makes my heart ache." She paused, read it again. He waited quietly. "'I think you should not tell chief about him stay away maybe soon he go work another village,' and the word could mean boss. So daughter wants to tell boss something about some man, mother says don't, stay away, maybe he will leave, get a job somewhere else."

"June, that's one of the killers, maybe the man who did both. I just know it. So you see why I'm hoping you can get something."

"So she told him, told Victor, and the killer had to kill him, then her."

"Or maybe the killer just *thought* she had told him. And it could be two killers, we can't forget that."

"Honey..." the word now in occasional use by both "...why don't you just go back to them, the cousins, take your translator, ask them if they have any idea what she...that would be their aunt! Ask them what their aunt meant, who they could have been writing about."

"Considered and rejected. It's either one of two things. One, they don't know anything more than the nothing they've given us so far, in which case all my interpreter and I would get is more of the same, the letter wouldn't mean a thing, or two, they know something or at least suspect it, but are afraid, terrified. Fear of death is pretty powerful stuff, and they saw their cousin murdered literally at their feet."

"So why will they tell me?"

"Because you aren't going to ask them, not directly. June, if that's what's going on, fear of someone, I have no chance. But maybe you could ask them something like 'was she happy here' or 'did she feel safe here' or 'who could do such a thing to a nice young person like that'...maybe catch one of them off guard. Hell I don't know, June, sometimes people just let some things slip. Or maybe they'll confide in you because you aren't part of the police system. Sometimes immigrants from places like Cambodia, or Russia, other places, they see the police and the mayor and the federal government and the army, the FBI, see it as all one and the same."

"You aren't?"

"Well of course we are, southern sheriffs and California Highway Patrol and the US Air Force, we're all on the same payroll, comes out of a secret printing press two levels below the vault at Fort Knox."

"I knew it. Front page story tomorrow."

"You're not dating anyone else, are you?"

June stared, blinked. "What!?"

"Yeah, I thought not. Me too. I mean, I'm not, too. Either. So what if we talked about living together. Just talked about it."

"Where?"

"Talk where or live where?"

"Live, funny guy."

"One of the things we would talk about. I think probably we should decide if we want to, and then talk about where. That seems to be the logical order as I see it."

"Your drive for logic and order may be more than I can stand on a day-to-day basis, but I will consider considering it."

"Ball in your court, let me know if you want to talk about it."

He had left the engine idling in the usual police fashion. Now he turned back to the wheel, put the car in gear and pulled away. They rode in silence almost all the way back to her office, the sky beginning to clear, the rain dropping off to a gentle sprinkle. When they were a block away June spoke.

"You know how you shouldn't go grocery shopping when you're hungry, come home with all kinds of calories and fun stuff you don't need. Well I think this living together decision process is the same kind of thing."

"We won't decide while we're hungry."

"Sort of. I don't think we should talk about it when we're finishing up a bottle of wine, or in bed...."

"Finishing up."

"So very cute. But yes, that's right. Not while we're in bed, or cozy on the couch."

"So where?"

"Riding around in police cars works. Diners, not fancy restaurants with candlelight, but diners. Park bench, but no holding hands. Clear, dispassionate thinking."

"Fine." They pulled up in front of the building. They turned towards each other and said, in perfect unison, "Tonight?"

He raised his eyebrows and smiled, a sort of 'gotcha' smile. She said "Wait, reconsidering... not tonight, Bulldog. I've got some thinking to do."

"Then ball your court on that too. Let me know when you want to sleep over, I'll change the sheets."

Salath Doeung had agreed to come to her office, and then she would drive them both to the interview. He was thin, with bright eyes and a warm smile, and showed up wearing a slightly rumpled tweed jacket over a light blue long-sleeved shirt, no tie, blue jeans and penny loafers, white athletic socks. Very cool.

June greeted him warmly. He called her Ms. Replyn. She guessed he was about ten years younger, but that seemed to widen the gap, so she suggested first names. He smiled his acceptance.

"Let's go, we can talk on the way." As she drove, June asked him to tell her a little bit about himself before she gave him details of the assignment.

"Well, as you can probably guess I wasn't born in Cambodia. Never been there, in fact, and to be honest I've got really mixed feelings. I mean, I know it's my homeland, my parents came here as teenagers, couldn't wait to learn English. They got married early, became citizens... they like to say I'm the result of their citizenship ceremony celebration. So I'd like to see it, but I'm a little scared."

"Scared of...."

"Dangerous people, strange diseases, people not liking Americans... I'm really not the bravest of people, like to feel safe. So I don't know. Maybe I'll go, maybe not. Probably have to, like paying dues. Got to do it but not crazy about the idea."

"Understandable. So you grew up speaking two languages?"

"Well, it was easier for my parents to speak Khmer, their native tongue, and relatives and people in the streets spoke it, but they really encouraged my learning English. College was a goal from the day I was born. Growing up, some of my friends were more fluent in one than the other, so it was always a mixture in the streets, on the playground. By the time I got ready to enroll my Khmer was very weak, very rusty. That's why I'm taking Khmer in college, I mean sure, it's an elective I should do well in, but I never want to lose the ability to speak or read it. And I'm taking culture and history courses too, so I can really know the country, for the knowledge itself but also if I do some day visit the homeland."

"You're an architecture student."

"Yes, fourth year of five. Urban development is my thing. I'd like to work on rebuilding some of our central cities, stop the sprawl, do the livable neighborhoods thing. You know, like old Europe, everyone walks to the bakery."

"Sounds lovely, but I don't know. What are you going to do about the suburbs?"

"Got-to-drive-everywhere-for-everything-burbs? I think the answer is make downtown, or the smaller communities, neighborhoods, more desirable, then people will move there. Folks that want the burbs will still go there, can't stop that, but I think we need to offer more, different choices, especially near the offices or factories, where the jobs are. Let people rediscover what this country had a few generations ago, real neighborhoods."

"Walk to the bakery neighborhoods."

"Yep. And church and to get a jar of mustard or an ice cream cone. All in walking distance."

"Interesting. I wish you lots of luck. Really."

"Thanks. It's hard work, tough courses, tough math, but I love it. So tell me about this assignment we're going on."

"Do you remember the recent story about the young woman, Rith Long, shot dead in front of her cousins, two young women? Morning, on the way to work? And she worked at a clothing factory where the owner hand been murdered several weeks ago?"

"Sure."

"Well that's who we're going to see, the cousins. I'm doing a story about the company, it'll be a feature story in the next few weeks. The line is how a small company keeps going after the sudden loss of its founder, its visionary. Actually not loss but murder, right there, so everyone is a little jumpy, a little suspicious."

"Cops got any ideas yet?"

June paused. This was crucial, the second, hidden reason they were making this visit. "Important question, Sal, let me finish what I was saying about the story, and then I'll answer it. OK, so now the story has changed... not so much changed as gotten deeper, scarier. Not just the unsolved murder of the founder, but also the murder of someone who works there. Aside from solving the cases, which is important, of course... there is the idea of my article. Now it is how does a small, successful firm keep going in the face of two murders, the fear, the suspicion.... but every day product has to go out the door. Every day. Actually, business is quite good, so they all have to keep going, making and shipping athletic wear, while this nine-hundred pound gorilla sits in the corner."

"Two gorillas." He gave a bashful smile. "Sorry."

"No, you're right, two gorillas, because maybe the murders are connected, seems likely, I guess, but no way of knowing for sure, not at this point. Which leads me to the police, to your question."

June slowed her speech a bit, used her most serious speaking voice. "What I'm about to tell you I'm asking you to keep confidential, at least until the killer, killers, are arrested."

He had turned in his seat and was looking at her with no trace of his usual smile. "Sure, certainly."

They were crossing over the 59th Street Bridge, coming into Queens.

"The police are pretty well stuck at this point. They've asked my help because I'm known around the factory, a familiar face. They've interviewed these two women, the cousins, but they got nothing. And we...they don't think they're holding back. It was early morning, the man, if it was a man, pops out from behind a tree, shoots twice, fast, turns and runs, they stand there screaming. Maybe five seconds, they're not even sure if he or she is wearing a coat, and they aren't sure about a hat. Nothing to identify. Zero clues. What the police want from us..." at this point she turned a moment and made hard eye contact, then looked back at the street "...is to listen for something special, unusual. That's extra, something extra for the police, if it happens. We really are going there to interview the two cousins about Rith Long, about what she was like, her hopes and dreams, what kind of a cousin was she, what kind of co-worker."

"For your feature article?"

"Not sure. It may get combined in a City Desk story. If – guess I should be optimistic – when they catch the bad guy this may appear as a side-bar, tell about the victim, make her real in the eyes of the readers, at the arrest, or maybe when the trial starts. That's why we're going to see them, this isn't a subterfuge, I want you to know that. But if you hear something.... I don't know how to describe it. The police have asked us, and I guess that really means you, to keep alert to something that might be a clue. Maybe there was a fight, or maybe somebody threatened someone. And maybe there was a relationship between her and Victor Pritkin."

"Relationship? Sex, you mean? You think this is about jealousy?"

June didn't answer right away, she was driving slower, referring again to the directions she had printed in her reporter's notebook. She nodded to herself, seeing that she was still on the right track and only a few blocks away.

"Sal, you said "think." I'm going to answer it that way. I don't think so. There's no proof, no reason, just women's intuition, but I don't think so. It's too small a shop, and his family, two of his children, work there, so it would have been hard to hide." June paused, then said as much to herself as to her passenger "Of course, they may have known, and they could be hiding it from me." She shrugged slightly.

They were going through an area of older homes, almost all two story duplexes on small lots. On a corner was a small grocery with words in English and Khmer.

June pointed, indicating. "Is that Khmer?"

"Sure is. Alphabet and language. Eggs, chickens, fish... and prices. You knew to call it Khmer, not Cambodian."

"Reporter me. Check facts."

He smiled his broad smile as they pulled up in front of the house. It had a front porch that went the width of the house, and pillars that went up to the second floor where they held up a balcony with a four-foot wall around it, a playpen for toddlers or a place for adults to sit and soak up the sun.

They walked up the stairs and onto the porch, and the front door opened. A young woman opened it and smiled politely. She said a few words of greeting and Sal responded. He introduced her, Sopheara Moeun, to June. The door was held open and they were ushered in. The word redolent occurred to June; the house smelled richly of broth, chicken, spices. The young woman called out something, and a few moments later a second young woman came from another room, the four then going into a front room that was originally a parlor or library, but now held a television and three couches, two in serious disrepair, and what looked like three rolled-up sleeping bags. June was introduced to the second woman, Rith Long's other cousin, Sopharath Moeun. "Sopheara, Sopharath" June said in her head, looking at the sisters, fixing the similar names with the right faces. A man June guessed to be about twenty was slouched in one of the couches, staring at the television with a bored look while a TV pitchman yelled that people should buy his used cars. One of the cousins said something to him; they exchanged a few brief, sharp-sounding words, then the man got off the couch, turned off the television, frowned at June, and slouched out of the room.

The couches were arranged along the walls, all facing the television, so there was a moment of awkwardness about who would sit where. June suggested the cousins and Sal sit on one couch, and she would sit on another at right angles to theirs, near the end where he sat so he could be in the middle. Awkward, but workable.

As soon as they sat Sal turned and, half over his shoulder, said that he was going to remind them who she was, and talk some about why they were here. June nodded. He then turned to the two young women and began talking, making a few gestures to indicate June. As he spoke the sisters began to smile shy, discreet smiles, then giggled a bit. One of them said something, he answered then she spoke again, then the other added a comment, then more giggling as he started to laugh. It dawned on June that Sal was about their age and that he was certainly a nice looking young man, so although sitting there as a reporter unable to understand a word, or even where the conversation was going, was making her crazy, still it was obvious that there was some flirting starting up that might make the eventual interview a lot easier. June sat there, patiently.

After a moment he turned to June. "Guess I should take a minute, do some translation. As soon as I started talking about us, about why you're here, they wanted to know what village I'm from because I talk so funny. When I told them I was born here they said that explains it, I have a heavy New York accent, they rarely hear Khmer New York style. Then they asked me if I knew the latest slang... it would be hard to translate, but it's a pun on cell phone users, a pun about ears...never mind, not important. But they think I'm strange, a New Yorker who isn't up on the latest."

"Quite all right. And I think they think you're cute."

"I do too."

"Can we get to work?"

Salath Doeung nodded and turned back to the two young women. He spoke to them and then both started talking at once. He held up a hand and spoke again, perhaps asking them to stop, and turned back towards June. "I should have thought of this before. Can you give me paper and pen, please?"

June produced a blank spiral notebook and pen from her large combination purse and briefcase. He thanked her, turned back to the two attractive sisters with similar faces and names, and for the next ten minutes they talked and talked, sometimes all three almost at once. To June it was a blur, but she saw that Sal was writing a lot, covering several pages, so she chose to let it go. When they paused Sopharath got up and walked out of the room, and Sal turned his body on the couch so he could face June more directly. He spoke, consulting his notes, and she wrote while he talked. She was thrilled to find that he had done an excellent job.

"Rith liked living in America, liked her job and bosses a lot. They were good to her and she feels they never cheated her out of any of her bonus. The people in this house.. they wouldn't tell me how many, but I think it is a way station for people just off the boats, that's what those sleeping bags are, I'll bet... but anyway, they all share in the expenses, the rent, and some have their own bedrooms, some share. She had her own."

June nodded, writing.

"But she didn't want to stay here, no desire to. In America, I mean. She wanted to get back to where everyone spoke her language. She had some limited English skills, more than her cousins, but really couldn't say much or read more than a few words. Apparently she loved to talk, kind of a gossip, I guess, not being mean, just... you know, liked to be connected. So the situation of being around people who were going places, doing things, and she couldn't talk to them about it...she didn't like it." He paused, flipped a page, continued. "She knew, they all know, they can never be rich here. So it is a decision about being here with all that this country offers but a factory worker with no chance to advance; or going back to Cambodia, won't have the electricity or running water everywhere, especially in the small villages, no movies, malls... but several years of sending that powerful American dollar back home and her family could be quite well off, she could go home and be a... what do they call those coming-out girls, Texas riches....?"

"Debutantes?"

"Yeah, rich family, debutantes, marble vases, like that. The family was, is, getting into chicken and egg farming, already have the land, and it's starting to pay off."

June almost said "I know" and then stopped herself. Instead she said

"So that was the plan, some years here, then home and tend chickens and be a lady of some wealth."

"Yes."

At that moment Sopharath Moeun returned carrying a wicker tray holding a small teapot and four cups, and four spoons with four small bowls containing a baked coconut rice pudding covered in chilled fruit. As Sopharath was serving June asked Sal if he had a chance to ask all the questions they had spoken about in the car. He shook his head no. June sat back in the couch, nodded slightly to him and raised her tea to drink, trying to indicate that this was his interview, she wasn't pressuring him.

The four sat in silence for a moment, sipping the hot green tea, eating the sweet, wonderful dessert, and then the conversation began again. June wrote some clarifying comments next to the notes she had hastily written as he was speaking. She took her time, her head down, not wanting to convey the least impatience. Silence, and she glanced up to see him writing. Then he said something else and the cousin's smiles disappeared. They paused, and then in lowered voices began to speak. June felt like screaming, she wanted simultaneous translation. What were they saying? But she waited, waited. Finally they paused, and he turned back to her.

"Two things. The first is that she had done a little dating here but no boyfriends, and she liked it that way, she thinks it isn't easy to be a married woman with little kids here, not if you don't speak English. Like I said before, she really wanted to go home, planned on it, and pretty much was at work or here or a local restaurant, not out late, no mysteries. As far as your guess, the one you mentioned in the car, I think your impression is right, correct."

June, head down, nodded slightly as she wrote.

"Second, someone at work, guy who unloads boxes and helps the cutter, assistant cutter I guess, had a fight with her about some boxes or materials or something. Something at work. They don't know what it was about because Rith didn't want to talk about it, most unusual, she liked to gossip. They had a fight, and after that she avoided him."

"Avoided scared or avoided mad at?"

He turned back and there was a brief flurry of Khmer.

"Scared, but she didn't want to talk about it."

"Did they tell the police about this, and if so, why not?"

Even as she said it she realized her mistake; anyone living here, especially in lower-income neighborhoods, knows the word 'police' no matter what their language background or skills. The sisters visibly tensed. He started to turn, but she stopped him.

"Wait, I just made a stupid error, they recognized the p-word and they're already on guard. I really want to know the answers, hope you can fix things."

He winked at her, a youthful show of confidence, and turned back to the two young women, who now sat holding their tea cups tightly in their laps, their backs straight. He spoke for some time, they both listening intently, occasionally glancing at June. Then he stopped, and no one spoke for almost a minute. Then Sopheara Moeun softly began to speak, said only a few words and her sister spoke sharply to her. Sopheara responded in a raised voice, Sopharath responded loudly, and suddenly both were standing on their feet, noses inches apart, screaming at each other. In the midst of this June noted that they carefully placed the teacups back on the tray, a gentle, delicate gesture while they shouted as loud as they could. Suddenly Sopharath whirled and looked at June with a startling combination of fear and anger, tears starting to run, and held out both hands, palms up, pleading, and said "You all make dead." Her right hand changed, index finger pointing, and pointed at herself and her sister, back and forth, pointing at each several times. "You all make dead, you all make dead." She ran from the room.

June wasn't sure what to do next, so she did nothing. She lowered her eyes, giving up any control, trusting that her interpreter, who had done so well so far, would know what to do.

He said something softly, and Sopheara sat down again. He paused, then turned to June. "They do know something, they may even know who did it. They are, as you can see, scared. They didn't say anything to the police for that reason, but now Sopheara feels that she has to make it right, has to help the Americans...I mean, the government, punish him."

June took her time, spoke slowly and gently, nodding at Sopheara Moeun, trying to be positive, reassuring, conveying not only through the words to be translated but with her demeanor and tone of voice. "Please tell her this. First, she is doing the right thing, honoring her cousin's memory, and that she is very brave. Second, I have.. friends... in the police department, and I promise her that they will be very careful, move cautiously, and not do anything that will.... No, that doesn't work. Sorry. Say this, say that I will explain the situation and ask the police to be very careful."

The Khmer began again, both speaking in soft voices for a short time. Then Sal leaned forward and gently patted Sopheara on the shoulder, looked her in the eyes and said something. She smiled shyly, got up and started to leave the room. She stopped in front of June and, while looking at her, said something in Khmer. Salath Doeung translated "I hope you are the one who wins." Then she was gone.

June looked at Sal, who said "So does your expense account cover more than my fee? Can you buy me a steak?"

It was such a turn, such a change from the intensity of the past few moments that June started to laugh out loud, then quickly put her hand over her mouth, concerned one of the cousins would hear and misunderstand. She nodded yes and gestured with her head toward the door.

CHAPTER THIRTEEN

Scooter's Saloon of Steaks was as advertised, lots of beef, a few pork and lamb dishes. Serious meat. A small salad with some goopy dressing, a large baked potato or maybe the home fries, and a large portion of the chosen meat. Dessert, if you have room. Maybe the specialty, an over-sized soup bowl with a generous slice of apple pie in the bottom, bowl and pie heated for a moment in the oven. Then two large scoops of vanilla ice cream are added just before it is brought to the table.

Scooter, who had been called Scooter on all but his school records and drivers license since kindergarten, was way beyond scooting; he was in his mid-fifties, five ten, not far from three hundred pounds. His doctor regularly issued warnings, and Scooter had cut down on beer and fried potatoes and heated apple pie bowls, actually weighing thirteen pounds less at his last visit. But the man loved, and lived, to cook and eat and work in his restaurant. When things were crazy he would help out in the kitchen, maneuvering his bulk between the others, mostly in their twenties, mostly less then half his weight. When things were slower he would be everywhere; emptying trash, bussing tables, making coffee, helping the cashier, chatting with the patrons.

Since it was early in the dinner rush there was plenty of room, and they were seated at once. June looked around. "Well, like I said, I never heard of this place. I have a friend that I'll bet would like it."

"Me and some of my friends come here about once every two, three months. We don't get this kind of food at home. Thank goodness, I should add. This is fun on occasion but, well, see the big man over there? That's Scooter. Big steaks and potatoes and sour cream makes one a scooter-type person. Asian food, Cambodian, Vietnamese, Thai, most Chinese, especially the authentic stuff... well, you know, lots of vegetables, bean sprouts, tofu, fish... the only fat is peanut oil, not much meat."

"And rice."

"And endless rice, rice like you can't believe. I'm always amused in the American grocery stores, the little boxes of rice. People buy rice and they get those little boxes or bags that hold, what, a pound or two? What is that? People from the rice-eating part of the world buy large bags, twenty pound sacks, they walk out of the store with them across their shoulders. Most Americans think nothing of those gigantic bags of dog food they haul out of grocery stores, same time they pick up their tiny rice box. To us it sure looks strange. Anyway, I come here, we do, a bunch my age, to eat American and get a little sick on the beef grease."

"I may just have a small salad."

He laughed. "No, no, the food here is wonderful, that's what keeps bringing us back, we just overdo it. Check out the hot apple pie bowl. Meal in itself."

"You said 'we.' Do you feel part of two cultures, going back and forth?"

"No, and I've thought about it. Not going back and forth, but comfortable in both. I really want to do that, be comfortable, and accepted, in both. And I'm learning some of the traditional recipes, often cook them at home rather than do the fast-food thing. I want to know and be fluent in my culture." He paused. "I'm not sure that's a correct use of the word fluent."

"Never mind, it works. You'll make some lucky girl a wonderful husband."

Again that broad grin. "How about Sopheara?"

"Cute, huh?"

"Cute, but she'd have to learn English."

The waiter approached. He ordered a T-bone, medium, baked potato with sour cream and butter and chives. She ordered the petite strip, also medium, and a plain baked potato. The waiter seemed disappointed but said nothing. Iced tea for both.

"Plain potato?"

"Pepper on it, that's enough. OK, now I am feeding you besides paying for your translation skills, do you think you could share what that dust-up was all about?"

"Dust-up?"

"Argument. Hollering. Like I'm going to holler on you in a minute if you don't tell me what was going on. I mean, what was that 'You all make dead'?"

He spoke while she took notes. "Rith Long had an argument with the man who helps the cutter. That's what they called him, the cutter."

"I think I know who she means, who the cutter is."

"Well, he has a helper, who I guess brings him boxes, gets things from the loading area or trucks. His name is Say Phan."

"That's one word, a last name...?"

"No, first and last. Two short words, in English spelled S A Y, just like the word say, and P H A N."

"Got it.. please go on."

"I'm a little unsure of the factory process ... sorry, they weren't...it seemed they aren't real familiar with how things are done, who does what, away from the sewing department they work in."

"You're doing fine. What did they argue about?"

"Well, like I said when we were in the house, Rith Long was kind of a gossip, fun person, liked to poke into everything. She apparently asked him, the helper, something about some boxes and he blew up at her, told her it was none of her business. Then she told her cousins, kind of off handed, just making fun of him, but when they started giving him glances in the break room he knew she had said something. So he cornered Rith and said if she ever talked about it again she might never see her home."

"How do they know he said that?"

"She sat them on her bed, swore them to secrecy, whispered it to them. Told them to never say anything or even look at him."

"Do they think he was the killer?"

"Maybe. And something they didn't tell the police, just didn't, don't know why.... the killer looked strange, a shiny face."

"Shiny face? What...."

"Mask? Stocking?"

June smiled, nodded in recognition. "Oh, that's good. That's real good."

"Annnnd....the reason he wore a stocking to disguise his face was..... he was afraid that Rith's cousins would recognize him, even though the sun wasn't up much, just getting light enough to see."

"If saving our crumbling cities doesn't work out you might consider becoming a detective."

"No no, not at all interested. The evil-doers use real bullets that can kill you and make you dead."

The plates of steaks and side dishes arrived, and they concentrated on eating for a few moments.

The young man pointed at his food with his fork, smiled his broad smile and shook his head slowly from side to side, a gesture of wonder and appreciation. "I think they are pretty sure it was someone they know, probably that cutter helper Say Phan, the one who got so hot, warned her..."

"Pretty sure?"

"Well, they never said it, but that whole blowup... just before it I had tried something like....like.... let's see. They had mentioned the shiny face. I said...what I said, asked really, was 'you could not recognize, could not know who it was' rather than 'it was too dark to see.' Not bad, huh?"

"I'm telling you, you may think you're an architect, but....."

"It was the reaction. They didn't say what the police reported, what it said in the papers. Your paper, I never read any other...."

"The steak is paid for. Not necessary to flatter."

"Well, I do like your sports section. Anyway, they didn't talk about it being too dark. When I said that, you see? They didn't talk about not being able to see him.... when I spoke about recognizing they both paused, kind of looked at each other, you know, checking... and then the roof came off."

"So your guess is they have a hunch who it is, your guess being they both strongly suspect it was Phan, but can't be sure, and don't want to be."

"And *really* don't want to be."

"'You all make dead.' I recently heard a comment about the power of the fear of death. Guess that's what's going on here."

He nodded in agreement. "They see how easy it is to get a gun and kill someone on the streets and disappear. No, worse than disappear, actually go right back to the job, just like nothing happened."

"Must be creepy, scary, seeing him every day. It's a wonder they don't quit."

"Well, I can only guess... didn't ask that, of course.... but my guess is that they like the job, don't have to struggle learning English, so I guess they just stay there and stay away from him."

"And quitting draws his attention to them, makes them stand out."

"And that. How's your steak?"

"Just fine. Yours?"

"Very American. Wonderful."

June reached for her notebook again.

"All right, before you go into a protein-induced coma, anything else?"

He paused a long time, got out the notebook she had given him, flipped through the pages, then looked up. "No, I really think I've given you everything about her, Rith Long. She was a pleasant, friendly, slightly gossipy girl...woman, young woman..... people liked her, she was certain she was going home and so apparently was good at not partying too much, not risking being pregnant. Her cousins said she talked about having a child, having children in Cambodia as a wealthy person, that would be nice, desirable, but not in America, not be lower income in America and with a child. Apparently there are some women at the shop in exactly that situation and Rith would say that she didn't want to have to struggle like that. She sounds like a very focused person, work a while, send money home, follow the money in a few years and live a good life, marry well, have children and sell chickens and eggs. Yeah, focused. Those two miss her a lot."

They ate again for a moment, June feeling virtuous about giving up the sour cream, the butter.

"Oh, yes, there was something else. When I asked them to tell me about the killing, and they said that, well, just what was in your paper, on TV, you know, the three are walking to work, a man, probably a man, jumps out from behind a tree, shoots and runs away, just like that, it happens so fast early in the morning. But then they mentioned the shiny face, and I picked up on that, asked them... but the other thing is I asked them if they think anyone heard the shots, any neighbor's lights on.... and then Sopharath said it was a big gun but it made no noise. Her sister agreed. No noise, no gunshot, maybe a little pop, a popping sound like a toy."

"They both said that?"

"Yes, and although I didn't ask for details I think they both know what a gun sounds like. I don't mean anything sinister, could have been with their father hunting back home, but they both seemed sure of it."

"I didn't know if silencers were real or just something in gangster movies. Guess they're real. Wonder why the police didn't get that?"

Sal shrugged. "It was kind of luck, I asked them if they thought any neighbors heard the shots. If I didn't ask it that way.... The police probably assumed it was a, I don't know, a regular gun."

"And maybe they planned on checking with all the neighbors anyway, so they didn't have to... have a reason to ask the sisters. Sal, you've done fine, and if you don't mind I'll give your name to the police as another translator."

He smiled his big smile. "Cool, thanks. I'll have to learn some new slang if I'm going to be translating for the young ones, but I'd love to. Yeah, thanks."

June smiled back at him. This had gone so very well.

CHAPTER FOURTEEN

"**W**hat happened?" the American screamed, face hot and flushed. "What the crazy fuck happened?"

"He look see some be wrong" said the Cambodian. "Some number on box, show weight… ya know, make weighed some extra times, I don know, he talked me night before, but so tired, I talk him wait next morning, I say meet you in morning, we figure out. He say that OK."

"You've caught the papers before, never been a question."

"Not my fault" came the answer, voice raised almost to a shout. "Got weighed again, box weighed one more time, make weigh on docks after take off ship, on dock, ya know? I tink, he tink, I don know, now it don match. Weight don match I talk fast, tell him, ya know, say let's see in morning, get papers OK."

"So you had to kill him?" The anger stayed intense, hot.

"All night tinkin what fuck I gonna do, all night, can't figure it no way. Look, we got sweet somabitch deal, we do. Sorry about old boss, nice guy, but deal more sweeter now, he not here, not ask what papers say, ask about weight. No questions no more. Good for both us, huh?"

"I don't know, I don't know."

"*I* know. This nice deal, folks in deal, not just you me. Tink this deal just end if you pissed? Got some other people, ugly somabitches, kick crap outta us we want make end this deal. Shit, we lucky they only kick crap. Somabitches kill you like be nothin' you want stop deal." The Cambodian stopped, put out a hand and laid it gently on the American's arm. "Hey, sorry 'bout old boss, really sorry, no shit. I only no see other way make stop, make stop all somabitch questions, ya know?"

The American looked at the Cambodian a long, hard moment, said "You didn't have to kill him" then walked away fast, out of the room, slamming the door.

"Yes I did" said the other to the closed door. "Yes I did."

CHAPTER FIFTEEN

June had made a promise to a clothing manufacturer months before, and suddenly there it was, up on her calendar. It was the introduction of yet another moderately priced line for the euphemistically named working woman, which meant secretary or administrative assistant or program manager, not the boss. The display was created to emphasize that market target. Instead of a runway there was a large office setting, the desks far apart, computers and fax and copy machines everywhere, their brand names well displayed. Product placement at its best. At the desks were models, attractive but not gorgeous women, mostly five six to five eight, taller than most of the population but not so tall as the superstar models. Each was dressed in one of the outfits, suits with pants or skirts, office-appropriate dresses. They were all busy at their keyboards, springing up every so often to fax or copy something. On the back of their outfits, just below their necks, were discreet tags with a number on it. The numbers were referenced in a brochure handed to all the visitors, who wandered through this make-believe office, watching the busy models pretending to work. After about ten minutes the designers, a twin brother-sister team, began speaking from a small stage into hand-held microphones.

The brother spoke first. "Again, ladies and gentlemen, thank you for coming to this premier of our new line of TWYNS clothing. As you watch these busy people work, please note that their clothing resists wrinkling. Observe that sitting does not put unwanted creases across their laps or under their knees. Our new TWYNS weave is marvelously crease resistant. But there's more!"

At this cue one of the models, wearing a tan pants suit with a cranberry blouse came to the stage. She was holding a cup of coffee.

Now the sister spoke while the brother demonstrated. "Let's say there is a typical office accident." At this the brother faked, with wide-eyed horror, tripping and stumbling into the model, who spilled the coffee in a dark stain down her jacket and one leg of her slacks. "Don't worry, the coffee is cold." That brought some polite chuckles from the audience. "Now watch this!"

The model picked up a towel, and dipped it into a basin of water. "That's plain water, folks, no chemicals," said the twin sister. The model took the damp towel and began blotting her clothing, the stain slowly fading. In a few minutes the area was wet but no longer dark, and as the brother began using a hair dryer from a short distance away the wet faded, leaving no trace of the coffee behind. "How about that" said the sister, turning to the audience in an obvious call for applause, which was politely provided by the assembled reporters, buyers, and industry hangers-on.

After the demonstration the models continued their pretend office work while the twins circulated, making sure everyone had a brochure, answering questions. June thought the clothing, crease and stain resistant and reasonably priced, worthy of a mention, although not an entire article as the twins had hoped, so she took the time to ask questions of the two owners. For a few hours she was back on familiar turf, two feet solidly planted in a world she knew and understood. As she left the show June thought that this was where she wanted to be, not reporting on crimes, on murder. Leave that to the city desk, they are welcome to it.

"Terry, I've got something for you."

"I know you do, girl."

"Oh, in that kind of a mood, are we. You know, it does irritate me that I'm sitting here blushing, hoping no one notices, and I'm sure you're just as cool as can be. I know I keep asking this, but how do you do that?"

"Secret police training. Can't say anything more."

"Well, secret policeman, I just guess I'll call the chief of detectives, see if anyone is interested in a clue."

"So the interviews went well."

"Sort of…not bad, really. I've got enough for a good human-interest story, work with Joe and get it out in a few days. Oh, and by the way, I know who killed Rith Long." She tried to be flip as she said it, but her voice caught a bit. "Oh Terry, I guess I can't be funny about this. I really think I know who did it."

"What do I have to do so you'll tell me?"

"No doubt at all, you are in the *mood*."

"Often am. So I have to....?"

"You know."

"Yes, I know. What time will you be over?"

"No, my place tonight. My power. I'm in charge. I'm the one with the clue, so I'm the one who says what's what."

"I'll be there by seven. Am I bringing anything for dinner?"

"Main course, whatever it is. I've got the rest."

"Then it's pork chops tonight, cook 'em in that iron skillet, all blackened and spicy."

"See you then."

June hung up, a bit of a glow from his eagerness for her, the promise of what was going to happen that night. She took a deep breath, pushed back her shoulders, tried to put Terry on a shelf for the rest of the day so she could get some work done. Two choices: deal with the stacks that had grown again in her in-baskets, plus the too-many emails, or go talk to Joe Strecta about the interview. No contest. She picked up her notepad and headed for his desk. She could call first, of course, but this way if he wasn't in she could leave a note, personal and handwritten, show him she was reaching out, being a partner.

Joe was in, on the phone, the phone propped up by one of those phone pads that stick on and make it easier to hold the receiver between head and shoulder while the hands were busy. He was rapidly jotting notes on a standard size lined pad, and as he listened and wrote he also looked up, gave June a warm welcoming look and a nod of his head and pointed with his free hand to the chair next to his desk.

June sat, waited. She briefly considered giving him a "call me" signal and going back to her desk, but decided against it, instead opening her notebook and reviewing, although she well knew what was there.

"Got to tell you, that is really something. I don't remember ever hearing the like. Look, can you get me the contact person, phone number? No, yeah sure, if I'm not in just leave it. Thanks. Thanks for calling, great story, and we're always looking for good news, don't want to always be reporting what the bad guys did. Yeah. Sure. Thanks again. Bye."

He hung up and turned to her. "Hey, June. What's up?"

"You working on a good news story?"

"Little strip mall, almost to the Connecticut line. Got some road repair going, then a water main busts. Have to close the stores for three days, no water, and even when they get water again, there is all this muddy road work... plus now water lines being dug up and replaced. So business dies. Just dies. Almost impossible to get in and out, temporary access roads, detour signs, barriers... a mess, and shoppers are real scarce. Small shops like that, most of 'em don't have business interruption insurance, and even if they do their problem is immediate, cash flow squeeze right now, insurance check down the line won't help today. Anyway, the landlord cuts the rents by one half for everyone. For three months. Wasn't even asked, just learned about how bad it was and made the decision. This guy" he said, nodding towards the phone "owns a little frame shop, just can't believe it. He's going to come up with somebody who can speak for the landlord, so I can get a direct statement."

"Nice. Real nice to hear about companies with a heart."

"Well.... yes, and I'll tell it that way, reader's love it. Of course, it isn't all heart. Maybe zero heart. The three months of lowered rent may save the tenants... this way the landlord keeps everybody open, the mall looking prosperous. Otherwise maybe one or two go under, empty storefronts, looks bad. Plus, if they lose a few stores it could take six months, maybe a year to find new tenants. So this was insurance, in a way. But unless I hear something like that when I talk to them I'll leave it out, see if I can write one column without a cynical reality check."

"Meaning you hope they do say it 'cause you sure want to write it."

"Man, I was hoping to sneak my cynical nature past you, but looks like I can't. So since I'm guessing you didn't come to see what old Joe is cranking out, and you've got a notebook there, you've got something for me. Do it, I'm all ears." He sat back in his chair, crossed his arms.

"Joe, here's my problem. Ever since I got the assignment about ComFitter my work situation has been nuts, and I'm getting tangled up in the murder, now murders. I'm doing some investigating, and that's way out of my normal field, so I can't do it fast... this is taking lots of time and concentration. Meanwhile my regular job stuff piles up, things to read, letters, email, story ideas, conference or show invitations. I've got some information about a company that developed a new lightweight lifejacket for the government, Marines actually. Now they're planning on making a version for the public. It's a good story. I've got to stop being lady detective long enough to write it, and clean out my mail, paper and E...."

"I believe you. What do you want to do?"

June smiled warmly at him. "Well, Joe Strecta, I guess I am going to have to give up all my prejudices and just plain like you, just figure out that you're a friend."

"I thought we covered this already."

"We did. Reaffirmation, that was."

"Great. So....."

"How about I write it up in a good draft, you polish or spin or edit to your delight, put two names on it."

"Sold. Why don't you just do a quick sketch right now, let me be thinking on it till I get your draft."

"Sure. But it'll be soon, I want to get this down while it's still fresh, and besides if I don't it will just nag me, interfere with my reading of GQ."

"Hunk mag. You women are all alike."

"Ignored. So, here it is." June glanced once more, briefly, and a few of the pages in her notebook then lifted her head and talked to him without referring to it again. She spoke swiftly, with some intensity. "Well, Rith was a pretty level-headed young woman. She was sending money home on a regular basis, which the family was using to buy chickens. They, the family, bought a little piece of land adjoining their home, and they are making a chicken and egg farm there. Her plan was to work just a few more years and then go home and be a poultry queen, be part of a fairly wealthy family. The difference between the dollar and their Riel is so great that it has tremendous buying power. Think about it. She wasn't making much, and while she didn't have many expenses she did have a rented room, had to buy food, some clothes... but whatever she could send home was so powerful that doing that, sending something each month, was setting the family up real good. She had friends, was a jokester and kind of a live wire, bit of a gossip, but not much in the way of real entanglements, no serious boyfriends. Real worried about getting pregnant."

"Because that would kill the dream."

"Sure, and because apparently she didn't want to be here, struggling to learn the language. She really wanted to go home, speak her native language, enjoy the farm."

"Poultry queen."

"Yep."

"This may be a bit too mushy for an old crime beat goat like me."

"I'll make sure to say murder and blood and guns and death in my draft, that work for you?"

"Funny."

"I've got a clue, too. Going to pass it on to the cops, want to hear it?" She had decided that she had to share something with him, keep him connected. After all, she works for the paper, that's where her paycheck comes from. But how much to say.....

"For publication or not?"

"I think not, not yet, might make their job harder." She shrugged. "You tell me, this is your world, but I bet they'd like us to hold off."

"Clue me."

"Clue you. The cousins told me that the man...likely a man, not sure... had a shiny face. They couldn't really see him, too early, just past dawn and some distance away, but they saw he had a shiny face."

"A shiny face." He said it in a flat monotone. "What, he shaves and puts on some kind of after shave before going out to kill this girl? What?"

"Stockings. A stocking over his face because, well, our guess...."

"Our? You been to your detective with this already?"

She let the 'your' go this time. "No, the kid who did the translating. Nice college kid, Cambodian parents, raised in New York. Sal. I think the cousins were dazzled. So our guess is that it's someone they're familiar with, likely work with. He disguised his face because even in dim light they'd recognize him."

"Nice. Makes sense. Got a question, though." He paused, she waited. "Did they get close enough to see if it was a distorted face, that is, shiny because of a stocking, or shiny because of sweat? Could have been a man with a sweaty face... or maybe a woman sweating who was wearing lotion, too much lotion, sweat. Look, I think the stocking....fits...sorry... but it could be makeup or sweat. Heat sweat, nervous sweat."

June sat looking at him a moment, then picked up her pen and began writing. When she looked up again she said "Valid points. I'm not sure.

Let me give you a name..... just in case there's a police report, arrest or something, and Terry doesn't spot it, so might help if you keep an eye out too. Name is Say Phan. S A Y, P H A N. He works with them at ComFitter, they think he's the one. Scared of him, really scared." She paused a moment, he waited. "About that shiny... sweat or stocking or... I need to ask Sal, maybe he'll have to talk to them again. I don't think he'll mind. It will give him an opportunity to put some moves on one of them.

"Or both."

"They're all so cute, seem so young, the three of them. Of course, he's in college, so this is just another one of those reminders that I'm rapidly aging."

"Are the doctors you go to older or younger than you?"

"Older...yes, older.

"Wait until the doctors are younger. I mean *lots* younger, you hope they aren't imposters from a tech school with a two year degree. That really ages you. I'm not impressed, June."

June laughed, got up, headed back to her desk. She immediately began writing the story, and found that she couldn't confine it to a rough draft format, but rather was writing a nearly finished human interest story. Having thought about it, and just now going over it with Joe, helped the words flow rapidly and smoothly. She was done in less than an hour, saved and emailed the story to Joe. She sat back, pleased, and was debating whether to take a break, grab a coffee and sandwich, when a clerk came by and added three-quarters of an inch to her second in-basket, now approaching the spill-on-the-floor point. June first took that as a signal to work rather than break, but then she decided she needed her caffeine and some protein to climb those mountains of paper. Off for a break, then the world of business fashion once again.

CHAPTER SIXTEEN

June left work promptly at five. She hurried home, stopping by the small neighborhood grocery for salad makings, a wonderful rice pilaf and an unopened carton of peach sorbet already at home from her last shopping trip. As she moved around the apartment, doing a little cleaning, some picking up, making sure the kitchen was ready, she thought again about their brief comments about living together. Just a few spoken words, now hanging silently in the air just outside of their conversations, waiting like an apple on a near tree, waiting for one of them to pluck and show the other.

She was glad, really deeply glad when he rang her buzzer. He came in and set down the groceries and gave her a long, hard kiss

She thought, but didn't say, "if this ain't love it sure looks like it."

"So do you want to talk a while or get right to the cooking chores?"

"Can you wait a bit? We could wine cheese and crackers while I tell all."

"Sure. I brought a Shiraz to go with the steak, want that?"

"No, we've still got some Riesling, it'll go nice with the cheese. Put your feet up, let me make us a snack."

June sliced thin slices of a Canadian cheddar and a mild gouda, added some wheat crackers and bite-sized pieces of a firm pear, brought them to where Terry was sitting, the wine poured.

"Who killed her?"

"His name is Say Phan, he is the assistant to the cutter, moves boxes of material around, other helping chores. They had an argument, something about some boxes, no details beyond that. But whatever it was he was really angry with her. Then she talked to her cousins about his reaction and they start looking at him funny, so he really blows up, tells Rith Long that if she doesn't shut up... the way it was translated was that she'll never see home again."

"The boxes...."

She leaned forward, intent, animated. "Terry, I've had an idea for some time. I didn't talk to you about it because I wanted something to hook it to, make more sense in my head before I told you. Terry, they have a scale in the loading dock, you know, inside. Why? Everything they sell, everything, is by piece, that's why they call them pieceworkers, that's why they have two people counting tags while they inspect. Very thorough

120

piecework system, nothing by weight. So the scale must be for something incoming."

"Unless they're from a former system, something they don't do anymore."

"No, I don't think so. First, because they're strapped for space, you've seen it, they're looking for a new place now. No way they'd keep a big box-shaped thing like that, using up floor space, if they didn't use it. Plus they would have sold it, smart business people, not going to let an asset just sit there. No, they use it. In fact, it was being used the day we met, it just didn't register."

"You were too busy flirting with me" he smiled.

"Whatever your ego requires. To continue, they use it to weigh incoming boxes. My guess is that they are sold fabric by weight. The boxes come sealed, some kind of strapping around them. That's what the tin snips are for. Weight is shown on the boxes, and also on the paperwork that goes with it."

He nodded agreement. "Got it. How do you know all this?"

"Some I observed while there, but I've seen similar systems. How do you know if you're getting what you paid for? Weigh it before you cut the wires, if it doesn't weigh right call them, get a customer representative to come check on it." She sat back, pleased with her dissertation.

"So this is a murder over short-weighting?"

"How about over-weighting? What if there was something else in the boxes, made them heavier than the weight of the fabric? You order, say, so many bolts of fabric weighing two hundred pounds. Says that right on the box, on the paperwork. Everything checks. But what they ship... deliver...is a box that weighs two hundred and twelve pounds. But the customer ordered only two hundred. Put it on the scale, scale would say two hundred twelve. But what if you took the twelve pounds out before you weighed it?"

"Then the scale would say two hundred, the correct amount the customer ordered, so the customer is happy, all is well."

"As long as no one looks at the paperwork and the scale at the same time *before* you extract the extra pounds." June put down her wine glass, began drawing pictures in the air. "So picture this. Small shop, everyone trusts everyone, and this Say Phan, this cutter helper is the guy who weighs the boxes and opens them. And I'll bet they don't weigh each time, just every third or fifth or maybe even tenth, depends on their experience. Never had a problem with a particular supplier, they might spot-check the weight only every tenth box. And maybe the extra twelve pounds are coming in only every once in a while, maybe one box out of ten, or fifteen or twenty. Could be real easy to hide, that occasional heavy box never gets weighed."

"Drugs."

"Easy guess. Something else? I don't know....twelve pounds of diamonds?"

"Not nearly as likely. No, I think you've got it. A small-time drug smuggling operation, a box with an extra cargo of heroin or cocaine or hashish every once in a while, no way to spot it."

"Drug-sniffing dogs? Customs?"

He shook his head no. "Got to do some research, but my quick answer is the sheer volume makes it really hard to spot the occasional small shipment. They can't have the dogs working over thousands of tons of shipments, so they concentrate on the known or suspected bad guys, maybe act on tips. And even if a box were caught, then what? No proof anyone at ComFitter ordered it—it is addressed to a company not a person. So they'd have to investigate or do a sting ... and any strange faces would be spotted. Even strange cars parked nearby... no, it would just be really hard to catch the intended recipient, the one who knew the dope was coming. And since it's only coming in once every so often you can bet the stuff is out of there in a few hours." He paused, then concluded "So if they follow the box to the factory, they can't prove who the intended recipient was... I mean, who's going to believe it was the revered father who started the company? If they snoop around the contact just shuts down operations for a while. And... if the feds or customs police wait more than a few hours, likely there's nothing to find, nothing at all, except some low cost sports clothing. Neat."

"You didn't list Marijuana."

"Probably not, too bulky. I mean, think of oregano, or parsley, along with some small twigs. Even if you compress it into a tight brick it still takes up a lot of space. Not enough profit for the risk, too low a street markup. No, grass is brought in by the truckload, or at least trunk load."

"So why the murders?"

"You're being the dazzling detective. Keep going."

"Food first. Let me get blackened pork chops working and I'll give it a try."

Terry nodded, smiled, finished off his glass of wine. "Yes, let's have dinner and talk some more and go to bed. Remember, there was something I had to promise to do in trade for hearing those clues."

He picked up the now nearly empty snack tray and walked toward the kitchen. June watched him. She drank her wine, looked at the bottle and saw it held only a small amount. She emptied it into her glass and drank quickly.

They worked together in the kitchen, and soon dinner was ready. The hot frying pan seared and blackened the pork chops that darkened from the soy sauce and Worcestershire mixture. The second bottle of wine was red and crisp, bright, a nice contrast to the meat. They began eating, then June said "Ready to hear my theory?"

"Certainly."

"Victor spotted something, something about the boxes, the weight. Now your guess is that the murderer came in with him or was let in soon after. All right, so the day before, maybe even just before closing, Say Phan and Victor are talking. Just a conversation, two men who work together, about some discrepancy. They agree to check into it the next morning."

"Why wait?"

"Because... as I said, end of the day. Or maybe things are really busy, easier to do it in the morning." She cut and ate a bite of her chop, he waited. "Let's say it is some kind of drugs. They could still be there in the building, that's a question, isn't it, how they get rid of it, get it out of there without it being spotted."

"Take the material out, leave the stuff in the boxes, throw away the boxes and do a slight-of-hand then? Guess I need to check on that, how old boxes are pitched. But I keep stopping you....."

"No, I like that, helps clarify. Sure, this makes sense. They decide to look into the weight discrepancy in the morning. The killer knows the dope is stashed..."

"The dope is stashed?"

"I don't know about you, but I sure smoked some pot in college."

"As did I. But that's for another discussion."

"Anyway, he's in a bind. The dope is still there, in the boxes, the paperwork doesn't match up, maybe Victor hadn't looked at the numbers for a long time, thinks this is just a fluke thing."

"Yeah, that fits with the earlier idea, right? If they expect two hundred pounds of fabric and get that amount there's nothing to be suspicious about."

"Say Phan thought he could do this forever, never have a problem. Now suddenly he's got a big problem, can't figure out what to do about Victor's questions, and in the end just kills him. Not really planned, just ran out of time and ideas."

"And the proof is....?"

"Search warrant for his apartment. There you find boxes and boxes of potent illegal drugs, money wrapped up in rubber bands, names of contacts and dealers. He confesses in minutes, and they promote you to captain. And you take me to Las Vegas."

"More than wonderful, except it can't happen, the search that is. Vegas we can talk about. No search because no warrant, not near enough to get a warrant on, and even if we did I'll tell you right now there won't be a gram of drugs in his place. Or a list of the bad guys."

"Money?"

"Stashed, fake I D and put it in a safe deposit box under a false name, or a storage locker, something like that."

June put her knife and fork down, sat back in her chair. "So it really works that way, sometimes you're pretty sure who the bad guy is, but can't wire tap or get a search warrant because there isn't enough hard evidence. Like on television. Or the movies."

"The Constitution of the United States of America. Wonderful document. Occasionally makes this police work a little difficult, it does."

"So we need to trick him. Or trap him."

"Well, I'm certainly hoping you'll keep this out of your story, any mention of Phan. Make it a little hard to trap him if he reads about it first in your fine paper."

"Nope, although I like having a big head start on that story. No, the first story will be just about her, and probably something about the police having no clues at the end. Joe and I are writing it together, but no mention of his name, or a clue, or a trap. This is getting exciting."

A long moment went by, Terry eating, June picking up her knife and fork and resuming. Then "Terry, what?"

Now he put down his utensils and folded his hands in front of him. She knew by now that was his "serious statement coming" posture. "June, there are two people dead, and you've identified a strong candidate for one, maybe both of the murders. That's.... I don't know, great. Spectacular. But you can't go any further with this, this is a police investigation, and if we're going to set a trap you can't be part of it. For lots of reasons."

"The newspaper."

"Yes, you'd be crossing a lot of lines, confusing to think about all of them, and of course I would too. Something goes wrong and we're both in big trouble."

"But I told you about it, this is my lead...."

"Already conceded. But think about it this way, you're an informant. Not the usual informant, you're far better looking than the others I use, for one thing."

"And we're sleeping together."

He paused. "Honey, that's right. And that's a complication. Neither one of us can let our personal and professional lives get any more mixed than they already are."

There didn't seem anything else to say. They finished dinner talking occasionally about their jobs, then news of the day, national events. The investigation, the murders, the suspect, were not mentioned again. But they were not gone, they nagged in silence.

As they were cleaning up Terry said "June, one more piece of business. I need Sal Doeung's phone number. Sounds like he did a good job for you."

"Sure, I've got it at work. I'll email you in the morning. You know, I'm going to keep after you to make sure I stay connected to this."

"Big story."

"Yes, scoop of the year. No, well sure I want the big story, but I'm connected to this, you understand."

"I understand."

"Can we stop working and start playing soon?"

"Lusty Lady."

"Potent Policeman."

CHAPTER SEVENTEEN

People usually say supply and demand, but perhaps it should be demand and supply; where there is demand there will be supply. It is the same for hot dogs, apple pie, porch swings, prostitution, gambling, cocaine, heroin. Where there is demand there will be supply, an undeniable force.

There are several factors that make stopping heroin such a difficult, if not impossible task. The initial source is a flower, a particular kind of poppy, that grows on hillsides and low mountain slopes in many places around the world, and if it were a legal crop could certainly grow on millions of such acres in America. Harvesting the resin is a relatively simple task, as is the production of the final drug. So it is not hard to make; good wine or cheese or fine chocolate take at least as much effort, usually much more. It is an easy commodity to produce, and of course can be shipped in small quantities. Unlike marijuana, where tens if not hundreds of pounds are necessary for a large profit to be generated, a pound or two of pure heroin will produce a significant profit. That's the big problem in stopping heroin; it isn't hard to cultivate or harvest or process or ship to the eventual customer in America or Canada or France or Britain. If not for the stressful and occasionally dangerous work performed by thousands of diligent customs agents and border guards and other officers of the law it would be much worse, but even with their efforts the drugs come through. They arrive in trucks and cars and boxes of candy and teddy bears and crates of dried figs and stomachs and vaginas and rectums. Demand supplied by supply, as constant as gravity.

There are two more factors that make the battle to reduce drug use so difficult. The first is that the markups as the drug moves along, from the harvesting of the resin to the individual street sales, are staggering. This means that people can be bribed, with officers and guards in various Asian or Middle Eastern countries being offered the equivalent of a whole year's wages to just look the other way for a while; and not in the local currency, but in American money, bricks of green money to take home and hide. An overwhelmingly powerful bribe. It also means a young unemployed American or Canadian can be offered five thousand dollars to drive a car across the border, that's all, just pick up a car in Vancouver and drive it to Seattle, half a day's work for five thousand dollars. Don't be nervous, tell the guards you're on vacation. Of course, if you get busted you're on your own, since the person who made the offer has only a first name. And if you make it through just turn over the keys and collect your money, try anything else and the bad guys will find you and torture you and kill you. And it also means that there is plenty to give away free, hook young people as they are hooked on cigarettes, acts of defiance, proof of adulthood, tobacco and marijuana and sex, heroin and cocaine to prove how tough and grown up they are. Only too late do they discover that they will do anything, *anything* to get their next fix. Sell their bodies, even sell their babies. Anything. And, tragically, that anything includes not only selling one's possessions or body or children, stealing from the family, robbery and burglary, but also getting others hooked, finding new customers for the dealer. The payoff, the commission, is free drugs.

The final factor is that the wide customer base allows for low cost individual sales. With tobacco, as cigarette prices go up more people are willing to suffer the withdrawal to break their legal drug addition. In contrast, by regulating the purity - more drugs per dose when the supply is plentiful, more additives when the supply is tight - the price of heroin and cocaine can be held fairly constant, nickel and the more common dime bags, five and ten dollars per purchase, several purchases a day. So an almost unstoppable flow of fives and tens and twenties comes from this alley and that apartment building, this small town and that city, a trickle here and a larger one there, until a great green flood of millions of dollars leaves the purchasing nation and goes to Mexico or Columbia or China or Afghanistan, Laos or India or Pakistan or other nations. Millions and millions of dollars, one purchase at a time. One addiction at a time. One child, teenager, young adult at a time.

CHAPTER EIGHTEEN

"Salath Doeung, please."

"This is Sal Doeung."

"Mr. Doeung, this is Detective Terry Stans. I'm working on the Rith Long and Victor Pritkin homicides, and June Replyn said you were very helpful. I'd like to know if you'd be interested in doing similar work for us, for the New York Police Department."

"Certainly. Absolutely."

"You have to understand that anything you do with us will have to be completely confidential, and can't be shared with anyone, including your family or Ms. Replyn."

"I understand."

"I'm not sure at this point what direction we're going in next, but we're going to do something soon. How available are you on short notice?

"I'm a stressed college student, help my parents part-time, so it just depends... I mean, I've got time, but it's hard to say for sure what days or times."

"I don't think that will be a problem. This is a cell phone number, right?"

"Yes, and I pretty much have it with me all the time."

"Good. I don't think this will be a drop everything and come now situation, but it could be if there is an arrest."

"Say Phan?"

A significant pause. "Mr. Doeung, can we both pretend you didn't say that? And can you work real hard to not repeat that name to anyone? You haven't, have you? Told anyone?"

"No sir, I'm sorry, no, only June."

"That's what I was hoping you'd say. I want to use you, but you have to keep everything confidential. Not partially or almost completely. Confidential. Period."

"Yes sir."

"As I said, I don't know where this is going next, but I'll certainly call if we need your translation services. Thanks. Goodbye."

"Goodbye."

The One Nine, the Nineteenth Precinct, Terry's station house, was a building almost one hundred years old. It had been remodeled numerous times over the years, always for space considerations, to move an interior wall or to run or replace electrical lines or plumbing. Aesthetics were always second, and often fell victim to whatever paint was in the warehouse, budgets ruling over all. So there were blue walls and beige walls, several patterns of linoleum and some well-worn wooden floors that might be original. At one time, more than thirty years ago, a decision was made to create space for a captain. The captain was the son of a factory foreman, a man who needed to keep an eye on production workers in a vast and noisy atmosphere of moving employees and powerful machines. His office was right in the middle of the factory floor, all four walls having windows from waist-high up. His son, the policeman, often visited his father and admired that office, loved the way his father could watch over, rule over, all he surveyed. Years later, promoted to captain and asked where he wanted his office for the upcoming renovation, said "Right in the middle of the floor." Now these many years later it was the office of a lieutenant, the present captain having chosen a more traditional corner office.

Lieutenant Corriling waved at Terry as he came into the office.

"Morning, Carl, what's up?"

"Got your note about the Long girl. So you've got a lead."

"Yeah, guy she worked with, name is Say Phan. P H A N. Cambodian, like her. The cousins who were with him think, maybe... guess she, Long, had some arguments with him, he threatened her."

"How'd you pick this up? You didn't have it from the cousins first time you talked, go back for another round?"

Terry paused, wanting to be very careful in his answer. "June Replyn, the reporter, is doing a story about Long. For some reason the cousins opened up to her, guess she asked the right questions. Anyway, she passed it on to me."

"I see. So it's going to be in the paper?"

"Not this, not about the guy. Article's just going to be about the girl, Long."

"You trust her."

"I trust her."

"So you got anything besides the cousins telling you about an argument?"

"Well, it's a bit stronger. She had two confrontations with the guy, asked some questions about boxes, he told her to shut up or he'd shut her up, something like that.... plus, no one else seems to have had a beef with her, just a nice kid, got along, except for this one guy. And the killer did it in front of the cousins, pretty clear message there.... no other candidates, Lieutenant. Hot arguments with him, threats, nobody else."

"So pick him up, I guess."

"Got a problem, give me your best... deal is, Carl, the guy's still on the job. So if he is our man, maybe did both, Long and Pritkin, maybe.... he's showing up for work every day. Could be he feels safe, no way to tie him to either murder, could be he knows if he splits he'll attract our attention. Soon as I call him in, can't do more than talk, he'll at least cover all his tracks, maybe split. I mean, who knows, he may be stupid enough to still have the gun, maybe paid a lot and can't let it go, got it under his pillow. Can't get a search warrant, no I D of the shooter, just stories of raised voices a coupla times. So I haul his ass in.... after which gun, wherever it is, maybe he and the gun, disappear."

"Sniff around more at work?"

"Not easy to do, and that's another thing."

"What?"

"I gotta get some coffee. Be right back."

Carl Corriling lifted an empty, oversized mug with WORLD'S GREATEST DAD on it in bright red, a new addition to his desk, and handed it to Terry. "Thanks."

"You're welcome, Dad. Guess I missed your birthday."

"You wait till you fuckin' have kids, see what kind of ties and mugs they get you. Hey, my kids love me, you got a problem with that?"

Terry smiled, shook his head, and went to his desk to retrieve one of the several identical white mugs he kept there. Then he walked to the coffee maker, a tall urn with a small glass dome, an ancient relic that still made great coffee. Everyone knew the secret was to thoroughly rinse the urn out on occasion, wipe it down, but never use soap. He filled both mugs and walked back to Carl's office.

"I got it. Got it figured."

"You got what figured?" said Terry, handing over the red-letter mug. He had stood before, this time he sat, balancing his mug next to his leg on the wide flat seat of the wooden chair. Years ago a purchasing agent got a deal from a school furniture supplier that was going out of business, a special close-out price for chairs designed for teachers' desks. The office was full of them, as were other stations.

The lieutenant took the mug, looked at it and paused in his response. "Shit, I gotta be careful, this is like drinking a pint and a half. I could triple my intake without knowing it, sleep worse than I do now."

"You could go the other way, cut down on it."

"I quit smoking. That's enough withdrawal for one lifetime, thanks. So let me tell you. You think the guy may have done both, but if you go snooping around anymore than you done already, the kids that work there are going to want to know what the fuck's up. No doubt they'd freak knowing the guy that maybe murdered their old man, could be the girl too, is on the payroll, right under their noses every day."

"Yeah, that's it. I mean, even if they didn't fire him, they probably couldn't help staring at him, tip him off."

"How you feel about not saying anything? I mean, here's this guy maybe whacked their old man, and a co-worker, guy uses a gun, and you don't tell them? They won't take that well when they find out."

"No, and he may get itchy, split just because. So I go round and round... he's got a passport, I'm sure, could head back to Cambodia in a flash unless we can get the feds to pull it, and maybe not do that in time. Gets to Cambodia of course he's gone, never see his ass again. So I don't want to spook him, but I don't want to leave him there a minute longer than.... shit, I don't even know what this is about, don't know if the crimes are connected."

"What's your guess?"

"Again from June. The argument was about boxes, something about the boxes the fabrics come in. Drugs, maybe."

"The old man found out?"

"Or was finding out, or about to, Phan has to kill him to stop him."

"So you're going to continue to work with your reporter, see if she can dig up anything else, enough to get a warrant."

"That's first choice."

"You make sure she doesn't slip up playing sleuth, mess this whole thing up, get herself shot. Lots of ways this could go sour. Or her editors could tell her to put more of this into print and she screws up the case. You're dating, right?"

"Yes."

"Don't get stupid on me, Terry. Don't get us caught in the wrong place and all written up in the headlines."

"I know the drill. Don't worry."

"Cops and reporters. Worse. Cops dating reporters. Don't worry, he says. Hey, keep me posted, right?"

"Right" Terry stood.

Terry took his coffee mug and left. After a moment the lieutenant said, into the empty room, "Coulda said 'be careful the reporter don't screw ya,' but thought that'd be poor taste."

CHAPTER NINETEEN

"**W**anna ride around in a police car?"

"Lights and sirens or that same old brown thing?"

"Yeah, I gotchur siren right here. So how soon can you get away?"

"Are we talking romance or work, hours and hours or fifteen minutes?"

"I like the ratio, fifteen minutes of work and hours of romance. Sorry, this is the world of work, got to talk to you about people getting killed, solving crimes, that kind of stuff."

"In front at four? Then I don't have to go back."

"Sure. I'll pick you up in my ugly car, take you to my ugly apartment. You probably don't like my suits much, either."

"I like it when you take them off."

"Compliment for me, thank you, but not for my clothes."

"They look like detective's suits, so they're fine. But you need something much nicer for elegant occasions. There's a big wool event coming up in London, maybe we go there, buy you a fine English twill or herringbone, two suits, a sport jacket, some slacks...."

"I think you're talking about my salary for the next two years."

"I'm a writer. They give you a deal, I write about how beautiful their materials are....."

"Is that legal? I am an officer of the court, please remember."

"Four."

"Four."

Terry pulled up a few minutes past four, and June was already in the doorway.

"So what's the plan?"

"Can we decide on my place or yours, and dinner, get that decided? I really need to talk to you, need your good thinking."

"Well, if you're willing to do the early commute this time, why don't we head out of town before traffic gets really bad, talk while we drive to some restaurant you discovered in your wanderings."

He paused a moment. "Seafood?

"Sure, but cooked. I gave up raw clams, don't want to take the risk."

"Got the place, Jersey Shore, seafood all caught on the incoming tide, no pollution."

"Sure. And uh-huh. Drive, policeman, and tell me what's on your mind."

Terry slipped the shift lever into drive and moved into traffic. He drove a little faster than she would have liked but was perfectly at ease doing so. On a few occasions she made a small, involuntary gasp when he executed a move; he would glance over at her and slow down slightly, but eventually the speed crept back up.

"June, here's the sitch. I've talked to my lieutenant, gave him this same speech. Told him where and how I'm stuck and that you might be able to help. Don't know what you've got to say to your managers, but I'm proceeding with approval, asking your help in solving the two murders."

June felt the intensity, the seriousness of his words, and responded in similar fashion. "I don't think there's a problem as long as I keep Tal informed... well, got to bring Joe in some, got to think about that. But sure, of course, how can I help?"

"Let's go on the assumption that it all fits together. You ever hear the crime investigation concept that you start with the last person known to have been with the victim? The idea that it turns out either that's the killer or he, or she, knows the killer?"

"Yes, I have heard that."

"Well, it's right a lot of the time, good rule to work off of. Another rule is go for the simple explanation. Like science. What's readily apparent, obvious, a logical path is likely the best explanation. In this case we have a logical path, so let's follow it. This guy, this Say Phan is employed at ComFitter. He's got a deal worked out somehow, with people to smuggle drugs on occasion from... where do most of the fabrics come from? Do you know?"

"China. Probably every box. Real cheap."

"China... doesn't fit the usual drug pattern, but... well, we'd have to trace the routes. Lots of places a small container of hashish or heroin could be slipped into a corrugated box."

"But they're strapped...."

"The straps aren't labeled, don't have a seal on them like a container would. Generic strapping, used around the world. Cut only one strap, lift up that end just enough to slip the box in, re-strap. Minutes." They were approaching the Lincoln Tunnel. Although it was after four the lines weren't too long or slow.

"Sorry, you were laying out the path."

"No, that's fine, I don't want to get so sold on this that I miss some reason that it can't work, waste a lot of hours that way. Please keep checking in, it helps. I want to be sure before I make my next move, which I think actually means your next move."

Neither spoke while they moved rapidly through the tunnel, not wanting to talk over the monotone hum of the constant stream of cars and busses and trucks. As they emerged on the Jersey side Terry continued.

"We've got a guy in a small factory who gets occasional shipments of drugs. Small time stuff, but still lots of money, many thousands a year. But he keeps working there, factory work. Why? Because it's easy to import the drugs there, almost no chance of detection, piece of cake. He's stashing money somewhere, but somewhere with no clue, like we talked about."

"When does he quit? " June asked. "Better, why doesn't he quit, like Rith Long was planning to? He could have hundreds of times what she's sent home. Couldn't he turn it into gold or diamonds, coins, go home and be a small-time king?"

"Sure, but maybe the decision isn't up to him. Maybe he's made a promise, maybe somebody has something on him, maybe he's paying off a debt, hard to say. Or could be you're right, but he hasn't reached his nut, his goal. I mean, who knows what his cut is for being part of an occasional, small-potatoes drug deal? Might not be all that much, he might not have much in that secret place yet. Remember, we don't know how long this has been going on, could be fairly recent."

They were driving south, heading towards Jersey City.

"Sure, sure....go ahead."

"One day Rith Long, this energetic young girl who likes to poke into things, likes to gossip, notices something. Something. Has to do with the boxes, who knows what she saw, said, but it's enough to set him off. Then she tells her cousins, they start giving him the eye, he kills her as a warning."

"Wait, Terry, I'm confused. Which came first, her saying something to Say Phan, the first time I mean... that or the murder of Victor Pritkin? I'm confused about the timeline."

"Hard to tell, June. Things happened close together. But let's call them A for Victor's murder, B for the first time Rith says something to Phan, C for her murder. Probably happened that way, but it could be B A C, couldn't it?"

June sat, looking out the window at the cars and trucks and airplanes and oil storage tanks, the industrial part of the Garden State streaming by. "Give me a minute."

A few minutes went by, he driving and thinking, she sightseeing and thinking. Then she spoke. "A B C. He's got drugs coming in from time to time... maybe some secret marking on the box, small mark but it tips him off...."

"That's good. That's very good."

"....and then something catches Victor's eye. He was always into everything, not the office work but all over the production and shipping, moving things along... so he spots something about the boxes and the weights and mentions it to Phan in complete innocence, Phan can't come up with anything better than killing him. End of story, back to smuggling, except it isn't the end of the story, this woman, this perky kid starts asking questions. Maybe she asked it offhand, not a big deal, just curious or snooping or even making small talk, who knows? To her it's a minor conversation, but to him it's alarm bells, he thinks she's going to connect him to the murder. So he warns her, then kills her."

"So very Bingo. Offer to join the force still open."

"Still rejected, unless I can redecorate the place."

"What's wrong... no, even I know the answer to that one. But I think that's it, I agree. Now we have to prove it, or at least get enough to hold him. He spooks and runs and it's all over."

CHAPTER TWENTY

The phone rang. A woman answered in hesitant English. "Hello?" In Khmer. "Is Sopheara Moeun at home? Please tell her Salath Doeung is calling."

In Khmer. "Salath! This is Sopharath! What do you want to talk to my sister about? More newspaper work?"

"I want to ask her why her sister asks so many impolite questions."

Sopharath giggled. "I think you like my sister, want to teach her American ways. I am correct, I know it."

"Sopharath, is your sister at home? May I please talk to her?"

"Sure, I will go tell her you want to talk to her. If I do that will you find a boyfriend for me too, one who could teach me how to speak American, teach me American ways of doing all the things?" Again a giggle.

"I am not anyone's boyfriend. But I will be glad to tell some of my friends about you."

"What will you tell them?" she cooed.

"I will tell them you are lovely and I will tell them you want an American boyfriend and I will give them your phone number. I will also tell them you are" switching to English "a pain in the ass."

"I know what that means! Maybe I don't know how to find my sister, so I will hang up now, you can call another day."

Again in Khmer. "If you hang up I won't tell my friends about you. I will make a promise to find you a Khmer-speaking American boy who will speak to you much nicer than I do."

"That is better."

"Now....."

"Yes, I will go find her. And listen to this, listen to what I have learned." Switching to heavily accented English, she giggled and said "Keep it zipped."

Salath heard the phone clunk down on the table before he could reply. In the background he could faintly hear the television, and then "This is Sopheara. Hello, Salath."

"My greetings. How are you, are you and your family well?"

"We got a letter from my family, they are doing well, thank you for asking. My sister and I are also in good health, although if she does not go away and stop standing next to me she soon will have a very sore nose and pulled hair."

Sal heard a shouted "Remember to find one for me" followed by laughter that trailed off as Sopharath left.

"I am sorry for my sister's rude behavior."

"I have a friend who speaks excellent English, in fact, he is an English literature major, wants to teach. His Khmer is pitiful. And he is a little crazy sometimes. I think they will like each other, and can give each other language lessons."

"That would be nice of you."

"Do you like to dance?

"Authentic Cambodian or American, the kind where a man and a woman jump around close without touching.?"

"Well... I meant the second kind, the American jumping kind, but do you know the traditional dances?"

"Of course. But is that why you called me? Do you want to know the next time my sister and I will be dancing in a festival? Want to see us dance at New Year?"

"I would enjoy seeing you dance American or Cambodian. And your sister. But for now I wanted to ask you to dance with me American style. Have you ever been to Club Loak Khae?"

"Many times. You go there? I don't remember seeing you."

"Sometimes. You just weren't looking for someone like me. Bet we walked right past each other."

"Then you weren't looking for someone like me."

"But now I am. Saturday night, this Saturday night, I would so much like to take you."

"Of course. But I want you to teach me English, so we speak English most of the time. That's what I want. Most of the men I know can't dance very good, so if you are like them I will give you dancing lessons in trade."

"I can dance very well, the girls like dancing with me, but I will still give you English lessons."

"I will be the person who judges your dancing, not the American women. What time will you pick me up?"

"Eight, if that is all right, judge."

"I should not tease you so much. I am very glad that you want to dance with me, and eight is a good time. I will see you then."

CHAPTER TWENTY ONE

The LOAK KHAE nightclub in Manhattan was cooking on Saturday night, as usual. American, British, Australian, German, and bands from other nations were played by the master of the turntables, tapes and disk players. All shared a common, deep thumping base beat, amplified by woofers and sub-woofers so that men could occasionally feel the vibrations in their testicles, women in their wombs. All were played *loud*.

The music, and the lyrics, if distinguishable, didn't matter, since only non-Cambodians spoke English inside the nightclub. LOAK KHAE was by, and for, Cambodians, and the Khmer was rich and full. People had to lean close and raise their voices to be heard, raised voices speaking the language of a nation thousands of miles away. There were occasional visitors from Thailand, China, Vietnam, and curious Americans and others, but they were the exception. If you didn't speak Khmer you were likely there with a date who did.

Salath Doeung and Sopheara Moeun walked into the crowded, loud, jumping club. There were strobe lights bouncing off walls and dancers and a mirrored ball, colored lights and trails of neon that snaked along the walls and the ceiling. People were laughing and talking, having learned the trick of part lip-reading, part tuning in tightly on the spoken word rather than the music. Beer, fruity wine coolers or mixed drinks in almost every hand, the mixed drinks nothing special, mostly gin-sevens or rye-and-ginger or whiskey with soda. Salath Doeung at once recognized some neighborhood friends, and Sopheara Moeun recognized some co-workers. They leaned towards each other. He spoke first.

"Some friends, I'd like you to meet them."

"Same. Friends. Over there."

"You sure we can't speak Khmer? Tell you what, let's spend a little time here, not too much, then we'll go some place quieter. Speak English there. My throat is already hurting."

Sopheara Moeun started to speak, then just stopped and nodded. Then she said in Khmer "Do you want to meet my friends first or your friends? Or just dance."

He caught a bit of a smile with that last line, so he said "Dance. Let's dance."

They found some room on the dance floor, a large hardwood circle that filled almost half the room. They both began stepping and jerking their arms and hips to the beat, and Sal executed a step-spin to show Sophie he had some moves. When he looked at her he saw that she wasn't watching him, but was really into her dancing, focused, so he settled down, dancing easy, and enjoyed the show. Sophie's breasts moved tightly, pointedly, beneath the silk dress, and her left leg kept popping in and out of the slit in her skirt. Sal allowed himself to really look at her body as she moved, and he decided that he liked the view. A lot.

As with all great mix masters, the DJ kept the music moving from one song to another, with a barely perceptible change in pace. Dance or drop, but the music plays on. After fifteen to twenty minutes of uninterrupted music there was a brief break, about five minutes, during which conversation became much easier, telephone numbers were exchanged, plans were made, decisions reached about leaving now or staying for another set. Then the music began again, occasionally with an alternate DJ. Sopheara and Salath had come in near the end of a set. When the music stopped he asked her if she would like something to drink and she requested a berry-flavored wine cooler. He got a beer, and they started a slow walk through the crowd. As he walked Sal saw one of his friends leaning against a wall. Although too far away to talk, they did wave at each other. Then his friend pointed at Sophie and gave an appreciative nod, touching his beer bottle to his forehead in salute. Fun to be with a pretty girl that your friends check out and approve.

They spent a few minutes meeting some of his friends and hers, mostly students for Sal and pieceworkers for Sophie, but when the music began again it was too hard to have any significant conversations, and it was obvious Sophie liked to dance, wanted to be on the floor. So they left their nearly-empty drinks on a table and returned to the wooden circle. Fine with Sal, spinning and stepping and watching her body slide inside the tight silk dress with the long leg split. Pleasant moments of letting fantasies float easy through his mind and tickle his libido.

Suddenly Sopheara stopped dancing, just stopped and stood still, a look of anger and fear on her face. Salath stopped too, asking "What's wrong, what's the matter?" He turned and looked where she was staring, and saw a man looking at her with a sideways glance as he walked by ten feet away. Sal turned back to her. "Who is that man, what's the matter Sophie?"

"That is the man who told my cousin he would kill her. He killed Rith. Say Phan. Say Phan, murderer."

Sal turned again, this time his whole body. He couldn't help it, he had to see, to know this man. At that Say squared his body so that he was facing them. All around them people jumped and danced and twitched to the beat and shook their bodies, stood in small circles and half-shouted at each other, the music played loudly and the bass thumped and the drinks were poured and drunk, but the three stood, staring, like points on a human obtuse triangle. Then Say Phan walked quickly up to Sopheara Moeun and Salath Doeung; they could have been any three of those present having a conversation, except the looks on their faces were not of joy or pleasure. All spoke Khmer.

"What are you staring at, boy?"

"We don't want any trouble with you." Sal had never been confronted with an authentic bad guy before, and although the sentence came out with some power his knees were trembling, a trickle of sweat starting down the inside of his left thigh.

"American, huh? Get lost." Say turned from him with a dismissive sneer. "And you, jungle beast, what is your problem? Maybe you should just go back to Cambodia, go home before something bad happens to you, bad like what happened to your cousin. Hear me, bitch dog?"

"Don't you talk to her like that" Sal shouted. He had no chance to react to the hard punch, the fist that hit him high on the cheekbone and knocked him to the floor, his head spinning. Say gave him a short, poking kick in the ribs and then said to Sopheara "It is best for you if you and your sister find other jobs." He spun and walked away, disappearing instantly in the crowd. A few people had stopped and gawked, but seeing one man on the floor and the other leaving it was obvious there wasn't going to be a fight, so they returned to their dancing. The bouncer wasn't even aware there had been an incident.

Sophie squatted next to Sal, touched him gently on his face. He sat up, started to rise and sat down for a brief moment, then rose again and stood. They walked to a cluster of small tables. They sat at a table and Sal bent forward, his eyes closed.

"Are you OK?" Sophie asked.

Sal managed a smile. "OK is English. Two languages in one sentence."

"You should call the police." Sophie was pale and trembling. "He hit you. We should tell the police he hit you."

"Sophie, I don't think the police care about one punch at a nightclub where everyone is drinking. They would laugh at us. But I think they should know he said the same thing could happen to you that did to your cousin. That's more important; he threatened you, and you have a witness."

"He didn't say he would do it, just that there is danger. Would the police care?"

Sal gently rubbed his cheekbone, moved his lower jaw from side to side. "No loose teeth, guess I'm going to be all right. Let's get out of here."

They left, both peering into the crowd, then looking carefully as they stepped outside, but no sign of Say Phan.

CHAPTER TWENTY TWO

The Following Monday.

As the man was dropped off in front of the restaurant everyone inside, staff and patrons, knew who was coming before he opened the door. His driver was sent away; a man so powerful and feared needs no bodyguard. The man, dressed in a fine herringbone wool suit, custom made for seventeen hundred dollars, walked directly to the table that, out of respect for his power and the fear he could generate with a frown was always empty, always his to enjoy, whether he appeared every day or not for weeks at a time. The waiter was replacing the spotless white tablecloth with another, smoothing it in place as the man sat. A moment later the restaurant's owner appeared with a tray upon which were clean silverware wrapped in a napkin, a separate folded napkin, a cup of coffee with one-half teaspoon sugar and a glass of Cabernet Sauvignon. No menu. The powerful man greeted the waiter and owner with a nod and a few soft words then ordered one of his favorites, always prepared and presented with extra care. No bill would be put on the table, but once a month the driver appeared and left behind ten one hundred dollar bills, which meant a splendid payment for the owner and a staggering tip for the waiter.

The restaurant, a neighborhood establishment with seating for forty-six, was just over half full, with a cook, a cook's helper, a busboy-dishwasher, the owner and two waiters present. The patrons stole tiny glances but for the most part kept their eyes away from the powerful man at the rear corner table, his back to the corner. People sitting facing that direction kept their eyes on their companions or their plates, not letting them rest on the fine suit or on the man of power and fear who wore it.

A man entered, a new face in the neighborhood. He was wearing wool slacks, a light tan shirt, a sport jacket but no tie. He sat at a table near the door, opened a newspaper he was carrying and read a few moments until the waiter arrived, leaving a menu, silverware and napkin, and a glass of water. The man glanced at the menu then returned to his newspaper. When the waiter returned the man placed an order and then continued reading, turning pages occasionally. When his meal arrived he ate for a while, then got up and went to the men's room. After a few moments he came out, walked to the corner table and shot the powerful man once right between his eyes, then turned and walked out, pausing a moment to drop a fifty dollar bill on his table. He walked out of the door and around the building to a car waiting in the parking lot, its motor running, a woman driving who put the car in gear as the man closed the door. They disappeared, having just earned a sizable fee.

Detective Terry Stans was frustrated and angry. All of the patrons had left the restaurant within moments of the shooter's exit. Neither the waiters nor the owner could remember who had been there, a strange lapse of memory for people who had served many of the same customers for more than twenty years. And they had no memory of the shooter, just an average man, average height, nothing special about his face, wearing a sport coat... gray? Blue? No, tan, yes, it was tan. No......

The table where the shooter had sat was still as he had left it, the owner understanding that clearing it could be a criminal offense. Though not quite as the shooter had left it. The fifty was gone.

The forensics detective called to him. "Terry, take a look at this." The woman was wearing white plastic gloves. She had taken a scalpel from her tool kit and had scraped something from the tablecloth. It rested on the shiny scalpel blade, a few flecks of what might be taken for bad dandruff.

"Jean, what is that?"

"Plastic, a thin polymer coating. Just before coming in the shooter puts it on his fingertips, maybe parts of his palm, too. Carries the stuff in a tube or jar, because it dries in an instant. Starts flaking off after a while, but for an hour or so the guy leaves no fingerprints. That's how he comes in and handles silverware and a glass and leaves nothing. Not a print, barely a partial. Slick, no pun intended. This hit was done by a professional's professional."

"Great, and the witnesses don't remember a thing. Well, one thing. It was a man. Most helpful" he snorted.

"Hey, you getting anywhere on that factory murder, the early morning one with the tool in the head?"

"Thanks bunches, Jean... I love working with people who remind me of my failures."

"Only Holmes solved them all, and he was a work of fiction. No, the reason I asked is I've been thinking about it. Can't figure how a guy gets killed in the middle of a large empty room unless he never heard the killer, possible on a cement floor I guess, or else it was someone he knew, friend, someone he works with. You've probably gotten there too."

"Yes, one or the other, I'm leaning towards the second. Problem is so far no obvious motive, haven't found anything that points to a suspect. Gonna keep digging, that's for sure. I want to solve that one, in part because it seems the victim was a good Joe, a regular guy who treated people well and paid his staff a decent wage, reputation for being honest. Yeah, want to solve that one. This...." He gestured, made a dismissive shrug. "I'll push it around some more for form's sake, but our man is long gone, far out of sight until he gets his next assignment. What a job. Probably works about an hour a year, if that, five to ten minutes a job, makes a hell of a lot more than you and me together."

"Yeah, but boring, same old thing, shoot in the face, shoot in the face, shoot in the face..."

"Sick forensics humor, just what I needed. See you tomorrow." Terry left his card with the waiter and the owner, just in case they remembered something else, and walked out the door.

When the phone rang June picked it up without taking her eyes off the computer screen, then cradled it under her chin and returned her hands to the keyboard. She had long ago learned to carry on a conversation and proofread at the same time. "Humanities, June Replyn."

"Hey June, this is Sal. Salath Doeung. Got a minute?"

"Sure, Sal. What's up?"

"Actually, swollen cheek. That's what I called you about."

"Sounds like you need a dentist, not a reporter."

"Or maybe a cop. This is serious."

June turned away from the screen, grabbed a notebook and pen. "I'm listening."

Sal told the whole story, June listening and making notes but not interrupting.

"So that's it. The punch isn't any problem, just some swelling, although seeing it inspired my mother to give me a lecture about hanging out in bars."

"But Soph..pheer..sorry..."

"Sopheara. She wants to be called Sophie. Wants me to teach her English."

"Your mother will approve."

"Thank you. Should I call you Auntie June?"

"Only if you want the other side of your face punched. Does Sophie want to go to the police?"

"We talked some about that. She's not sure. Not sure if she should just leave him alone, you know, better to stay away, or tell the police, or get away from him, find new jobs for her and her sister. Women who can sew well are in great demand all over New York, New Jersey, thousands of jobs."

"But he made a threat, I think the police should know that. Sal, he might really be a murderer, maybe he killed the owner too, who knows? You want to ignore a threat from a guy like that?"

"I guess the police could talk to him... but all he said was, well I don't remember exactly, but like I told you he never said 'I'll do this or that,' he didn't really warn her, he asked her if she didn't want to go back to Cambodia, be safe, not have the same thing happen to her."

"Sure sounds like a threat to me. What do you want to do, want me to do? Aren't you worried?"

"The guy scares me. Sure I'm worried."

"Tell you what. I don't know exactly the police rules, but you sure can't punch people, you could file a charge. Or maybe the police would think like me, hear the meaning of the words like I did, that he threatened Sophie. I don't think you have to say 'I'll shoot you' for it to be a threat, just saying something about bad things could happen to you is enough. Or maybe I've seen too much television... but I'll ask Detective Stans. Either way it seems that questioning him would be important. Look, Sophie is pretty sure, told both of us, he's the killer. If she's right.... let me make a call. I'll let you know what happens."

"Meanwhile Sopheara and Sopharath are working with the guy every day."

"Tricky, isn't it? The police, Detective Stans or someone else, may want to get right on it, but this might make it worse. I mean, if they call him in, ask him what he knows about Rith's murder, what mood is he going to be in when he leaves?"

"Or it might make him more careful, or he might get another job, or disappear... go back to Cambodia, maybe... not that I want the sisters to take chances, but if he knows the police are watching is he likely to kill again?"

"That makes sense. Tell them to be careful." She paused. "Not sure what they can do to be careful..... just stay away, I guess." Her voice shifted to a warmer, more casual tone. "And about the attractive Miss Sophie... I thought you liked her, saw that flirtation even though I couldn't understand a word."

"That does it. Goodbye, Auntie June." He hung up.

June smiled briefly, then immediately looked serious as she called Terry. She never called his office number, he was at his desk so intermittently that it was easier to just call his cell phone.

"Terry Stans."

"Terry, something big. That young man, Sal, the translator… he took out one of the cousins, the sisters that we interviewed, named Sopheara, Sophie. They go to this Cambodian club and Say Phan is there. They start staring at each other, glaring I guess, then Phan warns her, something about.. wait, I wrote it down...." She glanced at her notes. "As near as Sal can remember he, that is Phan, says something about shouldn't she go home, meaning Cambodia, before something bad happens to her too, then he punches Sal, puts him on the floor. Is that enough for you to question him?"

"Plenty. But we're back to the question about spooking Amy and Tony. So I should stop by his house. Do you know where he lives?"

"Dammit. I Should have thought of that. I'll call Sal back, ask him to ask Sophie, I'll tell you tomorrow, soon as I know."

"And another. Do I need an interpreter? How good is his English."

"Sophie will know. I'll have him ask both questions."

This is good, could be a break. Gotta run...I'll call you later. Bye."

"Bye."

It was disconcerting to June that they sometimes made arrangements for dinner, sometimes not, sometimes spent the night together, on occasion three or four nights in a row, sometimes not, but nothing was set or committed to. Plans were rarely made for more than a day or two ahead, unless they were doing something special on a weekend. They had met some of each other's friends, gone to a few parties together, but it was as if it could vanish, end at any moment, stop like it never started. June's perspective, of course. To Terry it was a fine, warm, loving, monogamous relationship, and he was comfortable in it, had even offered to talk about living together. He liked where they were and had no intention of leaving; to him it seemed far more likely they would continue to grow closer together. To Detective Terry Stans a quick short, "I'll call you later, bye" meant a solid relationship with no game playing. For Reporter June Mary Replyn the brief words reawakened concerns, questions about how fragile the relationship might be. It would astound him to know she feared the sudden end. It would astound her to know how comfortable, settled, almost permanent he thought they were.

By the time June called Sal back he was already gone, but she left him a message. He hadn't called back by the time she left to go home. She ate a lonely meal, and was actually in bed when Terry called.

"Hi. Sorry to be so late. Been listening to the news?"

"Beethoven's Seventh. Sorry."

"No, Beethoven is far preferable to the news almost any time."

"What's in the news, what did I miss?"

"Old-fashioned, clichéd gangland killing, crime boss shot while eating spaghetti. Killer walks into the restaurant, orders a meal, eats a little, gets up and shoots the guy. I mean, sits there eating knowing he's going to commit murder in a few minutes? Then he walks out, no one knows what he looks like, how tall, even the color of his skin. Amazing, isn't it? Anyway, I've been thinking about our case, about Sal's call. I'm going to talk to Say Phan at home, but I want to make sure he's there. So I think I'm going to park near his house a little past four, quitting time, see if I can catch him walking in the door. If I don't see him I'll figure he went somewhere for a drink or dinner, so I'll come back late."

"I didn't know you knew what he looks like."

"I saw him several times at the shop... there aren't many men, I'm pretty sure I'll recognize him."

"If he doesn't go right home it'll be another late night for you."

"Sleeping in tomorrow, already decided. Going to unplug the phones, cell phone off, get some serious sack time."

"Do that. I don't want an exhausted policeman on my hands this weekend. Exhausted policemen are no fun."

"I was thinking about doing nothing this weekend. Well, maybe a load of underwear, but that's it. Take-out or frozen food, read the newspapers, stare vacant-brain at the tube, nap on the couch."

"You want company or would that interfere?"

"Company is most welcome, as long as you aren't offended by sloth."

"Vacant-brain staring sounds most inviting. Maybe I'll pick up some frozen dinners."

"That would be fine, but make sure you get ones that take the same time to cook. I don't want to have to deal with two different cooking times."

"Will there be sex?"

"Sure. Another excuse for a nap."

"I am so flattered."

"June, I'm falling asleep, and I'm starved. Bad situation, gotta go. Eat some cheese, glass of milk, that's it. I'll call you as soon as I wake up. Hope you can get the address by then."

"Me too. Have a good rest. Goodnight, Bulldog."

"Night, June."

The first time they were naked together she saw the bulldog tattoo on his shoulder. "A dog? Not 'Mom' or a heart with an arrow through it?"

"That is not a dog. That is a bulldog. The bulldog. The mascot."

"I give. Mascot of..."

"May not have heard of it way down in Texas. Little eastern school called Yale."

"Yale? You went to Yale?"

"Your surprise is not flattering."

"No, no... I mean, I don't connect police work with an ultimate Ivy."

"Public Service, Sociology. Three point four five, a bit less partying and I could have made the three point five."

"Forgive me, forgive me...."

"Someday you'll have to tell me about your finals. 'Let's see, is it knit one purl two, or knit two purl one?'"

She slapped his bulldog, he roared, she giggled, they started again.

The next morning the message was waiting. "Hey June, it worked out fine. I called Sophie, she said she knew the street and house but not the address, but she got a friend to drive her by there. I thought that would be dangerous but she said she sat in the back, slouched down, and they kept moving, just slowed a bit, read the address and drove away. Then she called me back... it's two six oh seven Wurthrop Street, white house, two stories, near Chase Street. Queens, that is. Please let us know what's going on, going to happen. Oh, and the language... he'll do fine, one of the best English speakers in the shop, he and Daro, the head of the sewing room."

The phone rang several times, but none was Terry. It was ten-fifteen before he called.

"June Replyn."

"I am so rested and well fed."

"I hear your car... thought you were going to sleep in."

"Got up around eight, but hey, that's about nine hours, plenty of sleep. Took myself to the diner, had steak and eggs for breakfast, biscuits, orange juice, coffee. What a feed. I'm ready to get back into it. So, got an address for me?"

"Good news first, he speaks English enough for an interview, should be at least as good as Daro, the woman who found Pritkin. Remember her?"

"Yes, and I could interview her, so if he's about the same there shouldn't be a problem. What's the address?"

"I don't want you writing while driving. Call me when you get to the office, I'll tell you then."

"Cool."

"How soon?"

"Ten minutes."

"Good."

"Bye."

"Bye."

June turned back to her computer, back to the story she was working on. She was finding it easier and more natural to switch between the world of her day job, her paycheck job of reporting on the world of fashion business, and being part of a police search for two murderers, or one killer of two people. The drama and the fear, however, of the murders was taking more and more of her attention because people she knew were actively involved with the likely villain, and she feared for Sal and Sophie. And Terry. Who knows what could happen if Say Phan felt cornered?

She did manage to get into her writing, working on a story of how warehouses had become more of distribution centers, the goods staying in the facility not for weeks but for two days at the most, often less than one day, then shipped out to retail stores. Then Terry called again.

"Humanities, June Replyn."

"And the address is..."

"Work work work. Twenty-six zero seven Wurthorp Street, two story white house, near the corner of Chase Street."

"Two six zero seven Wurthrop. Well done. Want me to tell you what happens?"

"I want you not to get shot. Try not to get shot, OK? It would certainly spoil the weekend."

"Nap at home, nap in the hospital, same thing."

"That's not even a little bit funny. Be careful, will you please?"

"Certainly will. Always do. Look, I don't know when I'm going to catch up to him, but I'll call you soon as I'm done. It might be late, though, so don't worry."

"Most certainly will. Always do."

He paused. "We'll have a nice weekend."

"I look forward to folding your just-washed underwear while you take a nap."

"I have some underwear thoughts of you, too."

"Bye."

"You cute thing."

CHAPTER TWENTY THREE

End Of A Dream

Young Woman's Murder Still A Mystery

Rith Long came to America for a reason common to millions of New World immigrants for over four hundred years. She came to make money. At nineteen she followed two cousins, Sopheara Moeun and Sopharath Moeun from A-Saan, a small village in Cambodia. A village with no autos except the occasional visitor, usually in a rugged four-wheel drive vehicle. Within Rith's lifetime, electricity and running water came to the community, a peaceful place on the edge of the forest, not far north of Kampot, near the Gulf of Thailand.

Rith followed her cousins to America and joined them sewing sports wear, shorts and tops, for the ComFitter Company in Queens. People liked her. They describe her as energetic, funny, and a bit of a gossip. She dated and went to parties occasionally, but her goal was always to go home, back to A-Saan. Every two weeks she would take her paycheck, go to the Western Union office and cash it, sending a portion back to the office in Kampot where her family would go to claim it. The money was used to purchase a plot of land adjoining the family home and, more recently, to purchase chickens and the supplies necessary to set up a modern chicken and egg farm.

Two more years and Rith was going to go home and join the family business. She would be a woman in a wealthy family, supplying eggs and poultry to A-Saan and other communities, perhaps eventually owning a small truck making a regular run to Kampot. So Rith didn't make the effort to learn much English or to meet a husband. She was going home, going home to a place where people spoke Khmer as she did, where the forest smelled sweet, where her family was. Her dream never came true. Three weeks ago she was shot on her way to work, murdered in front of her cousins.

This is the second tragedy to strike the small company

on Bazervia street. Just over nine weeks ago the founder and manager, Victor Pritkin, was murdered at the factory. A spokesperson for the police would not confirm if there is evidence of a connection between the two murders. A $10,000 reward has been offered for information leading to the arrest and conviction of Mr. Pritkin's killer. It was announced today the company will offer a similar reward for the arrest and conviction of Ms. Long's killer. Anyone with information is encouraged to call 889 -0707.

CHAPTER TWENTY FOUR

Terry sat in his car two houses past Say Phan's home. He had parked on the same side of the street as the house, facing the corner of Chase street and the bus stop. Just past four-thirty a bus pulled up and let off three women and two men. The men separated, and one began walking in Terry's direction. Terry recognized the man from the factory, and opened the door of his car, stepping out quickly as Say Phan approached the walk that led up to his house.

"Mr. Phan? I'm Detective Stans, New York Police. I'd like to talk to you." Terry spoke in a strong but neutral voice, polite but firm, as he walked briskly toward the other man. Say Phan looked startled, tensed, and for the briefest moment Terry thought Say was going to run.

"What about?"

"Would you like to go inside?"

"No, talk here... what you want we talk about?"

The two men stood, strong straight postures, tense, uneasy.

"We received a complaint that you made a threat, made reference to the murder of Rith Long. What do you know about her murder, Mr. Phan?"

"What said? Who said?"

"You threatened Sopheara Moeun that the same thing would happen to her that happened to Miss Long. And you assaulted Mr. Salath Doeung. So I'm asking you again, Mr. Phan, what information do you have about the murder?"

"Never said, all be bullshit, told her dangerous place, this country, better she be safe in Cambodia." Say Phan seemed to listen to his words, accept his own argument. He spoke again, this time nodding agreement with himself. "Yes, like friend. Go home, be safe."

"You scared her."

"Be good I scare her. Not stay here, go home be safe. I tell her like friend." He wasn't budging.

"Why did you assault Mr. Doeung?"

"What is Az –salt?"

Terry suspected he knew perfectly well what the word meant, but played along. "Assault means to attack. You hit him."

Say Phan shrugged. He was relaxed now, and although standing up acted as if lounging. "One hit, not so hard. I can say him I am sorry, now sorry for hit him. Only one hit." He shrugged again and began to grin, as if a deal had been concluded in his favor. "Maybe you want come in, I make for us tea?"

"No, no thanks. Please answer the question. Why did you hit him?"

"He a boy, so young, I talk Sopheara, warn her be danger. He get in way, talk loud. I hit loud boy, sorry, hit him. Sorry. You want Say Phan call him say sorry that be OK. Just be we all drinking, all three, place noisy, loud, maybe Sopheara and boy not understand what I say. Big mix up, I call.... what is word saying so sorry, so much sorry?"

"Apologize?"

"Apologize. Just drink, mix up. No problem." The grin grew, almost a swagger now in his pose.

Terry continued to bore in, standing and speaking with an upright posture and firm but still polite voice. "What danger were you warning her of?"

A touch of indigence. "Told you. Danger in city, in America. Old boss killed at factory, Rith Long killed. Watch news from TV, all danger happens. Rape, shoot people, very much danger happens all days. Tell person I work with, girl, be danger, maybe go home, be safe." No, he wasn't budging.

"One more question. Did you kill Rith Long?"

The smile and swagger instantly disappeared, replaced by the tense, pre-flight posture. "No. NO! How you ask somabitch question to Say Phan? You say one more, that now make one more, all done with talking questions." He turned and walked quickly up the walk and steps to his home, stood on the side front porch with the peeling gray paint and took keys from his back pocket, unlocked the door and went in, closing the door hard. Throughout this Terry stood, unmoving, his eyes on Phan's back. After the door shut he stood a long moment staring at it, then he looked at each window for a hard, long moment, time devoted to each window, all the while a stern look on his face. The windows were all covered with either a thin lacey material or with the blinds pulled down. Terry had no way of knowing if he was being watched, but if so he wanted to be sure he sent a message. So he stood, and looked, and frowned, at the door and each window in turn, making the rotation several times, a total of almost two minutes. Then he returned to his car and took out his cell phone.

There was no answer at June's desk; when it started to roll into her voicemail he hung up and called her apartment. No answer there, either. He kept his eyes on the house, hoping he was being observed. Her phone message came on, after the beep he said "Call me." Just in case he called her office again and left the same two-word message.

Terry promised himself at least a half hour. After twenty minutes the cell phone chirped.

"Stans."

"No bullet holes, I hope."

"Friendly, pleasant conversation, at least until the end."

"What happened then, said the straight-woman."

"Straight-man is generic, doesn't have to be a man. Like foreman."

"To be debated another day. What happened?"

"I asked him if he killed Rith Long. Made for a real chill in the air."

"So no confession."

"Ahhhhh.... no."

"Where are you? I don't hear car noises or office noises. Or any noises."

"I am sitting in my car, motor off, just down from his house. I've been staring at the windows for about a half hour now, really boring, but I'm hoping to spook him. I'll bet he's watching me right now. Sure hope so. Hope he thinks I'm talking to my boss or maybe the prosecutor."

"How much longer are you going to be spooky?"

"This is enough. I'm ready to leave."

"Where you going?"

"Got a suggestion?"

"I've barely seen you this week. In fact, I think it's been a week since I allowed you to approach me. You losing interest?"

"Allowed me to approach you? Approach?"

"You're on a police-issue phone. Discretion is the better part of cell phones. You certainly don't want me saying fuck, do you?"

"Certainly do not. So how about I come over and approach you?"

"I need corned beef and cabbage. Just do. Meet me at the place on my corner."

"Don't know about the traffic. I'll call when I get closer. Whoever gets there first orders two corned beef and cabbage dinners. That will cut down on restaurant time, give us more time for approaching."

"Dinner and a bulldog. Done."

Terry hung up. He started the car, slipped it into Drive and barely touched the gas peddle, moving past the house at about three miles per hour. He didn't accelerate to a normal speed until he pulled away from the stop sign at the corner.

The detective would have been pleased if he could have known how well his performance worked. Very pleased. As soon as Phan was inside he walked toward one of the windows, looking out through the thin lace. He stood back from the window, and since the room was dim and it was bright outside he knew he couldn't be seen. But it was a shock that made him jump back further into the room when he saw, not as he expected, the detective getting into his car and driving away, but rather standing where Phan had left him, his hard gaze moving slowly over the house. When that gaze hit his window Phan's eyes opened wider and his breath and pulse became more rapid. Even when the eyes moved to another window, and another, Say Phan's pulse raced. What was that detective doing? Why was he looking at the house, the windows? Why? Inside the room the man was close to panic. Then Terry turned and walked away, and Phan began to relax. He had a front bedroom, and since he couldn't watch Terry all the way to his car without coming right up to the window, he ran to the stairs and sprinted up, unlocking his bedroom and rushing inside. He had a good view of the brown unmarked police car from the middle of his room, and stood there waiting for the car to start and drive away. But it didn't start; a half minute, a minute, two minutes. Five minutes! Phan pulled his wooden desk chair toward him and sat, watching. He didn't know what to think, what to make of this. When the sun glinted off the windshield all the watcher could see was glare, but when a cloud passed he could see inside, although not well. He thought the detective was holding a hand up to his face, probably talking on a phone, but the image wasn't clear and Say couldn't be sure. His pulse slowed but not to normal. He was, indeed, spooked.

Finally the car started. But instead of driving away it sort of glided, barely moving, in front of and past the house. To the man inside the room it was a chilling salute, a warning.

Say Phan sat a moment, then stood up and realized that he had shut but not locked the door behind him. He went to the door, paused, then changing his mind slipped out of the room, checking his back pocket to make sure he still had the key, set the door to lock and closed it. Then he went downstairs and out into the weedy backyard, walking to the alley, looking both ways, then around the house, looking up and down his street, around again to the back yard. He returned to the house, to his room, let himself in and locked the door behind him. He then walked over to his dresser, pulled out the bottom drawer and reached down under the piles of sweaters and faded jeans. He took out a folded grocery store plastic bag, unwrapped it, pulled out the gun.

Say Phan sat lotus-style on the floor, turning the gun over and over in his hands. It was all metal except for the hard, scratch-resistant plastic grips. Hard metal, shiny, smooth, an instrument of terrible, terrifying beauty, function and form perfectly blending. The grooves that had been cut to allow the silencer to screw on were well done, high quality, no burrs or uneven edges. The silencer, the illegal addition, lay on the floor next to his left foot. He picked it up and spun it on, the machine oil allowing the gun and silencer to join quickly and smoothly. The gun and silencer had cost him more than ten weeks pay, and he was reluctant to throw away such an investment. But the money wasn't primary, he wanted to keep it for a far stronger reason: nothing in his life, not coming to America, not his first job that paid him in American dollars, not a naked woman urging him on, had given him the feeling of power and control and manhood and domination that this beautiful, deadly instrument did, this fine tool of death. He unscrewed the silencer and carefully laid it next to him, reached into the drawer and took out the cotton rag that the gun had been wrapped in, and carefully wiped the gun, as much in reverence as cleaning. He knew almost nothing of American laws, but he did know that the police can't come in your house and look around when they feel like it, he had heard such discussions more than once drinking with friends. But why would the policeman ask him if he had killed Rith Long? Not hide it or try to be tricky but just say it to him, "Did you kill Rith Long?" Just said it, asked him as if he expected the answer to be yes. What to do?

Hiding the gun anywhere else in the house would just stall things a while at best, because Phan had no doubt the stern man would come back with ten policemen, a hundred, in their blue uniforms, and they would look until they found it, in his room or the basement or attic. Worse, there were people in and out of the building all the time, his bedroom was locked as were others, but the rest of the house was as open as a Greyhound waiting room. It was not unusual to come home and see a new face on the porch or watching television or eating hot, spicy soup in the dining room or kitchen. But were the police coming? Could he keep the gun under his clothes in this bottom drawer for one more hour or day? A week, a year? Forever? Were the police coming soon or never at all?

He wiped the silencer, then wrapped them both up carefully in the rag and stored them again, next to the box of bullets and the extra clip that were included with the purchase. About three dozen bullets missing, most used at a target range, of course without the silencer. A few used for real, with the silencer.Say Phan felt hungry, but didn't want to open a can or eat lunchmeat or search through the shared-expenses refrigerator or hassle with someone else in the kitchen. Instead he walked two blocks to a pizza shop he visited fairly often, ordered a small pizza with a large soda, ate then walked home. He thought about returning to, but didn't really expect, the sight of a dozen police cars pulled up in front of the house, some parked on the lawn. But no police, just the sounds of a late workday afternoon. He watched television, went to bed for a restless, disturbed sleep, got up and got ready for work and went to work. All the time, almost every minute, the gun, the question of the gun, rolled and tumbled and nagged in his mind.

CHAPTER TWENTY FIVE

All day Say Phan felt everyone was looking at him, though he knew it was his imagination. He was jumpy and kept giving himself lectures, kept trying to calm himself down. Suddenly he came to a decision. He felt better, more in control. At the end of the day Phan clocked out and left as usual, but instead of turning toward the bus stop walked to a neighborhood store, a narrow dark building with wood floors that sold beer, milk, lunch meat, eggs, aspirin, cough remedies, and hundreds of other grab-and-go items, more expensive than at a grocery store but much closer and quicker for the people in the surrounding community. At the back of the store was a pay phone, one of a dwindling number in public places. Say Phan got the dial tone, dropped the coins. He dialed a number. A phone was picked up, a greeting was started, but the caller cut him off.

"Got to talk."

"What about?"

"Got to talk. Cop in suit, what, detective, come my house, want know what I make tell him. Ask me I kill Rith Long. Just ask me. He tough somabitch, just ask me I kill."

"What did you tell him?"

"I say, 'no, you did!' What you think fuck I say? I say, 'no, not kill Rith Long.' Shit!"

"A detective. What was his name?"

"Ah, Stanley, Stang...."

"Stans? Terry Stans?"

"That the somabitch."

"What do you want to talk about? And where are you calling from?"

"What you care where I call from?"

"Are you on a cell phone?"

"No. Now fuck listen. I need hide gun, not keep my house, maybe they search, I dunno. I need hide, need you hide it."

"Oh no, oh no. I hide a murder weapon? Listen, Say, you did this, not me. You didn't talk it over with me, ask what else you could have done. I might have been able to help, maybe something we could have done with her. I don't know what, something, but now you've killed two people and want me to keep the gun? Why don't you just throw it in the river?"

"Not throw in river. Keep my gun. You hide for month, two, three, police give up, you give back. Maybe enough money I go back Cambodia then."

"Wait, let me understand this. If I hide the gun for a month or two...."

"Or three..."

"Or three, no more than three, understand? Then when I give it back to you you'll take your money and gun and get out, go back to Cambodia? Is that a promise? If I keep it, when I return it you get the hell out of my life, go home?"

"Maybe you help, give Say Phan some money you make from deal too?"

"Don't give me that. We had an agreement on the split. You remember telling me what you wanted, how much before you went back a rich man? You've got that and more unless you've been throwing it away... got enough now to be a big player in Cambodia. In fact, why don't you get out, just head back right now?"

"I not work, cops look for me right away, soon I buy ticket they arrest me, search. Got to work like no problem, work every day, smile at dog bitches like no problem. Go in three months. Quiet. Want to take gun with me. Like my gun. Have money in Cambodia, be like king, power, need keep gun make protect money. Not call police like easy like Queens. Maybe not trust police my country."

"All right, wait a minute, wait a minute, let me think."

"Not think, just come alley behind my house, so dark, come maybe nine, I give you, you hide. That be all."

"Shit. All right! But I want your promise that you and your money and your gun will be the hell out of here in three months. Three months, then your ass is back in Cambodia for good."

"Sure be for good. We get shipment two, three times maybe in three months, I take my money, maybe some of yours...."

"That is not going to happen. You've got plenty."

"You don't have move the shit, hide it, cut hands on boxes, worry about dope being found. You just collect money."

"That's the way the world works. Look, in three months you'll be able to leave nice and quiet, take your gun and your money, go be a big rich man in your country. Deal? Deal on you going home when it cools down?"

A pause, then a bit reluctantly "Good deal."

"See you at nine."

They hung up.

CHAPTER TWENTY SIX

The summer sun had just set, the sky still holding a glow, but the alley was quite dark. The nearest streetlights were blocked by two-story houses or trees or both, so only a dim reflected light, enough only to see the vaguest shapes, shown on the gravel alley that led the full length of the block, flanked by small garages, garden plots, fenced-in yards, green plastic trash containers provided by the city.

At nine o'clock a car pulled into the alley and glided slowly, the driver peering into the dim shadows. The headlights on bright setting showed the world directly ahead but made the backyards, visible out the side windows, seem even darker except where the occasional light was on over a back door. Suddenly Say Phan appeared next to the driver's door. The driver turned off the lights and motor.

"Scared me, coming out of nowhere like that."

"Make sure you in car, not detective."

"So where is it?"

"Come put car here, no problem, house for sale. I get." He faded into the shadows again.

The driver sighed, started the car again but didn't turn the lights on; there was enough light to see the parking spot Say Phan had indicated. The car pulled into the spot and then the motor was turned off again. The driver got out of the car.

Say appeared again, jumpy. "It over here. You take, drive away." He turned to go.

"Wait a minute. I want to know what you're giving me. You split and I will too and some kids can find it, I don't give a damn."

"OK, OK, look."

There was just enough light to see a plastic bag laying on the ground under a bush. The driver reached down and opened the bag, which contained a gun and silencer and extra clip carefully wrapped in an oily rag. The driver flipped the rag open. Saying "I never saw one of these before" the driver picked up the silencer and spun it onto the barrel of the gun. "Interesting."

"Here" Say Phan said nervously, reaching into a jacket pocket and pulling out a paper bag. "Box, rest of bullets. Hurry now going."

The driver nodded, put the box of bullets in a jacket pocket, then turned and shot Say Phan four times in the chest, picked up the oily rag, wiped and wiped and wiped the hard metal and plastic surfaces, even the trigger, carefully, even wiped the plastic bag where it had been opened, then dropped the gun right onto the body, poured out the bullets from the box, ignored the untouched clip, threw the rag away, stuck the empty bag and box in a pocket, walked to the car, started it, backed into the alley, turned on the lights and drove away.

CHAPTER TWENTY SEVEN

"Humanities, June Replyn."

"June, Joe Strecta. Heard the news?"

"No, what's up."

"What's down. Say Phan, shot close range in the chest, close to his house. Neighbors recognized him."

"Dead, I assume."

"Very dead."

"Oh, man, three murders now. Three murders! Hate to run, Joe, but there's a detective I've got to call."

There was a long pause on the other end. June was about to speak again when he said "June, you certainly can tell me to shove it, but if you can stand it, I would like to be avuncular for a moment before you make that call. What a fun word. Avuncular."

"Avunc away."

"I want to warn you about two things. The first is about getting deeper into something where there is a dangerous killer, at least one, maybe more, and there you are poking around and investigating. If he, hell he or she, who knows, if *they* think you're on to something why not kill you next?"

"What, you want me to just drop it?"

"No, I guess not, but I'd like you to be careful. Please."

"That's sweet, and you're sweet, and I'll be careful, but this really is a police thing now. Guess my feature story will have to be on hold until the murders stop. Sorry, this isn't funny. But really, I don't expect to be at the factory or doing any interviews... but thanks for caring. And the second?"

Again a long pause. She switched the phone to her other ear, waited. "Just a gentle, avuncular, well meaning warning about something that is absolutely none of my business. I want to warn you about loving a cop."

"Ohhhhh... Oh my goodness. What warning, why?"

"Because they lead a life that is totally different from ours. They work, especially detectives, in a place of slime and crud and danger and the threat of death. It makes them... never mind, I was going to generalize far too much. But they have a tough life, a tough job, crazy hours, pressure.... the divorce rate among our nation's finest is sadly rather high. Not to blame anyone, in fact I couldn't have higher respect for people in that line of work. Bless them all, and sincere thanks for being there, on the job... but sometimes, on more occasion than one would like, love is a casualty."

June sat, listening. He waited a moment then continued. "I think it's also hard on the spouses, mostly women of course, hard to kiss goodbye and be praying inside that there won't be that terrible knock on the door, praying that your husband... or wife... will be alive at the end of the day. Can you imagine living with that? Not me. I'm sure that busts up some of them, too."

June spoke softly. "Yeah, I imagine they get used to it or lose it, make an adjustment or have to get out. Yeah, sounds tough, sounds tough. But you know, uncle, I just can't help loving that man of mine."

"I think there's a song in there somewhere."

"Got to call that man right now. I'll see if he can scoop us a scoop, share with you before deadline."

"Hope I didn't offend you just now, June. It really isn't my business...."

"Oh, shit, Joe, I'm starting to cry. Glad you can't see me. Thanks for caring, thanks for the warnings, I love you too. Now go to hell, will you?"

"Standing by for scoops."

"Bye.

June reached in her second right hand drawer, the one where she kept her tissues and breath mints and hand lotion and dental floss and antacid tablets. And chocolate. She wiped her eyes and blew her nose, threw away her tissue and picked up the phone. It rang only twice.

"Stans."

"Terry, I just heard. Can you share anything, anything we can use?"

"Looks like four shots. Wait, I didn't say that. Don't use that number, June, we aren't giving that out yet."

"Got it, just shot, murdered."

"Something else. The gun was still with the body. Lucky for us nobody made off with it."

"Who found him?"

"That's the lucky part. Little kids, they go screaming into the house, the grandfather lives with them, he comes out and sees, tells them to call 911 while he stands there, older guy but big and strong, just stands there telling everybody to keep away."

"Sounds like an ex-cop."

"Retired railroad man, actually, but must have watched a lot of cop shows on TV. Did just the right thing, protected the crime scene."

"So, anything special we can use?"

"Well.. since the murder weapon has been found, it was right there on his chest, bullets scattered like some kind of confetti... June, it was fitted with a silencer."

"A silencer!"

"Don't know yet, but it could be the gun from the Long shooting.

Already on the way to the lab."

"OK, paper first. Can I use that?"

"Sure, it doesn't help the killer, whoever did this sure knows where the gun was left and how it was rigged. Looks like just shot and dropped it."

"Fingerprints?"

"We're checking, but I think it was wiped clean. Oily rag we found nearby, gun oil, not motor oil, gun may have been wrapped in it... anyway, I don't think we're going to pull any prints off it."

"So we can say the gun had a silencer, and that bullets were scattered near the gun, and that it looks like the prints were wiped off."

"Yes."

"And about links to the Long murder?"

"You haven't reported that the cousins said they heard no noise, right?"

"Not yet, didn't have a place to stick it into a bigger story, and it didn't make sense to run it alone, since there wasn't anything else to report about the murder at that time."

"Let's find out if it's the same gun. If it is you can go with that, tie it all together. We'll have to issue it for everyone, you know."

"Sure, but only the part about it being the same gun, right? Not what the cousins said, because we did that, not you."

"That's fine. We'll tell everyone, have to, that the gun was used in both. Your extra piece will be what you found out as a reporter. Just make sure you say that, say that it was in the course of an interview conducted by the paper, so we don't get accused of playing favorites."

"But won't you get in trouble for missing that?"

"No. Not a big deal clue, and it looks like it's moot now."

"So what do you think happened?"

"What do *you* think happened?"

She was ready, didn't hesitate. "Say Phan killed the owner, Pritkin, for some reason. Maybe has to do with drug smuggling. Then Rith Long starts bugging him, snooping, gossip, he kills her to shut her up and warn the others. Then.... well, lots thinner here, but sometime during the night he meets someone else caught up in this, and the reason is because you sat outside his house, Phan's house, spooked him. It worked. It worked so well he called his buddy and said you've got to hide this gun for a while, I can't keep it under my mattress any longer. They meet, Phan hands over gun and bullets, double-cross occurs."

"Bingo, lady. I think so too."

"So who killed the killer?"

"I answer that only upon agreement that this is not for printing, attribution, or even repeating. In other words, this is between us. All right?"

"Yes, Terry, yes, but I'll bet I can answer my own question. I just don't like the answer. Remember the first time I visited you at your office, we talked about the murder, the first one... now three..." She shook her head. "Three murders. Anyway, I looked at the pictures and read the report and you gave me a ninety-five on my guess about what happened. Remember?"

"That I do. And I remember why you didn't get a perfect grade."

She felt the chill as she said the words. "His children. One of his children killed Say Phan." She paused. "Maybe killed Dad?"

"Maybe, but I don't think so. No, my guess is the earlier one. It fits. One of the children is working a deal with Say Phan, smuggling something, probably drugs. Old man gets suspicious, not really suspicious, he's too innocent, just mentions that something isn't square, paperwork doesn't work. Phan says he'll meet him in the morning, they'll fix it, he runs out of ideas and just kills him. In a panic, I guess. Then he shoots the factory gossip. Then he does just what I want when I questioned him, gets so spooked he calls his partner... one of the children, that's what it looks like, says please hide the gun. Partner says yes, does the deed."

"Why didn't Phan just throw the gun away?"

"Now I'm really guessing, but probably because it cost a lot and it's a hell of a weapon. Phan wanted to keep it for both reasons."

"OK, of the trio, which one?"

"Or more than one."

June shook her head in sadness. Yes it could be more than one. "Dinner first, guessing later?"

CHAPTER TWENTY EIGHT

Terry arrived at June's apartment laden with fresh trout, almonds, and other fixings for a trout almondine dinner with small potatoes and a salad. "Fish is brain food, right? At least that's what I always heard."

"Brain food because..."

"Got to figure out the puzzle, the who done it, then how to trap him. Or her."

"The girl didn't do it."

"Girl? How come you get to say girl? If I did it I'd be in deep shit."

"Charming phrase. Well, charmer, we get to say that and you don't because you're a man. Women get to call each other girls until they're in their nineties. No, make that *especially* in their nineties."

"So why didn't Amy do it? No, I mean how do you know Amy didn't do it? Do you think women can't pull triggers? Believe me, they can. And stick knives in people and set them on fire and run over them in cars. Back up and do it twice. So.....? " He was toasting the almonds, in butter in a frying pan, carefully watching the heat so they didn't burn.

"I just don't see it. Why would she?"

"Well, if you want to do it that way... actually, the motive is the same for all three. Greed. Money. If drugs are being smuggled in along with the fabrics it's because drugs are highly profitable. So who likes money? Who wants more money than he or she has? All three, I would guess." Terry had removed the almonds and set them aside. Now he cut the heads off the two trout, rinsed the fish inside and out, put lemon pepper seasoning and a touch of garlic powder in the cavities, then stuffed in the almonds. He added a few shakes of low sodium soy sauce to the butter and put the fish in the pan over medium heat.

June watched him work on the trout. "So her motive is money."

"Money is the root of all evil. It's true, it's true. Sure rape, murder over jealousy or betrayal, those crimes happen. But most crimes are because of, in pursuit of, money. You have it, I don't, I want it. Or, there is lots more money available if I break the law then if I don't. Selling drugs, extortion, prostitution, pimping, gambling, make a lot more profit than legal enterprise, more than a legitimate business makes. Sometimes a staggering lot more."

June nodded. "Until the criminal is arrested or killed."

"Operative word being until. Some people think they'll never get caught, or think it will be a long time before they are. And many just aren't afraid of prison, they plead guilty to a lesser, get a dime, get paroled in seven and start again." He paused, adjusting the heat down a little, carefully flipping the fish to brown on the opposite sides. "Did you know Amy is separated from her husband?"

June was surprised. "How did you learn that?"

"I asked."

"Smirking does not become you."

"You gonna make the salad or just pout because I interview better than you do?"

"Point *not* conceded. So she's splitting from her husband. Would an extra hundred thousand or so help her get on her feet if they divorce? Sure would. Especially if she can keep it hidden, boxes of cash he never finds out about." June started washing and cutting vegetables. "So she suddenly buys a fab four bedroom and Maserati after they divorce? Wouldn't that bring his attorney down on her, and maybe the cops and the IRS?"

"If it is Amy I would expect her to be much more subtle, add the money in a little at a time. In fact, how to use drug money, actually getting to use it, is one of the problems people in the business face. At the very top they can usually hide in plain sight, lots of shell corporations and legitimate businesses to wash money through, and layers and layers of corporate entities and corporate lawyers. Bank accounts in the Caymans or Switzerland. You must have read about such men, they're all men... they live large and dare their federal government to prove something. Mostly they live in Columbia, a few other places. Can't do that anymore in America, though, can't live large with no legitimate income, too easy to crack down here. But in other countries, especially those with fractured governments and civil wars, like Columbia...." Terry carefully slid the spatula under the fish and put them in turn on their plates. "But lower down, the street dealers and their supervisors, well sometimes we bust people who have boxes and boxes of money, mostly tens and twenties. I remember this small-time dealer had about thirty thousand, all wrapped up in rubber bands, stacked in boxes from the grocery. Thirty thousand!"

They finished their preparations, turned off the kitchen lights and began taking the plates to the table. "So these are people without checking accounts or jobs who don't know how to convert the money into cars or houses?"

"Cars are easier. There are ways of buying a car for cash, even lots of cash in small bills. And of course clothes and gold chains. Got to have the gold chains. And diamond-trimmed watches. So you buy one expensive car and all the gold you can wear. Then what, a house? Buy a three-hundred thousand dollar house with small bills? And banking it is tough. If you own a business like a pizza joint you can show up at the bank with small bills every day. Of course the pizza joint has a corporate tax I D number. But what if you have no business, no tax I D, yet a couple'a times a week you show up with hundreds of dollars in tens and twenties? Good way to attract attention, and these boys want no attention past the street corner."

They sat down, Terry opened the wine while June served them both salad from a wooden bowl. "Terry, I don't understand. Why the car and gold if they don't want attention?"

"It's because they want the local people to be impressed and afraid at the same time. Some of them live most of their lives in an area that's maybe ten square blocks. Very big scary rich fish in a tiny pond. I mean, yes, it is New York, or Chicago or lots of cities, but they stay in one small area where they know everyone and no one asks questions or calls the cops. Rent an apartment, maybe a house, pay rent in cash every month. These boys don't go to Wall Street to do their banking. But in the same way, if you're middle class like Amy it can be real hard to spend the money. You have to work it into your spending slow and steady."

Terry poured the wine, they lifted the glasses and looked into each other's eyes, clinked them and drank. Then they both attacked the trout.

June looked up first. "You think it was Amy, don't you?"

Terry paused, split a small potato, ate half. "No, I'm not leaning towards her more than her brothers, but it could be. It could be her. OK. Quick takes, start with Amy. Loved her father, angry at Phan for killing him."

"Same for her brothers."

"True. Same motive for all. Maybe the divorce is pushing her back to square one financially, back to where she was before she got married. But now she's older, and angry about how things are working out. Saw the chance for some fast bucks."

"Tony."

"Ah, Tony. Straight arrow, wife and kids and mortgage. Settled, comfortable, secure."

"Motive being...."

"Your turn. I need to eat. I sure can cook, can't I?"

"Second reason I keep you around. OK, motive for Anthony Pritkin. Motive, motive....give me a moment."

They ate in silence for several minutes. The fish was perfect, easily coming way from the spine and small bones. Finally June spoke, softly, carefully considering her words. "Because he was trapped. Is trapped. Bird in gilded cage. Maybe he saw himself as a corporate powerhouse, major business tycoon, or at least money manger, senior vice president of fat money for zillion dollar corporation. Instead he settles for the easy way out. So he's comfortable, but just a guy in a small shop in Queens, not a suite in Manhattan."

"Could be. Certainly a possibility."

"Or could be he counts his blessings every day. Steady income, can't get fired, company won't go out of business as long as people wear tee shirts and shorts. A good life, a growing company, a secure future. Maybe the Joe next door to him gets laid off, so while Tony's telling him how sorry he is, at the same time he's thinking 'I'm sure glad that can't happen to me.' Could be he really is what he seems to be, mister straight arrow manager."

Another quiet moment, eating, drinking wine and sips of ice water. Later would be coffee and vanilla ice cream with strawberries sliced on top.

June said "And then there's Peter."

"And then there's Peter. Gone from humble truck driver to small-time transport tycoon. Expensive car, expensive apartment. Hot women, and they're expensive too, real expensive."

"How do you know about hot expensive women?"

"Dating one. You think the trout were cheap?"

"Uh-huh. Got your expensive trout. And you've no doubt read about such women in books, strictly research, I'm sure. Moving right along... so what about Peter? Are his new riches kind of obvious, you aren't sure it's him just because he's so flashy?"

"You can look at it from either view. It's like something's a cliche because it is so often true. Sure, he's an obvious candidate, most likely of the three, I guess, because he's the most flamboyant. Flashy's a good word. He throws money around. Maybe drug money. Or view from the other side, maybe the money is all honestly earned, he's just a big kid, a hard-working big kid who likes his toys....."

"All kinds of toys..."

"Yes dear. So could be he is legit or isn't. Might be a dealer. After all, he's got trucks going to the docks, ships coming from everywhere, then deliver all over New York and New Jersey and Connecticut. And if customs spots something... well, he's just the trucker."

"So he's a strong maybe."

"Or Amy or Tony, and they've got it hidden away, spending a little now, stashing the rest for later. Peter living large might be a clue, or might be just someone who spends it as fast as he makes it, and he's really making it all honestly."

Again they ate in silence for a few minutes, each turning over the possibilities, the arguments for and against the three children of the murdered man, the murdered father. That child of the father was probably dealing in drugs, had almost certainly pulled the trigger in that dark alley. The man who killed Say Phan. The woman who killed Say Phan. One of them killed the killer.

June came wide awake at three in the morning. Maybe police work, being around murder and dangerous people, became somewhat routine, which was why Terry was so sound asleep, a softly breathing log next to her. What a shame to wake him. So she got up, went to the bathroom and turned on the light, used the toilet and flushed it, washed her hands, being just a bit noisier than she had to. When she returned to bed he got up, power of suggestion used the toilet too, and as he got into bed she started talking.

"How are you going to figure this out? Where do you go from here?"

"Tomorrow's Thursday, isn't it? We don't sleep late on Thursdays, we work on Thursdays. You want to ask me questions at three in the morning do it on weekends."

"The problem I see is that approaching any one of them casts doubt on the other. Or alerts the killer. Do you ask Amy about Tony? Tony about Amy? How do you go after Peter?"

"We're going to do this now, aren't we?" He sighed, turned on his back, doubled the pillow under his head.

"Come on, just a little. Where do you start? Who do you start with?"

"Man oh man... all right, give me a minute. Purple rat fuck, three in the morning and I have to solve crime riddles. Where do I start.... How about this? First we get some dogs to sniff around, see if there's any drug traces, see if that part of the picture fits."

"Because if not then..."

"If there are no drugs involved none of this makes sense, unless they were smuggling diamonds, which I really doubt. No, if there aren't any drugs I'm going to transfer to vice, spend the rest of my career busting sex vendors."

"So you take dogs to the factory with their permission or with a search warrant. Which is it?"

"Same problem, right? Asking their permission means we have to tell them why, which is a tip-off, but that's just a discussion point, we're not near enough to get a search warrant. Can't ask for a search warrant for evidence drugs were at the factory on the premise that nothing else makes as much sense. Doesn't work that way."

"So....."

"Sleep. Go to sleep." He paused, still on the folded pillow, eyes open. She waited. "Maybe not the dogs. Maybe the squeeze play, a little pressure. Do the tough cop thing like I did with Say Phan. Hope someone can't handle the pressure."

"What squeeze play?"

He turned his head, looked at her. "Here, squeeze this."

"Three in the morning?"

He reached out, cupped her in his hand.

CHAPTER TWENTY NINE

Terry asked them to come to his office. He was counting on basic human nature; no one likes being in a police station. People get nervous, rattled, say things. They agreed on a morning meeting, eight.

The room looked like a movie set. Four walls, one with a large mirrored window, obviously a one-way mirror. Unlike much of the rest of the station all four walls were the same color, a flat beige. In the room was a heavy metal table with a dark green top of uncertain material and six of the hard wooden chairs from the school furniture close-out. A room low on charm but high on utility.

Amy and Tony arrived at the same time; they must have ridden together. While Terry was greeting them they heard the whine and burble of Peter's sports car, and he came in the door a few moments later. Terry offered coffee but there were no takers. All three were acting impatient, jumpy. Just what Terry wanted. He guided them back to the beige room then said "Sorry, forgot my notes, I'll be right back." He stepped outside the room and moved to the window. Looking in he saw them sitting, fidgeting, not talking to each other. No one likes being in a police station.

The detective waited another minute, then pulled his notepad out of his coat pocket. Holding it in his hand he went back into the room, saying "Sorry, left it on my desk. OK, let me tell you what we've got so far." The "we" was deliberate, it made it sound like the system, the Man, not just Terry Stans.

He laid his notepad on the table but didn't open it. Another nerve-rattler, a small one, but disconcerting. "Here is what we are certain of, or certain enough to take to court." He leaned forward, strong and positive, and ticked them off on his fingers. Pleasantly neutral, but all business. Hard business. "First, Say Phan killed your father and killed Rith Long. Second, the reasons are connected. Your father, and Rith, both saw something that sparked their attention, something that seemed wrong." He paused, only a few seconds but it seemed much longer to the three listeners. "Third, someone killed Phan because that person, Say Phan's killer, was involved in a crime with him, and had to shut him up. Things had gotten out of hand, two murders, and it was time to get rid of him before anything else happened. Fourth" and again he paused, and looked hard for a moment at each of them, staring as he had stared at the windows of Say Phan's house

168

"fourth, the linking crime for all of this was, is, drugs."

Six eyes went wide.

And now the bluffing started. Bluffing based on knowledge of what was normal, the usual way of doing business in the drug trade. "Say Phan was receiving occasional shipments of hard drugs, heroin or cocaine, maybe both. Most likely pure or near-pure heroin tucked inside boxes of material. He would somehow get them out, the packets, and hide them, maybe in the parking lot. We may never know that part, but we do know without a doubt that drugs were being smuggled into the factory in those boxes. We think your father saw something on the paperwork, maybe the boxes got weighed before and after the drugs were inserted, again, we'll never know for sure. But our guess is that he saw something and mentioned it to the man who opens almost all the boxes, Say Phan. So Phan says, 'yes that is unusual, why don't I meet you tomorrow and we'll figure it out. Meet you nice and early.' They meet, Phan kills him."

"Why there? In that way?" said Peter.

"Yes, why didn't he just shoot him?" said Tony. "I'm sorry, that sounded ugly, I meant...."

"No, that's a good question, Tony" Amy said.

Terry nodded. "Yes, a good question. I think he bought the gun after the first... after he killed your father. But maybe not. See, I think he panicked. I think he worried and thought about it all night, wondered what he could say, how he could fool the boss. Never planned on killing him, so even if he already had the gun it didn't occur to him to use it. Just guessing, but it makes sense. 'What to tell him, what to say,' Phan doesn't sleep all night. They meet early, and as they're walking back your father is saying things about the paperwork and we have to check this and that and he, Phan, realizes that there's no way to fool this guy who built the company from the ground up, so he just does it. Probably didn't even really think about it, just did it. Murder in a panic. It happens."

Amy asked "Why Rith?"

"That one we're even surer about. She poked into his affairs, got nosy, said things. So he killed her, partly to shut her up, partly to scare, warn and scare, I guess, her cousins and any one else who might want to get nosy."

Tony leaned forward. "And his killer? And the drugs, the heroin?"

"He couldn't do it alone. He needed someone to make things as smooth as possible, handle money, help him avoid detection as much as possible... someone who could handle things he couldn't, make it happen. All he did was open boxes and hide the dope somewhere, collect a fee. He wasn't the brains."

"I'll be a mother-fucking son of a bitch. *Son of a bitch!*"

They all turned and looked at Peter.

"You think it's one of us! You think one of us was bringing in drugs, working with the asshole who killed our father."

Terry looked him hard in the eyes.

"Motive? Money, lots of it. Opportunity? Your trucks deliver the boxes. Amy is there all day making things hum. Tony is there all day too. Yes, Peter, I think one of you killed your drug smuggling partner."

No one knew what to do with their eyes. Look at Terry, look at each other, look at the floor, look at the mirror and wonder if someone was behind it, watching.

"Yeah, well fuck this shit. If you weren't a cop I'd break your fucking jaw" said Peter, loudly, getting up and almost running out the door. The others watched him go.

Amy arched her eyebrows high, inhaled, blew it out slowly. "Now what?"

"Now I keep investigating, asking questions, hoping for a break. Unless someone confesses, that is."

"There are other possibilities, aren't there?" asked Tony.

"Which are…."

"That you're wrong, that the partner is one of our vendors or a trucking company other than Pete's or the people who bring the junk for the vending machines….."

Amy joined in. "How about the janitorial crew? Here every day."

Terry nodded in agreement. "All possible, all possible. I just don't think so."

"How about a family crime? Two of us, or even all three?" Amy tried to smirk, but couldn't manage it.

"Maybe, maybe." He was so cool, his voice and face level and calm and neutral. A stone face, and the brother and sister could only blink at it.

Amy started to get up, then half out of her chair, her knees still bent, her hands on the table, she said "Anything else?"

"No, not now."

The stone face stayed unchanged, the other two stood, walked out of the room, out of the police station.

CHAPTER THIRTY

"You did it, didn't you? You killed Say Phan. Why?"

"Are you crazy? You're crazy!"

"You know that won't work. We haven't been able to lie to each other since we were kids. I knew it the second that detective said it was one of us. That is some cold-hearted son of a bitch."

"Cold-hearted, got that right. Wonder if he ever gets any?"

"You killed a man. What are we going to do about it?"

"Just leave me alone."

"*Leave you alone?* This is murder! Or was it self defense. You can say it was self defense, he pulled out the gun, you grabbed it, it went off."

"Hard to claim self defense after four shots."

A long pause.

"Stans never mentioned four shots. It wasn't in the paper, either. You did it. You did it, and you are mixed up in murder and drugs. What are you going to do?"

"I, and you... *we* are going to keep our mouths shut and go about our daily lives and see if he can find anything, prove anything. I think he can't."

"Well 'daily lives' can't include dope smuggling. You have to stop everything. You can't risk... they could confiscate the whole factory, couldn't they? I think I read that, they can just take it as part of a criminal enterprise. Then what? You can't risk the courts closing the company down because the dope's coming in that way. And the cops have got to be watching."

Another long pause.

"You're right. But turning these guys off isn't easy. They take this business very seriously. I'll try."

"You can't try, you have to do it. NOW!"

"Funny, I had a similar discussion with Say Phan, not long before he died."

A short pause, a look of shock and amazement.

"Was that a threat? Did you just threaten to kill me?"

"No no no ….. just rambling. No threat. I love you. I just have to figure out what to do, what to do…. can we both just keep quiet for a while?"

"That's not the problem. The problem is keeping quiet forever."

"There is no proof. Just let it go, let it go. Bury it in the back of your mind and let's get on with the rest of our lives. That's all I'm asking."

"I won't go to the cops if you stop the dope."

"Deal. And, well, I don't know if it makes you feel any better.... different... about what happened, but Say Phan did kill Dad."

They hugged, briefly, uncomfortably.

CHAPTER THIRTY ONE

"Yeah?"

"It's me. We have to meet."

"Where you calling from?"

"I'm not stupid. Pay phone."

"OK, where?"

"Alley Pond Park. Near the entrance. Saturday, ten?"

"Yes."

Saturday

It was now the fullness of late summer; already at ten in the morning there was a high, hot sun. The early flowering trees and shrubs had shown and dropped their flowers, and it was time for marigolds, day lilies, geraniums, snap dragons. The trees and bushes were now solid green, thick and full. A man sat on a bench, waiting. At a few minutes before the hour he was approached.

"We have to stop."

The man on the bench was use to panicky people full of fear, greedy people watching their world spin apart. He didn't care; his loyalty was to the people who paid him very well to be obedient and thorough, and who would torture and kill him without blinking if he strayed. He stayed seated, calm and cool, the other standing. "What seems to be the problem?" said the man on the bench.

"The cops are all over this. I'm a suspect, all three of us. They're watching us, probably got the phones tapped. Can't handle any shipments, not now, maybe not for a long time."

"What are you going to do about the shipments already on the way?"

"Cancel them! I don't know, divert, lose them. Throw them in the fucking ocean, but they can't go to the factory."

The man spoke calmly in tones of logic, with just enough edge in his voice to terrify.

"There are two five-pound shipments coming, same as always. One will be here in two or three days, the other in another ten days or so. I'll see what I can do about *temp-o-rarely* halting future shipments, but those ten pounds are in the pipeline and they are on their way. On ships in the

173

middle of the ocean. To try to intercept them would raise suspicion. The boxes are sealed, the papers in order. We're talking about a lot of money, a lot of money. You have to retrieve those shipments, or get someone new to do it." He paused. "Sorry about the loss of your partner. I wonder who could have shot him?"

"I can't retrieve them! Don't you understand?"

The man on the bench had seen such panic many times. It was almost an early death rattle. "Then you will find the quality of your life significantly diminished. Significantly." He rose, put a hand on the other's shoulder in what to a distant observer would seem to be a gesture of friendship. It was not. He looked hard into the other's terrified eyes. "Significantly."

CHAPTER THIRTY TWO

A stretch of four-lane highway winding through the State of New York, heading west, many miles from Manhattan. The driver was drinking whiskey straight from a small bottle, speeding up, driving erratically. A highway patrol officer, sitting at the start of the ramp that returned traffic to the highway from a rest stop, saw the car go by and immediately turned on his rollers and gave chase. The driver looked in the rear view mirror, held the gas pedal flat against the floor, and was going well over a hundred when the car left the highway and hit a rail designed to deflect impact, but the speed and weight of the vehicle were too great and the car flipped and rolled and was bent hideously out of shape when it came to rest at the bottom of a cement-lined drainage ditch. The driver, not wearing a seat belt, was killed instantly.

The highway patrol car pulled slowly into the driveway. Libby Pritkin looked out the window and felt terrible cold fear. Tony had been so distracted lately, worried looking, not sleeping well. Had he been too distracted to drive carefully? How badly was he injured?

Two officers got out, their uniforms clean and well pressed, their shoes shining as if painted high gloss black. Her eyes took it all in while her mind fought to calm the rising terror. She rushed to the door, opened it before they climbed the steps.

She knew it was bad by the gentle way the officer said her name. "Mrs. Anthony Pritkin?"

"Is it Tony? How bad is it?"

"You may wish to sit down, Mrs. Pritkin."

Libby backed into the living room and they followed. She backed until she found the sofa, sat down hard and reached down at her sides and held the cushions so hard her hands hurt, but she kept squeezing and squeezing them.

"I'm Officer Johnson, this is Officer O'Malley. We're very sorry, but your husband was killed in a single-car accident about an hour ago. He was on Interstate 81 just north of Binghamton."

"Interstate 81? Binghamton? What was he doing there?"

"We don't have any information on that. He was alone, no one else was involved or injured."

Officer O'Malley spoke. "Can you call someone? Relative or neighbor? We can wait, or take you somewhere if you need a ride."

"His sister. They work together." Libby got up, dialed the number, praying Amy would be in as usual. She was. "This is Amy Pritkin."

"Oh Amy…" and then it hit her, hit her so hard she couldn't talk, the tears streaming down and her body twisting, she stumbled and sat down hard on the floor. The officers came to her but she shook her head no and held the phone up to them. "You tell her" she whispered, then sat, her arms around her knees, rocking, crying.

"What! Libby? What…."

"Ma'am, this is officer Johnson with the highway patrol. I'm sorry to inform you, your brother Anthony was killed in an accident today. Can you come be with your sister-in-law?"

"It will take me about half an hour. Can you wait with her?"

"I'm going to see if there is a neighbor who can come over, but we won't leave her alone."

"Thank you. I'm leaving now."

While driving Amy called Peter, speaking into the hands-free microphone mounted over the rear-view mirror. He wasn't in and she thought briefly of calling his cell phone, sure he would answer, but decided that it was easier to just leave a message. No reason to hurry. "Like when Dad died" she thought. No reason to hurry, plenty of time to grieve.

It was difficult to carry the terrible knowledge, to not tell, never tell Peter or Libby or anyone that Tony was involved in drug smuggling and murder. Better to let them think, wonder, but there was no reason to ever say the words. "Yes, we had a talk, he confessed everything, he and Say Phan were smuggling drugs and he killed Phan. That's why he killed himself. You don't think it was an accident, do you?" No, no reason to say it.

When Amy arrived she found Libby had been joined by three neighbors and her children. The oldest, Tony Junior, a little over four, was crying and bewildered. Libby had dry, red eyes, and was holding the baby, sitting in a soft, large chair. The baby was peacefully asleep. Amy came in, picked up Junior and hugged him hard, kissed him, smoothed his hair, gently set him down again. He walked next to his mother's chair, reached up and held her arm. Libby smiled at him. Amy sat down on an ottoman at Libby's feet. Libby held the baby in one arm, extended the other towards Amy so they could hold hands.

They spent the next half hour fussing over the children and speaking in soft tones. Reassuring words, promises from Amy and her friends to help and support Libby, praise for Tony as a husband and father. Other neighbors, and some of Libby's friends, appeared with fresh hot casseroles and plates of fruit and cheese. They would walk in composed but a few cried the instant they saw Libby's face. It was crushingly sad, everyone being brave and helpful and loving and just as sad and broken-hearted as they could be.

The roar and squealing tires approached, they and the burbling exhaust announced Peter's arrival. Parking spaces near the house were gone, so he parked several houses down and ran back. Peter burst through the door and walked quickly to where Libby sat, bending over and kissing her forehead, touching the still-sleeping baby, giving Tony Junior a hug and kiss.

"Can we go for a car ride Uncle Peter?"

Peter smiled at him. "Sure, Junior, sure. In a little while."

Amy could feel the tension, the pull of the unspoken words between sister and brother. Moments later the baby, Susan, woke up and instantly began to complain about her wet diaper and empty belly. This gave everyone a focus, an almost palpable relief of something else to talk about. They commented on Susan's crying style and how red her little face got. One friend took Susan so Libby could get out of the soft chair, hard to do while holding a baby. Libby and the friend went off to change the diaper, two neighbors headed for the kitchen to find and open and warm the baby food jars. Peter gave Amy a look, then turned and headed for the front door. She followed him onto the front lawn.

"It was no accident, was it? He killed himself because he did it, right? Drugs and killed that guy, right?"

She wanted to tell him he was wrong, had made that promise to herself, but lying was simply not possible. Too much pointed towards Tony. And they were siblings, a lifetime of sharing. Amy knew she could never carry off the bluff, so she said "Libby can never know. We can't tell her anything."

"But the cops, the papers....."

Amy gasped. "The papers... you're right! I've got to make a call."

She started back towards the house but realized that wouldn't work, far too public, so she spun and went to her car.

"Humanities, June Replyn."

"June, it's Amy Pritkin. Is there really such a thing as off the record? Please, please don't lie to me." Her voice was urgent, intense.

June heard the intensity, answered in a quick, serious manner. "You have my word that this conversation is totally off the record, and will stay so until you say different."

"Thank you. I can't talk long. My brother Tony is dead, killed in a one-car crash. I think... my brother Pete and I believe he was the smuggler and the.... that..... "

"He shot Say Phan."

"Yes. Please, his wife, his children....."

"What are the police saying?"

"Driving fast, lost control. They may even suspect suicide, who knows? I got it from Libby, that's his wife, they just said he was exceeding the speed limit and appeared to have lost control. Maybe they were being gentle with a new widow."

"Let me think." She forced the wheels to spin fast. "Amy, if there are drugs in the car then there's no way I can keep it quiet, it will be on every station and in every paper. But if not, then right now there's nothing to report except the loss of life…" the wheels spun on "… but you know everyone is going to report that this is the fourth death associated with your company. Don't be surprised to see the word jinxed, although I won't use it."

"I understand."

"So we'll report it straight." Careful now, careful wording. "I'd like to call the detective, Terry Stans. I think he should know. Do I have your permission?"

Amy sighed. "Sure. Still off the record, aren't we?"

"Millions of miles."

"Detective Stans had the three of us in his office a few days ago, pretty much said that one of us, maybe more than one, were involved in running drugs through the factory, hidden in boxes of fabric. He didn't flat out say it, but the implication was there that one of us killed Say Phan."

The squeeze play. June hadn't asked, and he hadn't volunteered, but there is was. Confront all three at once, level the accusations. "Here's all I can promise. If no one else breaks the story then we won't either, I gave my word… but if they do then I have to write what I know. I'll get it from the police, or say it came from them, but I can't sit here while the other papers are printing those headlines." Another wheel spin. "But Amy, I need something from you. Television, the other papers, everyone, they're going to show up at your door. Satellite trucks parked in front of your factory and your homes…. four deaths, three murders and a maybe suicide, too much to resist. I want you to hold out for me. We still do the story. I'll still write it to honor your father, the way we talked about, and about the company carrying on. Except it's much more of a story now, same story but much more to it. I want it to stay mine. I'm asking you to do that for me."

"Yes, yes, a trade of promises…. shit, I'm crying into my cell phone, probably short out the damn thing. Gotta go. Thanks. I'll be in touch."

"Wait, please, was it in the city? The accident?"

"No, way out on the highway. A long drive to nowhere. Highway Patrol."

"That gives us some time. Look, I don't want to intrude, but I've got to talk to you again today. Give it a few hours, call me, will you? I'll forward this one to my cell phone, so anytime, any hour. If there's going to be something in the paper I'd like you to know first."

"Sure. Bye."

June sat back, stunned. Amy hadn't said it, but of course much more was at stake than the reputation of a dead man and the embarrassment of his widow. The future of ComFitter also hung in the balance. A good little company hit by four sad events and swirling rumors - of course there would be rumors - could survive, in fact, as Amy had said when they first met, business boomed because of purchases spurred by sympathy for the loss of her father. Could happen again. But a bad little company, a drug smuggling front where people got murdered, that company could falter, fail, because no one wanted to do business with them.

She called Terry. "Terry Stans."

"Terry, Tony Pritkin is dead. Single car crash, way out of town. Maybe suicide. Can you get details? Highway Patrol."

"Sure. What are you going to do with it?"

"Don't know yet. I think I can keep a lid on things, got a deal where Amy talks just to me, but I can't control the rumors, that's for sure. I mean, the company can 'no comment' all they want, but it's probably still going to get ugly."

"I'll call you soon."

She hung up and struggled to return to the story she was working, about people who rarely purchased anything but seconds when shopping for socks and underwear. A few minutes ago she was into it, writing about what seconds were, how great the discount, some quotes from people who believed it was the only way to shop. Now it seemed unimportant, almost silly. Never before had the two worlds been so starkly divergent. Murders and drugs and cops and smugglers and suicides and heartache in one; in the other law-abiding people who knew how to save some dollars buying white athletic socks with the label woven crooked. June almost physically wrenched herself away from the first, got back into the article, but felt she was writing in a fog, the words and sentences coming slowly, with an effort. Somehow she finished it, read it over, decided that she would park it for one day and read it again before sending it to production. She had to pee, and started to head for the ladies' but realized she needed her cell phone, just in case. So she forwarded her desk phone and took the cell phone with her. Terry, with perfect timing, called just as her bladder began to empty.

"Hello?"

"Not the usual greeting."

"Not the usual place. What's up?"

"Where are you?" At that moment the lady in the next stall flushed her toilet. "Oh, there."

"Say one cute, sexist thing and you will pay for it many times over."

"Not a word. He was going a hundred, maybe more, running away from a patrol car. Slammed into a rail, dead when they got to the car. Open whiskey bottle, too. Drinking, don't know yet if he was drunk. June, you know there's no way to stop that from being reported. Already on the radio, TV by five, maybe a bulletin now."

"Anything about drugs?"

"Nothing mentioned in the first report, but they haven't looked in the trunk, that'll take some work. I guess the car was a pretzel. You want my guess?"

"Bet it's the same as mine, but go ahead."

"He killed himself. Got a little drunk and drove fast and ran into that rail on purpose. There aren't any drugs in the car, or money, or a suicide note. I think he wanted his family to collect all the insurance they could, so he made it look like drunk driving."

"Yes. That's it. So it's over."

"Not quite."

"Why not?"

"Don't you have to flush?"

"I'll call you back," she said, clicking off the phone, finishing her chores.

Minutes later his phone rang.

"Terry St..."

"Why isn't it over?"

"Because there may be drugs still on the way. You know, it takes over two weeks, sometimes over three, for those shipments to get here, especially if the freighter has more than one stop. So there could be drugs being delivered today, tomorrow, in three weeks. And that's best case, if the word gets back to the starting point today to stop the shipments. Could be a month or more before we can assume that the incoming is clean."

"Oh, Terry, if you start checking them for drugs, checking around the factory, that'll get out, it could ruin them. Drugs and murder, their customers will be gone in a flash. Let me think.... tell you what. I trust Amy. I just do. If you can go along with that I've got an idea."

"I'm listening."

"That is the corniest cop-speak thing you ever said to me."

He sighed greatly. "I'm still listening."

"And suffering. OK, so I ask her if any shipments have come in since Phan was shot."

"No, you'd have to go back a few days, in case he hid the stuff somewhere then got killed before he could retrieve it."

"All right. So she can go there Sunday morning, check any unopened boxes, look outside. Shouldn't take her long, she calls you if she finds any drugs. If she finds nothing, you work it out with the customs people, tell them to watch for boxes coming in, x-ray them or open them or something. Do that for two, three months, word should get back to the shipper by then."

"You know, it strikes me that I've never had any proof of anything. I sweat Phan and he gets killed, I sweat Tony and he kills himself, but I have no proof Phan killed Pritkin or Long, no proof Tony killed Phan, no drugs, no witnesses to murder or drugs, nothing. And yet I feel like it is wrapping up, everything solved, we know who killed the three victims, and at least one small drug pipeline has been closed. Strange case. Strange, strange case. Going to write it up and hide it under a file cabinet."

"So you approve of my idea?"

"Pete wasn't involved?"

"I don't think so….."

"I don't think so either. We did a little checking. He really is very successful, making a great profit, paying himself a nice salary. Hard working playboy."

"So it was the family man. Husband and father and drug smuggler. Why?"

"Money. Why wasn't he content with what he made? We'll never know. But to answer your question, yes, I approve of your idea. We can alert the customs folks, make their job a bit easier. I'll explain to them that the receiver isn't in the picture any longer, but that some shipments may have been made that couldn't be stopped."

June waited at work a bit later than usual, and had just decided to give up when the phone rang. It was Amy.

"Did you learn anything?"

"Amy, there was an open bottle in the car. We'll report it like everyone else, a high-speed chase, a drunk driver, a single-car crash. The highway patrol haven't indicated they suspect suicide. Maybe they would suspect if he just ran off the road by himself, but he was being chased, looks like he made a bad decision, drunk and tried to run. So not pretty, but not suicide, and apparently nothing incriminating in the car. No, this will read as just a sad case of alcohol and poor judgment."

"Thank you."

"Amy" June said gently "if they open the trunk or look under a seat and find something incriminating, we have to run it, everyone will. But I don't think there is anything to find. I think he wanted the cops to see him speeding so it could end like it did." She sighed, then went on more briskly. "I worked something out. Can't tell you how, but here's the deal. You get over to the factory tonight, Sunday morning, some time when you think you won't be seen. Actually, it needs to be daylight. Look at all the boxes that have come in recently, open any that are sealed. Then look around outside. We think the packages were stored somewhere outside, maybe in the dumpster, then retrieved before the scrap dealers picked them up. If you find drugs, call Terry. From this point on all your incoming boxes will be checked by customs, it's just what's already there, maybe hidden, that's a problem."

"Thank you. You must know what this means to me, the whole family. Look, when I leave here tonight I'll go to the shop. It won't take me long to check the last two, three weeks of fabric, we haven't gotten that many shipments. And maybe I'll check the dumpster first light tomorrow, way before anyone gets there. Take a flashlight, be there at dawn. I want this to be over."

"Good. Call me."

"And…. well, you're being so helpful, such a friend, really, I'm reluctant to ask… but you said 'We think the packages were stored' and you called him 'Terry,' not Detective Stans… or is this my imagination working?"

"Not to be shared?"

"Keeping lots of secrets, we are."

"The cop and the reporter. Starting to look like an item."

"Invite me to the wedding."

"Far distant way from that. But having a good time."

There was silence at the other end. "Amy?"

In a small, quiet voice Amy said "There's one more thing. I guess you can tell your…Terry. Tell Terry. But I never said this, never did, understand? You and me and your cop, your detective. I don't know, maybe someday I'll tell Pete. Probably will."

Again silence, a long one, but this time June waited. Finally Amy spoke.

"He did it. He killed Say Phan, and it was about drugs. He confessed to me after we met with Terry. Goodbye." She hung up quickly.

And so now it all came together. Terry's theories and her theories and the murders and the suicide, it all made sense. And it was so sad, so very sad. A fine gentleman, founder of a business, dead. A young woman, pursuing a dream, planning on going home to her loving family, dead. A family man, father of two so young children, dead. Because of drugs. Drugs and money and greed. To her surprise June felt tears running down her cheeks.

CHAPTER THIRTY THREE

Amy checked the boxes of fabric, all of them, even the opened ones. She looked in the dumpster and around it, and walked around the property. Nothing. There had probably been a shipment the day her father was killed, and Say Phan got it off the property. And then Tony killed Say, then killed himself. At the end of her search she found herself sitting in her father's chair behind his beat up old desk. She shook her head in wonder, in sorrow, too tired to cry.

Terry alerted U.S. Customs, told them a dealer had been shut down but that he believed there were still drugs in the pipeline. He got a promise that the fabric would be released, no need to punish an innocent company waiting for its raw product, not knowing that one of its employees was a drug merchant. Two days later a ship that was being unloaded yielded a box of fabric with five pounds of nearly pure heroin. It was confiscated before it could be passed on and divided, from pounds to half pounds to quarter pounds to ounces to quarter ounces to grams to tiny bags sold on the street, cut, stepped on in street language, with baby formula or sugar or quinine or powdered milk, and everyone marking up in the process, everyone making a profit. Dime bags, ten dollars each, containing two hundred milligrams of heroin and other substances so that the contents of the bags are only thirty or forty percent pure. The five pounds of pure would have produced tens of thousands of dime bags. Tens of thousands of doses, injected into collapsing veins.

Eleven days later came another five pounds, drugs that were already on a ship the day Say Phan was murdered. Bureaucracy is a problem even in the drug world; another twenty-two days and yet another shipment, even though the receiver was dead. Then never again, although for the next four years all boxes bound for ComFitter were searched.

Libby pulled the dirty laundry out of the hamper, the family's clothes, some if it Tony's. At the bottom was one of his shirts wrapped around something. It was an envelope, addressed to her. The children were still up, so she took it and put it in her purse, unopened. That night, the children sound asleep, she got it out and sat at the kitchen table, turning it over and over in her hands. Finally she opened it, pulled the letter out. She sighed a deep, ragged sigh, unfolded it and read:

My dearest Libby, my true love;

I'm so sorry

She could get no further, the tears overwhelmed her. She folded the letter, put it back in the envelope, took it into the bedroom, put it under her pillow. She got ready for bed, the letter waiting, waiting. Libby told herself to be strong, do it, read the letter. She checked on the children, closed her door, put a box of tissues on the bed, and slipped the letter out from its hiding place.

My dearest Libby, my true love;

I'm so sorry to have ruined everything. By ending things this way you will have insurance money and the house will be paid for.

I got mixed up in drugs. I thought I could make some extra money without getting in too deep, we could have some expensive vacations, send the kids to private schools, retire early. I didn't realize how fast these things can go wrong, or that once they do there is only one way out.

Move the left side of my workbench away from the wall. You will see a small hole. Put your finger in and pull. There is about seventy thousand dollars hidden there. This is drug money, very ugly money, and you probably don't want to touch it. But if you keep it, invest it quietly and wisely, it will pay for two expensive college educations. So I urge you, for the sake of the children, to do so. Obviously it is your choice. Guess that's the last bad joke I'll ever tell you.

Sweetheart, you were wonderful, all I ever wanted or needed. Too bad for me I realized that too late.

Tony

Libby ached anew, as she never had before. Angry and frustrated and beyond heartbroken, she picked up his pillow, pounded it and hugged it and cried and cried and cried.......

June called Terry. "I'm ready to talk about talking about it."
"See, you think I won't know what you mean. But I do. You're ready

to talk about living together."

"And you?"

"Ain't been no woman 'cept you long time now, whatchu think?"

"Well that sounds just fine, Bulldog. Remember we agreed not to discuss this during a romantic event. How about you pick me up and we'll go to Central Park, get a hot dog, sit on a bench, talk?"

"Can't get more romantic than that, I think. Guess we have some differences. Probably not a deal breaker."

"Noon?"

"Sure."

"And can you show me how handcuffs work?"